ONCE G — P9-DTB-943

(A RILEY PAIGE MYSTERY—BOOK 1)

BLAKE PIERCE

Prologue

A new spasm of pain jolted Reba's head upright. She yanked against the ropes that bound her body, tied around her stomach to a vertical length of pipe that had been bolted to the floor and ceiling in the middle of the small room. Her wrists were tied in front, and her ankles were bound.

She realized she'd been dozing, and she was immediately awash in fear. She knew by now that the man was going to kill her. Little by little, wound by wound. It wasn't her death he was after, and it wasn't sex either. He only wanted her pain.

I've got to stay awake, she thought. *I've got to get out of here. If I fall asleep again, I will die.*

Despite the heat in the room, her naked body felt chilled with sweat. She looked down, writhing, and saw her feet were bare against the hardwood floor. The floor around them was caked with patches of dry blood, sure signs that she wasn't the first person to have been tied here. Her panic deepened.

He had gone somewhere. The room's single door was shut tight, but he would come back. He always did. And then he'd do whatever he could think of to make her scream. The windows were boarded, and she had no idea if it was day or night, the only light from the glare of a bare bulb hanging from the ceiling. Wherever this place was, it seemed that no one else could hear her screams.

She wondered if this room had once been a little girl's bedroom; it was, grotesquely, pink, with curly-cues and fairytale motifs everywhere. Someone—she guessed her captor—had long since trashed the place, breaking and overturning stools and chairs and end tables. The floor was scattered with the dismembered limbs and torsos of children's dolls. Little wigs—doll's wigs, Reba guessed—were nailed like scalps on the walls, most of them elaborately braided, all of them in unnatural, toy-like colors. A battered pink vanity table stood upright next to a wall, its heart-shaped mirror shattered into little pieces. The only other piece of furniture intact was a narrow, single bed with a torn, pink canopy. Her captor sometimes rested there.

The man watched her with dark beady eyes, through his black ski mask. At first she had taken heart in the fact that he always wore that mask. If he didn't want her to see his face, didn't that mean that he didn't plan to kill her, that he might let her go?

But she soon caught on that the mask served a different

1

purpose. She could tell that the face behind it had a receded chin and a sloped forehead, and she was sure the man's features were weak and homely. Although he was strong, he was shorter than she, and probably insecure about it. He wore the mask, she guessed, to seem more terrifying.

She'd given up trying to talk him out of hurting her. At first she had thought she could. She knew, after all, that she was pretty. *Or at least I used to be,* she thought sadly.

Sweat and tears mixed on her bruised face, and she could feel the blood matted into her long blond hair. Her eyes stung: he had made her put in contact lenses, and they made it harder to see.

God knows what I look like now.

She let her head drop.

Die now, she begged herself.

It ought to be easy enough to do. She was certain that others had died here before.

But she couldn't. Just thinking about it made her heart pound harder, her breath heave, straining the rope around her belly. Slowly, as she knew she was facing an imminent death, a new feeling began to arise within her. It wasn't panic or fear this time. It wasn't despair. It was something else.

What do I feel?

Then she realized. It was *rage*. Not against her captor. She'd long since exhausted her rage toward him.

It's me, she thought. *I am doing what he wants. When I scream and cry and sob and plead, I'm doing what he wants.*

Whenever she sipped that cold bland broth he'd feed her through a straw, she was doing what he wanted. Whenever she blubbered pathetically that she was a mother with two children who needed her, she was delighting him to no end.

Her mind cleared with new resolve as she finally stopped writhing. Maybe she needed to try a different tack. She had been struggling so hard against the ropes all these days. Maybe that was the wrong approach. They were like those little bamboo toys—the Chinese finger traps, where you'd put your fingers in each end of the tube, and the harder you pulled, the more stuck your fingers became. Maybe the trick was to relax, deliberately and completely. Maybe that was the way out.

Muscle by muscle, she let her body go slack, feeling every sore, every bruise where her flesh touched the ropes. And slowly, she became aware of where the rope's tension lay.

At last, she found what she needed. There was just a little

looseness around her right ankle. But it wouldn't do to tug, at least not yet. No, she had to keep her muscles limber. She wiggled her ankle gently, gently, then more aggressively as the rope loosened.

Finally, to her joy and surprise, her heel popped loose, and she withdrew the whole right foot.

She immediately scanned the floor. Only a foot away, amid the scattered doll parts, lay his hunting knife. He always laughed as he left it there, tantalizingly nearby. The blade, encrusted with blood, twinkled tauntingly in the light.

She swung her free foot toward the knife. It swung high and missed.

She let her body slacken again. She slid downward along the post just a few inches and strained with her foot until the knife was within reach. She clutched the filthy blade between her toes, scraped it across the floor, and lifted it carefully with her foot until its handle rested in the palm of her hand. She clutched the handle tight with numb fingers and twisted it around, slowly sawing at the rope that held her wrists. Time seemed to stop, as she held her breath, hoping, praying she didn't drop it. That he didn't come in.

Finally she heard a snap, and to her shock, her hands were loose. Immediately, heart pounding, she cut the rope around her waist.

Free. She could hardly believe it.

For a moment all she could do was crouch there, hands and feet tingling with the return of full circulation. She poked at the lenses over her eyes, resisting the urge to claw them out. She carefully slid them to one side, pinched them, and pulled them out. Her eyes hurt terribly, and it was a relief to have them gone. As she looked at the two plastic disks lying in the palm of her hand, their color sickened her. The lenses were bright blue, unnatural. She threw them aside.

Heart slamming, Reba pulled herself up and quickly limped to the door. She took hold of the knob but didn't turn it.

What if he's out there?

She had no choice.

Reba turned the knob and tugged at the door, which opened noiselessly. She looked down a long empty hallway, lit only by an arched opening on the right. She crept along, naked, barefoot, and silent, and saw that the arch opened into a dimly lit room. She stopped and stared. It was a simple dining room, with a table and chairs, all completely ordinary, as if a family might soon come home to dinner. Old lace curtains hung over the windows.

A new horror rose up in her throat. The very ordinariness of the

3

place was disturbing in a way that a dungeon wouldn't have been. Through the curtains she could see that it was dark outside. Her spirits lifted at the thought that darkness would make it easier to slip away.

She turned back to the hallway. It ended in a door—a door that simply had to lead outdoors. She limped and squeezed the cold brass latch. The door swung heavily toward her to reveal the night outside.

She saw a small porch, a yard beyond it. The nighttime sky was moonless and starlit. There was no other light anywhere—no sign of nearby houses. She stepped slowly out onto the porch and down into the yard, which was dry and bare of grass. Cool fresh air flooded her aching lungs.

Mixed with her panic, she felt elated. The joy of freedom.

Reba took her first step, preparing to run—when suddenly she felt the hard grip of a hand on her wrist.

Then came the familiar, ugly laugh.

The last thing she felt was a hard object—maybe metal—impacting her head, and then she was spinning into the very depths of blackness.

4

Chapter 1

At least the stench hasn't kicked in, Special Agent Bill Jeffreys thought.

Still leaning over the body, he couldn't help but detect the first traces of it. It mingled with the fresh scent of pine and the clean mist rising from the creek—a body smell that he ought to have been long since used to. But he never was.

The woman's naked body had been carefully arranged on a large boulder at the edge of the creek. She was sitting up, leaning against another boulder, legs straight and splayed, hands at her sides. An odd crook in the right arm, he could see, suggested a broken bone. The wavy hair was obviously a wig, mangy, with clashing hues of blond. A pink smile was lipsticked over her mouth.

The murder weapon was still tight around her neck; she'd been strangled with a pink ribbon. An artificial red rose lay on the rock in front of her, at her feet.

Bill gently tried to lift the left hand. It didn't budge.

"She's still in rigor mortis," Bill told Agent Spelbren, crouching on the other side of the body. "Hasn't been dead more than twenty-four hours."

"What's with her eyes?" Spelbren asked.

"Stitched wide open with black thread," he answered, without bothering to look closely.

Spelbren stared at him in disbelief.

"Check for yourself," Bill said.

Spelbren peered at the eyes.

"Jesus," he murmured quietly. Bill noticed that he didn't recoil with disgust. Bill appreciated that. He'd worked with other field agents—some of them even seasoned veterans like Spelbren—who would be puking their guts up by now.

Bill had never worked with him before. Spelbren had been called in for this case from a Virginia field office. It had been Spelbren's idea to bring in somebody from the Behavioral Analysis Unit in Quantico. That was why Bill was here.

Smart move, Bill thought.

Bill could see that Spelbren was younger than him by a few years, but even so, he had a weathered, lived-in look that he rather liked.

"She's wearing contacts," Spelbren noted.

Bill took a closer look. He was right. An eerie, artificial blue

5

that made him look away. It was cool here down by the creek late in the morning, but even so, the eyes were flattening in their sockets. It was going to be tough to nail down the exact time of death. All Bill felt certain of was that the body had been brought here sometime during the night and carefully posed.

He heard a nearby voice.

"Fucking Feds."

Bill glanced up at the three local cops, standing a few yards away. They were whispering inaudibly now, so Bill knew that he was supposed to hear those two choice words. They were from nearby Yarnell, and they clearly weren't happy to have the FBI show up. They thought they could handle this on their own.

The head ranger of Mosby State Park had thought differently. He wasn't used to anything worse than vandalism, litter, and illegal fishing and hunting, and he knew the locals from Yarnell weren't capable of dealing with this.

Bill had made the hundred-plus-mile trip by helicopter, so he could get here before the body was moved. The pilot had followed the coordinates to a patch of meadow on a nearby hilltop, where the ranger and Spelbren had met him. The ranger had driven them a few miles down a dirt road, and when they'd pulled over, Bill could glimpse the murder scene from the road. It was just a short way downhill from the creek.

The cops standing impatiently nearby had already gone over the scene. Bill knew exactly what they were thinking. They wanted to crack this case on their own; a pair of FBI agents was the last thing they wanted to see.

Sorry, you rednecks, Bill thought, *but you're out of your depth here.*

"The sheriff thinks this is trafficking," Spelbren said. "He's wrong."

"Why do you say that?" Bill asked. He knew the answer himself, but he wanted to get an idea of how Spelbren's mind worked.

"She's in her thirties, not all that young," Spelbren said. "Stretch marks, so she's had at least one child. Not the type that usually gets trafficked."

"You're right," Bill said.

"But what about the wig?"

Bill shook his head.

"Her head's been shaved," he replied, "so whatever the wig was for, it wasn't to change her hair color."

"And the rose?" Spelbren asked. "A message?"

Bill examined it.

"Cheap fabric flower," he replied. "The kind you'd find in any low-price store. We'll trace it, but we won't find out anything."

Spelbren looked him over, clearly impressed.

Bill doubted that anything they'd found would do much good. The murderer was too purposeful, too methodical. This whole scene had been laid out with a certain sick style that set him on edge.

He saw the local cops itching to come closer, to wrap this. Photos had been taken, and the body would be removed any time now.

Bill stood and sighed, feeling the stiffness in his legs. His forty years were starting to slow him down, at least a little.

"She's been tortured," he observed, exhaling sadly. "Look at all the cuts. Some are starting to close up." He shook his head grimly. "Someone worked her over for days before doing her in with that ribbon."

Spelbren sighed.

"The perp was pissed off about something," Spelbren said.

"Hey, when are we gonna wrap up here?" one of the cops called out.

Bill looked in their direction and saw them shuffling their feet. Two of them were grumbling quietly. Bill knew the work was already done here, but he didn't say so. He preferred keeping those bozos waiting and wondering.

He turned around slowly and took in the scene. It was a thick wooded area, all pines and cedars and lots of undergrowth, with the creek burbling along its serene and bucolic way toward the nearest river. Even now, in midsummer, it wasn't going to get very hot here today, so the body wasn't going to putrefy badly right away. Even so, it would be best to get it out of here and ship it off to Quantico. Examiners there would want to pick it apart while it was still reasonably fresh. The coroner's wagon was pulled up on the dirt road behind the cop car, waiting.

The road was nothing more than parallel tire tracks through the woods. The killer had almost certainly driven here along it. He had carried the body the short distance along a narrow path to this spot, arranged it, and left. He wouldn't have stayed long. Even though the area looked out of the way, rangers patrolled through here regularly and private cars weren't supposed to be on this road. He had wanted the body to be found. He was proud of his work.

And it *had* been found by a couple of early-morning horseback

7

riders. Tourists on rented horses, the ranger had told Bill. They were vacationers from Arlington, staying at a fake Western ranch just outside of Yarnell. The ranger had said that they were a little hysterical now. They'd been told not to leave town, and Bill planned to talk to them later.

There seemed to be absolutely nothing out of place in the area around the body. The guy had been very careful. He'd dragged something behind him when he'd returned from the creek—a shovel, maybe—to obscure his own footprints. No scraps of anything left intentionally or accidentally. Any tire prints on the road had likely been obliterated by the cop car and coroner's wagon.

Bill sighed to himself.

Damn it, he thought. *Where's Riley when I need her?*

His longtime partner and best friend was on involuntary leave, recovering from the trauma of their last case. Yes, that had been a nasty one. She needed the time off, and the truth be told, she might not ever come back.

But he really needed her now. She was a lot smarter than Bill, and he didn't mind admitting it. He loved watching her mind at work. He pictured her picking away at this scene, detail by minuscule detail. By now she'd be teasing him for all the painfully glaring clues that had been staring him in the face.

What would Riley see here that Bill didn't?

He felt stumped, and he didn't like the feeling. But there wasn't anything more he could do about it now.

"Okay, guys," Bill called out to the cops. "Take the body away."

The cops laughed and gave each other high-fives.

"Do you think he'll do it again?" Spelbren asked.

"I'm sure of it," Bill said.

"How do you know?"

Bill took a long deep breath.

"Because I've seen his work before."

Chapter 2

"It got worse for her every day," Sam Flores said, bringing up another horrific image on the huge multimedia display looming above the conference table. "Right up to when he finished her off."

Bill had guessed as much, but he hated to be right.

The Bureau had flown the body to the BAU in Quantico, forensics technicians had taken photos, and the lab had started all the tests. Flores, a lab technician with black-rimmed glasses, ran the grisly slide show, and the gigantic screens were a forbidding presence in the BAU conference room.

"How long was she dead before the body was found?" Bill asked.

"Not long," he replied. "Maybe early evening before."

Beside Bill sat Spelbren, who had flown into Quantico with him after they'd left Yarnell. At the head of the table sat Special Agent Brent Meredith, the team chief. Meredith cut a daunting presence with his broad frame, his black, angular features, and his no-nonsense face. Not that Bill was intimidated by him—far from it. He liked to think that they had a lot in common. They were both seasoned veterans, and had both seen it all.

Flores flashed a series of close-ups of the victim's wounds.

"The wounds on the left were inflicted early on," he said. "Those on the right are more recent, some inflicted hours or even minutes before he strangled her with the ribbon. He seems to have gotten progressively more violent during the week or so that he held her captive. Breaking her arm might have been the last thing he did while she was still alive."

"The wounds look like the work of one perpetrator to me," Meredith observed. "Judging from the mounting level of aggression, probably male. What else have you got?"

"From the light stubble on her scalp, we're guessing her head was shaved two days before she was killed," Flores continued. "The wig was stitched together with pieces of other wigs, all cheap. The contact lenses were probably mail order. And one more thing," he said, looking around at the faces, hesitant. "He covered her with Vaseline."

Bill could feel the tension in the room thicken.

"Vaseline?" he asked.

Flores nodded.

"Why?" Spelbren asked.

Flores shrugged.

"That's your job," he replied.

Bill thought about the two tourists he'd interviewed yesterday. They had been no help at all, torn between morbid curiosity and the edge of panic at what they had seen. They were eager to get back home to Arlington and there hadn't been any reason to detain them. They had been interviewed by every officer on hand. And they'd been duly cautioned to say nothing about what they'd seen.

Meredith exhaled and laid both palms on the table.

"Good work, Flores," Meredith said.

Flores looked grateful for the praise—and maybe a bit surprised. Brent Meredith wasn't given to making compliments.

"Now Agent Jeffreys," Meredith turned to him, "brief us on how this relates to your old case."

Bill took a deep breath and leaned back in his chair.

"A little over six months ago," he began, "on December sixteenth, actually—the body of Eileen Rogers was found on a farm near Daggett. I got called in to investigate, along with my partner, Riley Paige. The weather was extremely cold, and the body was frozen solid. It was hard to tell how long it had been left there, and the time of death was never exactly determined. Flores, show them."

Flores turned back to the slide show. The screen split and alongside the images on the screen, a new series of images appeared. The two victims were displayed side by side. Bill gasped. It was amazing. Aside from the frozen flesh of the one body, the corpses were in almost the same condition, the wounds nearly identical. Both women had their eyes stitched open in the same, hideous manner.

Bill sighed, the images bringing it all back. No matter how many years he was on the force, seeing each victim pained him.

"Rogers's body was found seated upright against a tree," Bill continued, his voice more grim. "Not quite as carefully posed as the one at Mosby Park. No contact lenses or Vaseline, but most of the other details are the same. Rogers's hair was chopped short, not shaved, but there was a similar patched-together wig. She was also strangled with a pink ribbon, and a fake rose was found in front of her."

Bill paused for a moment. He hated what he had to say next.

"Paige and I couldn't crack the case."

Spelbren turned to him.

"What was the problem?" he asked.

"What *wasn't* the problem?" Bill countered, unnecessarily defensive. "We couldn't get a single break. We had no witnesses; the victim's family couldn't give us any useful information; Rogers had no enemies, no ex-husband, no angry boyfriend. There wasn't a single good reason for her to be targeted and killed. The case went cold immediately."

Bill fell silent. Dark thoughts flooded his brain.

"Don't," Meredith said in an uncharacteristically gentle tone. "It's not your fault. You couldn't have stopped the new killing."

Bill appreciated the kindness, but he felt guilty as hell. Why couldn't he have cracked it before? Why couldn't Riley? There were very few times in his career he had been so stumped.

At that moment, Meredith's phone buzzed, and the chief took the call.

Almost the first thing he said was, "Shit."

He repeated it several times. Then he said, "You're positive it's her?" He paused. "Was there any contact for ransom?"

He stood from his chair and stepped outside the conference room, leaving the other three men sitting in perplexed silence. After a few minutes, he came back. He looked older.

"Gentlemen, we're now in crisis mode," he announced. "We just got a positive ID on yesterday's victim. Her name was Reba Frye."

Bill gasped as if he'd been punched in the stomach; he could see Spelbren's shock, too. But Flores looked confused.

"Should I know who that is?" Flores asked.

"Maiden name's Newbrough," Meredith explained. "The daughter of State Senator Mitch Newbrough—probably Virginia's next governor."

Flores exhaled.

"I hadn't heard that she'd gone missing," Spelbren said.

"It wasn't officially reported," Meredith said. "Her father's already been contacted. And *of course* he thinks it's political, or personal, or both. Never mind that the same thing happened to another victim six months ago."

Meredith shook his head.

"The Senator's leaning hard on this," he added. "An avalanche of press is about to hit. He'll make sure of it, to keep our feet to the fire."

Bill's heart sank. He hated feeling as though he were over his head. But that's exactly how he felt right now.

A somber silence fell over the room.

11

Finally, Bill cleared his throat.

"We're going to need help," he said.

Meredith turned to him, and Bill met his hardened gaze. Suddenly, Meredith's face knotted up with worry and disapproval. He clearly knew what Bill was thinking.

"She's not ready," Meredith answered, clearly knowing that Bill meant to bring her in.

Bill sighed.

"Sir," he replied, "she knows the case better than anyone. And there's no one smarter."

After another pause, Bill came out and said what he was really thinking.

"I don't think we can do it without her."

Meredith thumped his pencil against a pad of paper a few times, clearly wishing he was anywhere but here.

"It's a mistake," he said. "But if she falls apart, it's *your* mistake." He exhaled again. "Call her."

Chapter 3

The teenage girl who opened the door looked as though she might slam it in Bill's face. Instead, she whirled around and walked away without a word, leaving the door open.

Bill stepped inside.

"Hi, April," he said automatically.

Riley's daughter, a sullen, gangly fourteen-year-old, with her mother's dark hair and hazel eyes, didn't reply. Dressed only in an oversized T-shirt, her hair a mess, April turned a corner and plopped herself down on the couch, dead to everything except her earphones and cell phone.

Bill stood there awkwardly, unsure what to do. When he had called Riley, she had agreed to his visiting, albeit reluctantly. Had she changed her mind?

Bill glanced around as he proceeded into the dim house. He walked through the living room and saw everything was neat and in its place, which was characteristic of Riley. Yet he also noticed the blinds drawn, a film of dust on the furniture—and that wasn't like her at all. On a bookshelf he spotted a row of shiny new paperback thrillers he'd bought for her during her leave, hoping they'd get her mind off her problems. Not a single binding looked cracked.

Bill's sense of apprehension deepened. This was not the Riley he knew. Was Meredith right? Did she need more time on leave? Was he doing the wrong thing by reaching out to her before she was ready?

Bill braced himself and proceeded deeper into the dark house, and as he turned a corner, he found Riley, alone in the kitchen, sitting at the Formica table in her housecoat and slippers, a cup of coffee in front of her. She looked up and he saw a flash of embarrassment, as if she had forgotten he was coming. But she quickly covered it up with a weak smile, and stood.

He stepped forward and hugged her, and she hugged him, weakly, back. In her slippers, she was a little shorter than he was. She had become very thin, too thin, and his concern deepened.

He sat down across the table from her and studied her. Her hair was clean, but it wasn't combed, either, and it looked as if she had been wearing those slippers for days. Her face looked gaunt, too pale, and much, much older since he'd last seen her five weeks ago. She looked as if she had been through hell. She had. He tried not to think about what the last killer had done to her.

She averted her gaze, and they both sat there in the thick silence. Bill had been so sure he'd know just what to say to cheer her up, to rouse her; yet as he sat there, he felt consumed by her sadness, and he lost all his words. He wanted to see her look sturdier, like her old self.

He quickly hid the envelope with the files about the new murder case on the floor beside his chair. He wasn't sure now if he should even show her. He was beginning to feel more certain he'd made a mistake coming here. Clearly, she needed more time. In fact, seeing her here like this, he was, for the first time, unsure if his longtime partner would ever come back.

"Coffee?" she asked. He could sense her unease.

He shook his head. She was clearly fragile. When he'd visited her in the hospital and even after she'd come home, he'd been frightened for her. He had wondered if she would ever make her way back from the pain and terror she'd endured, from the depths of her longtime darkness. It was so unlike her; she'd seemed invincible with every other case. Something about this last case, this last killer, was different. Bill could understand: the man had been the most twisted psychopath he had ever encountered—and that was saying a lot.

As he studied her, something else occurred to him. She actually looked her age. She was forty years old, the same age he was, but back when she was working, animated and engaged, she'd always seemed several years younger. Gray was starting to show in her dark hair. Well, his own hair was turning too.

Riley called out to her daughter, "April!"

No reply. Riley called her name several times, louder each time, until she finally answered.

"What?" April answered from the living room, sounding thoroughly annoyed.

"What time's your class today?"

"You know that."

"Just tell me, okay?"

"Eight-thirty."

Riley frowned and looked upset herself. She looked up at Bill.

"She flunked English. Cut too many classes. I'm trying to help dig her out of it."

Bill shook his head, understanding all too well. The agency life took too much of a toll on all of them, and their families were the biggest casualty.

"I'm sorry," he said.

Riley shrugged.

"She's fourteen. She hates me."

"That's not good."

"I hated everybody when I was fourteen," she replied. "Didn't you?"

Bill didn't reply. It was hard to imagine Riley ever hating everybody.

"Wait'll your boys get that age," Riley said. "How old are they now? I forget."

"Eight and ten," Bill replied, then smiled. "The way things are going with Maggie, I don't know if I'll even be in their lives when they get to be April's age."

Riley tilted her head and looked at him with concern. He'd missed that caring look.

"That bad, huh?" she said.

He looked away, not wanting to think about it.

The two of them fell silent for a moment.

"What's that you're hiding on the floor?" she asked.

Bill glanced down then back up and smiled; even in her state, she never missed a thing.

"I'm not hiding anything," Bill said, picking up the envelope and setting it on the table. "Just something I'd like to talk over with you."

Riley smiled broadly. It was obvious that she knew perfectly well what he was really here for.

"Show me," she said, then added, glancing nervously over at April, "Come on, let's go out back. I don't want her to see it."

Riley took off her slippers and walked into the backyard barefoot ahead of Bill. They sat at a weathered wooden picnic table that had been there since well before Riley moved here, and Bill gazed around the small yard with its single tree. There were woods on all sides. It made him forget he was even near a city.

Too isolated, he thought.

He'd never felt that this place was right for Riley. The little ranch-style house was fifteen miles out of town, rundown, and very ordinary. It was just off a secondary road, with nothing else but forests and pastures in sight. Not that he'd ever thought suburban life was right for her either. He had a hard time picturing her doing the cocktail party circuit. She could still, at least, drive into Fredericksburg and take the Amtrak to Quantico when she came back to work. When she still *could* work.

"Show me what you've got," she said.

15

He spread the reports and photographs across the table.

"Remember the Daggett case?" he asked. "You were right. The killer wasn't through."

He saw her eyes widen as she pored over the pictures. A long silence fell as she studied the files intensely, and he wondered if this might be what she needed to come back—or if it would set her back.

"So what do you think?" he finally asked.

Another silence. She still did not look up from the file.

Finally, she looked up, and when she did, he was shocked to see tears well up in her eyes. He had never seen her cry before, not even on the worst cases, up close to a corpse. This was definitely not the Riley he knew. That killer had done something to her, more than he knew.

She choked back a sob.

"I'm scared, Bill," she said. "I'm so scared. All the time. Of everything."

Bill felt his heart drop seeing her like this. He wondered where the old Riley had gone, the one person he could always rely on to be tougher than him, the rock he could always turn to in times of trouble. He missed her more than he could say.

"He's *dead*, Riley," he said, in the most confident tone he could muster. "He can't hurt you anymore."

She shook her head.

"You don't know that."

"Sure I do," he answered. "They found his body after the explosion."

"They couldn't identify it," she said.

"You know it was him."

Her face fell forward and she covered it with one hand as she wept. He held her other hand across the table.

"This is a new case," he said. "It's got nothing to do with what happened to you."

She shook her head.

"It doesn't matter."

Slowly, as she wept, she reached up and handed him the file, looking away.

"I'm sorry," she said, looking down, holding it out with a trembling hand. "I think you should go," she added.

Bill, shocked, saddened, reached out and took the file back. Never in a million years would he have expected this outcome.

Bill sat there for a moment, struggling against his own tears.

16

Finally, he gently patted her hand, got up from the table, and made his way back through the house. April was still sitting in the living room, her eyes closed, nodding her head to her music.

*

Riley sat crying alone at the picnic table after Bill left.

I thought I was okay, she thought.

She'd really wanted to be okay, for Bill. And she'd thought she could actually carry it off. Sitting in the kitchen talking about trivialities had been all right. Then they had gone outside and when she had seen the file, she'd thought she'd be okay, too. Better than okay, really. She was getting caught up in it. Her old lust for the job was rekindled, she wanted to get back in the field. She was compartmentalizing, of course, thinking of those nearly identical murders as a puzzle to solve, almost in the abstract, an intellectual game. That too was fine. Her therapist had told her she would have to do that if she ever hoped to go back to work.

But then for some reason, the intellectual puzzle became what it really and truly was—a monstrous human tragedy in which two innocent women had died in the throes of immeasurable pain and terror. And she'd suddenly wondered: *Was it as bad for them as it was for me?*

Her body was now flooded with panic and fear. And embarrassment, shame. Bill was her partner and her best friend. She owed him so much. He'd stood by her during the last weeks when nobody else would. She couldn't have survived her time in the hospital without him. The last thing she wanted was for him to see her reduced to a state of helplessness.

She heard April yell from the back screen door.

"Mom, we gotta eat now or I'll be late."

She felt an urge to yell back, *"Fix your own breakfast!"*

But she didn't. She was long since exhausted from her battles with April. She'd given up fighting.

She got up from the table and walked back to the kitchen. She pulled a paper towel off the roll and used it to wipe her tears and blow her nose, then braced herself to cook. She tried to recall her therapist's words: *Even routine tasks will take a lot of conscious effort, at least for a while.* She had to settle for doing things one baby step at a time.

First came taking things out of the refrigerator—the carton of eggs, the package of bacon, the butter dish, the jar of jam, because

17

April liked jam even if she didn't. And so it went until she laid six strips of bacon in a pan on the stovetop, and she turned on the gas range under the pan.

She staggered backward at the sight of the yellow-blue flame. She shut her eyes, and it all came flooding back to her.

Riley lay in a tight crawlspace, under a house, in a little makeshift cage. The propane torch was the only light she ever saw. The rest of the time was spent in complete darkness. The floor of the crawlspace was dirt. The floorboards above her were so low that she could barely even crouch.

The darkness was total, even when he opened a small door and crept into the crawlspace with her. She couldn't see him, but she could hear him breathing and grunting. He'd unlock the cage and snap it open and climb inside.

And then he'd light that torch. She could see his cruel and ugly face by its light. He'd taunt her with a plate of wretched food. If she reached for it, he'd thrust the flame at her. She couldn't eat without getting burned ...

She opened her eyes. The images were less vivid with her eyes open, but she couldn't shake the stream of memories. She continued to make breakfast robotically, her whole body surging with adrenaline. She was just setting the table when her daughter's voice yelled out again.

"Mom, how long's it going to be?"

She jumped, and her plate slipped out of her hand and fell to the floor and shattered.

"What happened?" April yelled, appearing beside her.

"Nothing," Riley said.

She cleaned up the mess, and as she and April sat eating together, the silent hostility was palpable as usual. Riley wanted to end the cycle, to break through to April, to say, *April, it's me, your mom, and I love you*. But she had tried so many times, and it only made it worse. Her daughter hated her, and she couldn't understand why—or how to end it.

"What are you going to do today?" she asked April.

"What do you think?" April snapped. "Go to class."

"I mean after that," Riley said, keeping her voice calm, compassionate. "I'm your mother. I want to know. It's normal."

"Nothing about our lives is normal."

They ate silently for a few moments.

"You never tell me anything," Riley said.

"Neither do you."

That stopped any hope for conversation once and for all.

That's fair, Riley thought bitterly. It was truer than April even knew. Riley had never told her about her job, her cases; she had never told her about her captivity, or her time in the hospital, or why she was "on vacation" now. All April knew was that she'd had to live with her father during much of that time, and she hated him even more than she hated Riley. But as much as she wanted to tell her, Riley thought it best that April have no idea what her mother had been through.

Riley got dressed and drove April to school, and they didn't say a word to each other during the drive. When she let April out of the car, she called after her, "I'll see you at ten."

April gave her a careless wave as she walked away.

Riley drove to a nearby coffee shop. It had become a routine for her. It was hard for her to spend any time in a public place, and she knew that was exactly why she had to do it. The coffee shop was small and never busy, even in the mornings like this, so she found it relatively unthreatening.

As she sat there, sipping on a cappuccino, she remembered again Bill's entreaty. It had been six weeks, damn it. This had to change. *She* had to change. She didn't know how she was going to do that.

But an idea was forming. She knew exactly what she needed to do first.

Chapter 4

The white flame of the propane torch waved in front of Riley. She had to dodge back and forth to escape being burned. The brightness blinded her to everything else and she couldn't even see her captor's face anymore. As the torch swirled about, it seemed to leave lingering traces hanging in the air.

"Stop it!" she yelled. "Stop it!"

Her voice was raw and hoarse from shouting. She wondered why she was wasting her breath. She knew he wouldn't stop tormenting her until she was dead.

Just then, he raised an air horn and blew it in her ear.

A car horn blared. Riley snapped back to the present, and looked out to see the light at the intersection had just turned green. A line of drivers waited behind her vehicle, and she stepped on the gas.

Riley, palms sweating, forced the memory away and reminded herself of where she was. She was going to visit Marie Sayles, the only other survivor of her near-killer's unspeakable sadism. She berated herself for letting the flashback overwhelm her. She had managed to keep her mind on her driving for an hour and a half now, and she had thought she was doing fine.

Riley drove into Georgetown, passing upscale Victorian homes, and parked at the address Marie had given her over the phone—a red brick townhouse with a handsome bay window. She sat in the car for a moment, debating whether to go in, and trying to summon the courage.

Finally, she exited. As she climbed the steps, she was pleased to see Marie meet her at the door. Somberly but elegantly dressed, Marie smiled somewhat wanly. Her face looked tired and drawn. From the circles under her eyes, Riley was pretty sure that she'd been crying. That came as no surprise. She and Marie had seen each other a lot during their weeks of video chats, and there was little they could hide from one another.

When they hugged, Riley was immediately aware that Marie was not as tall and robust as she'd expected her to be. Even in heels Marie was shorter than Riley, her frame small and delicate. That surprised Riley. She and Marie had talked a lot, but this was the first time they had met in person. Marie's slightness made her seem all the more courageous to have survived what she'd been through.

Riley took in her surroundings as she and Marie walked for the dining room. The place was immaculately clean and tastefully furnished. It would normally be a cheery home for a successful single woman. But Marie kept all the curtains closed and the lights low. The atmosphere was strangely oppressive. Riley didn't want to admit it, but it made her think of her own home.

Marie had a light lunch ready on the dining room table, and she and Riley sat down to eat. They sat there in an awkward silence, Riley sweating but unsure why. Seeing Marie was brining it all back.

"So . . . how did it feel?" Marie asked tentatively. "Coming out into the world?"

Riley smiled. Marie knew better than anyone what today's drive took.

"Pretty well," Riley said. "Actually, *quite* well. I only had one bad moment, really."

Marie nodded, clearly understanding.

"Well, you did it," Marie said. "And that was brave."

Brave, Riley thought. That was not how she would have described herself. Once, maybe, when she was an active agent. Would she ever describe herself that way again?

"How about you?" Riley asked. "How much do you get out?"

Marie fell silent.

"You don't leave the house at all, do you?" Riley asked.

Marie shook her head.

Riley reached forward and held her wrist in a grip of compassion.

"Marie, you've got to try," she urged. "If you let yourself stay stuck inside like this, it's like he's still holding you prisoner."

A choked sob forced its way out of Marie's throat.

"I'm sorry," Riley said.

"That's all right. You're right."

Riley watched Marie as they both ate for a moment and a long silence descended. She wanted to think that Marie was doing well, but she had to admit that she seemed alarmingly frail to her. It made her fear for herself, too. Did she look that bad, too?

Riley wondered silently whether it was good for Marie to be living alone. Might she be better with a husband or boyfriend? she wondered. Then she wondered the same thing about herself. Yet she knew the answer for both of them was probably not. Neither of them was in any emotional frame of mind for a sustained relationship. It would just be a crutch.

"Did I ever thank you?" Marie asked after a while, breaking the silence.

Riley smiled. She knew perfectly well that Marie meant for having rescued her.

"Lots of times," Riley said. "And you don't need to. Really."

Marie poked at her food with a fork.

"Did I ever say I'm sorry?"

Riley was surprised. "Sorry? What for?"

Marie spoke with difficulty.

"If you hadn't gotten me out of there, you wouldn't have gotten caught."

Riley squeezed Marie's hand gently.

"Marie, I was just doing my job. You can't go feeling guilty about something that wasn't your fault. You've got too much to deal with as it is."

Marie nodded, acknowledging her.

"Just getting out of bed every day is a challenge," she admitted. "I guess you noticed how dark I keep everything. Any bright light reminds me of that torch of his. I can't even watch television, or listen to music. I'm scared that someone might sneak up on me and I'll not hear it. Any noise at all puts me in a panic."

Marie began to weep quietly.

I'll never look at the world in the same way. Never. There's evil out there, all around us. I had no idea. People are capable of such horrible things. I don't know how I'll ever trust people again."

As Marie cried, Riley wanted to reassure her, to tell her she was wrong. But a part of Riley was not so sure she was.

Finally, Marie looked at her.

"Why did you come here today?" she asked, point-blank.

Riley was caught off guard by Marie's directness—and by the fact that she didn't really know herself.

"I don't know," she said. "I just wanted to visit you. See how you are doing."

"There's something else," Marie said, narrowing her eyes with an uncanny perception.

Maybe she was right, Riley thought. Riley thought of Bill's visit, and she realized she had, indeed, come here because of the new case. What was it she wanted from Marie? Advice? Permission? Encouragement? Reassurance? A part of her wanted Marie to tell her she was crazy, so she could rest easy and forget about Bill. But maybe another part wanted Marie to urge her to do it.

Finally, Riley sighed.

"There's a new case," she said. "Well, not a *new* case. But an old case that never went away."

Marie's expression grew taut and severe.

Riley gulped.

"And you've come to ask if you should do it?" Marie asked.

Riley shrugged. But she also looked up and searched Marie's eyes for reassurance, encouragement. And in that moment she realized that was exactly what she had come here hoping to find.

But to her disappointment, Marie lowered her eyes and slowly shook her head. Riley kept waiting for an answer, but instead there followed an endless silence. Riley sensed that some special fear was working its way inside Marie.

In the silence, Riley looked around the apartment, and her eyes fell upon Marie's landline phone. She was surprised to see it was disconnected from the wall.

"What's the matter with your phone?" Riley asked.

Marie looked positively stricken, and Riley realized she had hit a real nerve.

"He keeps calling me," Marie said, in an almost inaudible whisper.

"Who?"

"Peterson."

Riley's heart jumped up into her throat.

"Peterson is dead," Riley replied, her voice shaky. "I torched the place. They found his body."

Marie shook her head.

"It could have been anyone they found. It wasn't him."

Riley felt a flush of panic. Her own worst fears were being brought back.

"Everybody says it was," Riley said.

"And you really believe that?"

Riley didn't know what to say. Now was no time to confide her own fears. After all, Marie was probably being delusional. But how could Riley convince her of something that she didn't altogether believe herself?

"He keeps calling," Marie said again. "He calls and breathes and hangs up. I know it's him. He's alive. He's still stalking me."

Riley felt a cold, creeping dread.

"It's probably just an obscene phone caller," she said, pretending to be calm. "But I can get the Bureau to check it out anyway. I can get them to send out a surveillance car if you're scared. They'll trace the calls."

"No!" Marie said sharply. "No!"

Riley stared back, puzzled.

"Why not?" she asked.

"I don't want to make him angry," Marie said in a pathetic whimper.

Riley, overwhelmed, feeling a panic attack coming on, suddenly realized it had been a terrible idea to come here. If anything, she felt worse. She knew she could not sit in this oppressive dining room a moment longer.

"I've got to go," Riley said, talking. "I'm so sorry. My daughter's waiting."

Marie suddenly grabbed Riley's wrist with surprising strength, digging her nails into her skin.

She stared back, her icy blue eyes holding such intensity that it terrified Riley. That haunting look seared into her soul.

"Take the case," Marie urged.

Riley could see in her eyes that Marie was confusing the new case and Peterson, blurring them together into one.

"Find that son of a bitch," she added. "And kill him for me."

Chapter 5

The man kept a short but discreet distance from the woman, glancing her way only fleetingly. He placed a few token items into his handbasket so that he'd look like just another shopper. He congratulated himself on how inconspicuous he was able to make himself. No one would guess his true power.

But then again, he'd never been the kind of man who attracted much attention. As a child, he'd felt practically invisible. Now, at long last, he was able to turn his own innocuousness to his advantage.

Just a few moments ago, he had stood right next to her, scarcely more than two feet away. Rapt in choosing her shampoo, she hadn't noticed him at all.

He knew plenty about her, though. He knew her name was Cindy; that her husband owned an art gallery; that she worked in a free medical clinic. Today was one of her days off. Right now she was on her cell phone talking with somebody—her sister, it sounded like. She was laughing at something the person was saying to her. He burned red with anger, wondering if she were laughing at him, just as all the girls used to. His fury increased.

Cindy wore shorts, a tank top, and expensive-looking running shoes. He'd watched her from his car, jogging, and waited until she'd finished her run and came into the grocery store. He knew her routine for a non-working day like this. She'd take the items home and put them away, take a shower, then drive to meet her husband for lunch.

Her good figure owed a lot to physical exercise. She was no more than thirty years old, but the skin around her thighs wasn't tight anymore. She'd probably lost a lot of weight at one time or another, perhaps pretty recently. She was undoubtedly proud of that.

Suddenly, the woman headed toward the nearest cash register. The man was taken by surprise. She had finished shopping earlier than usual. He rushed to get in line behind her, almost pushing another customer aside to do so. He silently berated himself for that.

As the cashier rang up the woman's items, he inched up and stood extremely close to her—close enough to smell her body, now sweaty and pungent after her vigorous jog. It was a smell that he expected to become much, much better acquainted with very soon. But the smell would then be mixed with yet another odor—one that fascinated him because of its strangeness and mystery.

The smell of pain and terror.

For a moment, the lurker felt exhilarated, even pleasantly light-headed, with eager anticipation.

After paying for her groceries, she pushed her cart out through the automatic glass doors and out into the parking lot.

He felt no hurry now about paying for his own handful of items. He didn't need to follow her home. He'd been there already—had even been inside her house. He had even handled her clothing. He'd take up his vigil again when she got off work.

It won't be long now, he thought. *Not long at all.*

*

After Cindy MacKinnon got into her car, she sat there for a moment, feeling shaken and not knowing why. She remembered the weird feeling she'd just had back in the supermarket. It was an uncanny, irrational feeling of being watched. But it was more than that. It took her a few moments to put her finger on it.

Finally, she realized it was a feeling that someone had meant her harm.

She shivered deeply. During the last few days, that feeling had been coming and going. She chided herself, sure that it was completely groundless.

She shook her head, ridding herself of any vestiges of that feeling. As she started her car, she forced herself to think of something else, and she smiled at her cell phone conversation with her sister, Becky. Later this afternoon, Cindy would help her throw a big birthday party her three-year-old daughter, complete with cake and balloons.

It would be a beautiful day, she thought.

Chapter 6

Riley sat in the SUV beside Bill as he shifted gears, pushing the Bureau's four-wheel-drive vehicle higher into the hills, and she wiped her palms on her pants legs. She didn't know what to make of the sweatiness, and she didn't know what to make of being here. After six weeks off the job, she felt out of touch with what her body was telling her. Being back felt surreal.

Riley was disturbed by the awkward tension. She and Bill had barely spoken during their hour-plus drive. Their old camaraderie, their playfulness, their uncanny rapport—none of that was there now. Riley felt pretty sure she knew why Bill was being so aloof. It wasn't out of rudeness—it was out of worry. He, too, seemed to have doubts about whether she should be back on the job.

They drove toward Mosby State Park, where Bill had told her he had seen the most recent murder victim. As they went, Riley took in the geography all around her and slowly, her old sense of professionalism kicked in. She knew she had to snap out of it.

Find that son of a bitch and kill him for me.

Marie's words haunted her, drove her on, made her choice simple.

But nothing seemed that simple now. For one thing, she couldn't help worrying about April. Sending her to stay at her father's house wasn't ideal for anybody involved. But today was Saturday and Riley didn't want to wait until Monday to see the crime scene.

The deep silence began to add to her anxiety, and she desperately felt the need to talk. Wracking her brain for something to say, finally, she said:

"So are you going to tell me what's going on between you and Maggie?"

Bill turned to her, a surprised look on his face, and she couldn't tell if it was due to her breaking the silence, or her blunt question. Whichever it was, she immediately regretted it. Her bluntness, many people told her, could be off-putting. She never meant to be blunt—she just had no time to waste.

Bill exhaled.

"She thinks I'm having an affair."

Riley felt a jolt of surprise.

"What?"

"With my job," Bill said, laughing a bit sourly. "She thinks I'm

27

having an affair with my job. She thinks I love *all this* more than I love her. I keep telling her she's being silly. Anyway, I can't exactly end it—not my job, anyway."

Riley shook her head.

"Sounds just like Ryan. He used to get jealous as hell when we were still together."

She stopped short of telling Bill the whole truth. Her ex-husband hadn't been jealous of Riley's job. He'd been jealous of Bill. She'd often wondered if Ryan might have had some reason. Despite today's awkwardness, she felt awfully good just being close to Bill. Was that feeling solely professional?

"I hope this isn't a wasted trip," Bill said. "The crime scene's been all cleaned up, you know."

"I know. I just want to see the place for myself. Pictures and reports don't cut it for me."

Riley was starting to feel a bit woozy now. She was pretty sure it was from the altitude, as they climbed still higher. Anticipation had something to do with it, too. Her palms were still sweating.

"How much farther?" she asked, as she watched the woods get thicker, the terrain more remote.

"Not far."

A couple of minutes later, Bill turned off the paved road onto a pair of rough tire tracks. The vehicle bounced along jarringly, then came to a stop about a quarter of a mile into the dense woods.

He switched off the ignition, then turned toward Riley and looked at her with concern.

"You sure you want to do this?" he asked.

She knew exactly what was worrying him. He was afraid she'd flash back to her traumatic captivity. Never mind that this was a different case altogether, and a different killer.

She nodded.

"I'm sure," she said, not at all convinced that she was telling the truth.

She got out of the car and followed Bill off the road onto a brushy, narrow path through the woods. She heard the gurgling of a nearby stream. As the vegetation grew thicker, she had to push her way past low-hanging branches, and sticky little burrs started bunching up on her pants legs. She was annoyed at the thought of having to pick them off.

At last she and Bill emerged onto the creek bank. Riley was immediately struck by what a lovely spot it was. The afternoon sunlight poured in through the leaves, mottling the rippling water with kaleidoscopic light. The steady gurgling of the stream was soothing. It was strange to think of this as a gruesome crime scene.

"She was found right here," Bill said, leading her to a broad, level boulder.

When they got there, Riley stood and looked all around and breathed deeply. Yes, she had been right to come here. She was starting to feel that.

"The pictures?" Riley asked.

She crouched beside Bill on the boulder, and they started leafing through a folder full of photographs taken shortly after Reba Frye's body had been found. Another folder was stuffed with reports and photos of the murder she and Bill had investigated six months ago—the one that they had failed to solve.

Those pictures brought back vivid memories of the first killing. It transported her right back to that farm country near Daggett. She remembered how Rogers had been staged in a similar manner against a tree.

"A lot like our older case," Riley observed. "Both women in their thirties, both with little kids. That seems to be part of his MO. He's got it in for mothers. We need to check with parenting groups, find out if there were any connections between the two women, or between their kids."

"I'll get somebody on it," Bill said. He was taking notes now.

Riley continued poring through the reports and photos, comparing them to the actual scene.

"Same method of strangulation, with a pink ribbon," she observed. "Another wig, and the same type of artificial rose in front of the body."

Riley held up two photographs side by side.

"Eyes stitched open, too," she said. "If I remember right, the technicians found that Rogers's eyes had been stitched postmortem. Was it the same with Frye?"

"Yeah. I guess he wanted them to watch him even after they were dead."

Riley felt a sudden tingle up her spine. She'd almost forgotten that feeling. She got it whenever something about a case was just about to click and make sense. She didn't know whether to feel encouraged or terrified.

"No," she said. "That's not it. He didn't care whether the women saw him."

"Then why did he do it?"

Riley didn't reply. Ideas were starting to rush into her brain.

She was exhilarated. But she wasn't yet ready to put any of it into words—not even to herself.

She laid out pairs of photographs on the boulder, pointing out details to Bill.

"They're *not* exactly the same," she said. "The body wasn't as carefully staged back in Daggett. He'd tried to move that corpse when it was already stiff. My guess is this time he brought her here before rigor mortis set in. Otherwise he couldn't have posed her so …"

She suppressed the urge to finish the sentence with "nicely." Then she realized, that was exactly the kind of word she'd have used when she was on the job before her capture and torture. Yes, she was getting back into the spirit of things, and she felt the same old dark obsession growing inside her. Pretty soon there'd be no turning back.

But was that a good thing or a bad thing?

"What's with Frye's eyes?" she asked, pointing to a photo. "That blue doesn't look real."

"Contacts," Bill answered.

The tingle in Riley's spine grew stronger. Eileen Rogers's corpse hadn't had contact lenses. It was an important difference.

"And the shine on her skin?" she asked.

"Vaseline," Bill said.

Another important difference. She felt her ideas snapping into place with breathtaking speed.

"What has forensics found out about the wig?" she asked Bill.

"Nothing yet, except that it was pieced together out of pieces of cheap wigs."

Riley's excitement grew. For the last murder, the killer had used a simple, whole wig, not something patched together. Like the rose, it had been so cheap that forensics couldn't trace it. Riley felt parts of the puzzle coming together—not the whole puzzle, but a big chunk of it.

"What does forensics plan to do about this wig?" she asked.

"The same as last time—run a search of its fibers, try to track it down through hairpiece outlets."

Startled by the fierce certainty in her own voice, Riley said: "They're wasting their time."

Bill looked at her, clearly caught off guard.

"Why?"

She felt a familiar impatience with Bill, one she felt when she always found herself thinking a step or two ahead of him.

30

"Look at the picture he's trying to show us. Blue contacts to make the eyes look like they're not real. Eyelids stitched so the eyes stay wide open. The body propped up, legs splayed out freakishly. Vaseline to make the skin look like plastic. A wig pieced together out of pieces of little wigs—not human wigs, *doll's* wigs. He wanted both victims to look like *dolls*—like naked *dolls* on display."

"Jesus," Bill said, feverishly taking notes. "Why didn't we see this last time, back in Daggett?"

The answer seemed so obvious to Riley that she stifled an impatient groan.

"He wasn't good enough at it yet," she said. "He was still figuring out how to send the message. He's learning as he goes."

Bill looked up from his notepad and shook his head admiringly.

"Damn, I've missed you."

As much as she appreciated the compliment, Riley knew that an even bigger realization was on its way. And she knew from years of experience that there was no forcing it. She simply had to relax and let it come to her unbidden. She crouched on the boulder silently, waiting for it happen. As she waited, she picked idly at the burrs on her pants legs.

What a damned nuisance, she thought.

Suddenly her eyes fell on the stone surface under her feet. Other little burrs, some of them whole, others broken into fragments, were lying amid the burrs she was plucking off now.

"Bill," she said, her voice quavering with excitement, "were these little burrs here when you found the body?"

Bill shrugged. "I don't know."

Her hands shaking and sweating more than ever, she grabbed a bunch of pictures and rifled through them until she found a front view of the corpse. There, between her splayed legs right around the rose, was a group of little smudges. Those were the burrs—the very burrs she had just found. But nobody had thought they were important. Nobody had bothered to take a sharper, closer picture of them. And nobody had even bothered to sweep them away when the crime scene was cleaned up.

Riley closed her eyes, bringing her imagination fully into play. She felt lightheaded, even dizzy. It was a sensation that she knew all too well—a feeling of falling into an abyss, into a terrible black void, into the killer's evil mind. She was stepping into his shoes, into his experience. It was a dangerous and terrifying place to be. But it was where she belonged, at least right now. She embraced it.

31

She felt the killer's confidence as he lugged the body down the path to the stream, perfectly sure that he wasn't going to get caught, in no hurry at all. He might well have been humming or whistling. She felt his patience, his craft and skill, as he posed the corpse on the boulder.

And she could see the grisly tableau through his eyes. She felt his deep satisfaction at a job well done—the same warm feeling of fulfillment that she always felt when she'd solved a case. He had crouched on this rock, pausing for a moment—or for as long as he liked—to admire his own handiwork.

And as he did, he had plucked the burrs off his pants legs. He took his time about it. He didn't bother to wait until he'd gotten away free and clear. And she could almost hear him saying aloud her own exact words.

"What a damn nuisance."

Yes, he'd even taken the time to pluck off the burrs.

Riley gasped, and her eyes snapped open. Fingering the burr in her own hand, she noted how sticky it was, and that its prickles were sharp enough to draw blood.

"Gather these burrs," she ordered. "We might just get a bit of DNA."

Bill's eyes widened, and he immediately extracted a ziplock bag and tweezers. As he worked, her mind ran in overdrive, not done yet.

"We've been wrong all along," she said. "This isn't his second murder. It's his third."

Bill stopped and looked up, clearly stunned.

"How do you know?" Bill asked.

Riley's whole body tightened as she tried to bring her trembling under control.

"He's gotten too good. His apprenticeship is over. He's a pro now. And he's just hitting his stride. He *loves* his work. No, this is his third time, at least."

Riley's throat tightened and she swallowed hard.

"And there won't be much time now until the next one."

Chapter 7

Bill found himself in a sea of blue eyes, none of them real. He didn't usually have nightmares about his cases, and he wasn't having one now—but it sure felt like one. Here in the middle of the doll store, little blue eyes were simply everywhere, all of them wide open and sparkling and alert.

The dolls' little ruby-red lips, most of them smiling, were troubling also. So was all the painstakingly combed artificial hair, so stiff and immobile. Taking in all these details, Bill wondered now how he could have possibly missed the killer's intention—to make his victims look as doll-like as possible. It had taken Riley to make that connection.

Thank God she's back, he thought.

Still, Bill couldn't help but worry about her. He had been dazzled by her brilliant work back at Mosby Park. But afterward, when he drove her home, she'd seemed exhausted and demoralized. She'd barely said a word to him during the whole drive. Maybe it had been too much for her.

Even so, Bill wished that Riley was here right now. She'd decided it would be best for them to split up, to cover more ground more quickly. He couldn't disagree with that. She'd asked him to cover the doll stores in the area, while she would revisit the scene of the crime they'd covered six months ago.

Bill looked around and, feeling in way over his head, wondered what Riley would make of this doll store. It was the most elegant of the ones he'd visited today. Here on the edge of the Capital Beltway, the store probably got a lot of classy shoppers from wealthy Northern Virginia counties.

He walked around and browsed. A little girl doll caught his eye. With its upturned smile and pale skin, it especially reminded him of the latest victim. Although it was fully clothed in a pink dress with lots of lace on the collar, cuffs, and hem, it was also sitting in a disturbingly similar position.

Suddenly, Bill heard a voice to his right.

"I think you're looking in the wrong section."

Bill turned and found himself facing a stout little woman with a warm smile. Something about her immediately told him that she was in charge here.

"Why do you say that?" Bill asked.

The woman chuckled.

"Because you don't have daughters. I can tell a man who

33

doesn't have a daughter from a mile off. Don't ask me how, it's just some kind of instinct, I guess."

Bill was stunned by her insight, and deeply impressed.

She offered Bill her hand.

"Ruth Behnke," she said.

Bill shook her hand.

"Bill Jeffreys. I take it you own this store."

She chuckled again.

"I see you've got some kind of instinct, too," she said. "I'm pleased to meet you. But you *do* have sons, don't you? Three of them, I'd guess."

Bill smiled. Her instincts were pretty sharp, all right. Bill figured that she and Riley would enjoy each other's company.

"Two," he replied. "But pretty damn close."

She chuckled.

"How old?" she asked.

"Eight and ten."

She looked around the place.

"I don't know that I've got much for them here. Oh, actually, I've got a few rather quaint toy soldiers in the next aisle. But that's not the kind of things boys like anymore, is it? It's all video games these days. And violent ones at that."

"I'm afraid so."

She squinted at him appraisingly.

"You're not here to buy a doll, are you?" she asked.

Bill smiled and shook his head.

"You're good," he replied.

"Are you a cop, maybe?" she asked.

Bill laughed quietly and took out his badge.

"Not quite, but a good guess."

"Oh, my!" she said, with concern. "What does the FBI want with my little place? Am I on some kind of list?"

"In a way," Bill said. "But it's nothing to worry about. Your shop came up on our search of stores in this area that sell antique and collectible dolls."

In fact, Bill didn't know exactly *what* he was looking for. Riley had suggested that he check out a handful of these places, assuming the killer might have frequented them—or at least had visited them on some occasion. What she was expecting, he didn't know. Was she expecting the killer himself to be there? Or that one of the employees had met the killer?

Doubtful that they had. Even if they had, it was doubtful that they would have recognized him as a killer. Probably all the men that came in here, if any, were creepy.

More likely Riley was trying to get him to gain more insights into the killer's mind, his way of looking at the world. If so, Bill figured she'd wind up disappointed. He simply did not have the mind that she did, or the talent to easily walk into killers' minds.

It seemed to him as if she were really fishing. There were dozens of doll stores within the radius they had been searching. Better, he thought, to let forensics just continue to track down the doll makers. Though, thus far, that had turned up nothing.

"I'd ask what kind of case this is," Ruth said, "but I probably shouldn't."

"No," Bill said, "you probably shouldn't."

Not that the case was a secret anymore—not after Senator Newbrough's people had put out a press release about it. The media was now saturated with the news. As usual, the Bureau was reeling under an assault of erroneous phone tips, and the internet was abuzz with bizarre theories. The whole thing had become a pain.

But why tell the woman about it? She seemed so nice, and her store so wholesome and innocent, that Bill didn't want to upset her with something so grim and shocking as a serial murderer obsessed with dolls.

Still, there was one thing he wanted to know.

"Tell me something," Bill said. "How many sales do you make to adults—I mean grown-ups without kids?"

"Oh, those are most of my sales, by far. To collectors."

Bill was intrigued. He'd never have guessed that.

"Why do you think that is?" he asked.

The woman smiled an odd, distant smile, and spoke in a gentle tone.

"Because people die, Bill Jeffreys."

Now Bill was truly startled.

"Pardon?" he said.

"As we get older, we *lose* people. Our friends and loved ones die. We grieve. Dolls stop time for us. They make us forget our grief. They comfort and console us. Look around you. I've got dolls that are most of a century old, and some that are almost new. With some of them, at least, you probably can't tell the difference. They're ageless."

Bill looked around, feeling creeped out at all the century-old eyes staring back at him, wondering how many people these dolls had outlived. He wondered what they had witnessed—the love, the anger, the hate, the sadness, the violence. And yet still they stared back with that same blank expression. They didn't make sense to him.

People *should* age, he thought. They should get old and lined and gray, as he had, given all the darkness and horror there was in the world. Given all that he had seen, it would be a sin, he thought, if he still looked the same. The murder scenes had sunk into him like a living thing, had made him not want to stay young anymore.

"They're also—not alive," Bill finally said.

Her smile turned bittersweet, almost pitying.

"Is that really true, Bill? Most of my customers don't think so. I'm not sure I think so, either."

An odd silence fell. The woman broke it with a chuckle. She offered Bill a colorful little brochure with pictures of dolls all over it.

"As it happens, I'm heading to an upcoming convention in D.C. You might want to go, too. Maybe it will give you some ideas for whatever it is you're searching for."

Bill thanked her and left the store, grateful for the tip about the convention. He hoped that Riley would go with him. Bill remembered that she was supposed to interview Senator Newbrough and his wife this afternoon. It was an important appointment—not just because the senator might have good information, but for diplomatic reasons. Newbrough really was making things hot for the Bureau. Riley was just the agent to convince him that they were doing all that they could.

But will she really show up? Bill wondered.

It seemed truly bizarre that he couldn't be sure. Until six months ago, Riley was the one dependable thing in his life. He had always trusted her with his life. But her obvious distress worried him.

More than that, he missed her. Daunted as he sometimes was by her quicksilver mind, he needed her on a job like this. During the last six weeks, he'd also come to realize that he needed her friendship.

Or, deep down, was it more than that?

Chapter 8

Riley drove down the two-lane highway, sipping on her energy drink. It was a sunny, warm morning, the car windows were down, and the warm smell of freshly baled hay filled the air. The surrounding modest-sized pastures were dotted with cattle, and mountains edged both sides of the valley. She liked it out here.

But she reminded herself she hadn't come here to feel good. She had some hard work to do.

Riley turned off onto a well-worn gravel road, and after a minute or two, she reached a crossroads. She turned into the national park, drove a short distance, and stopped her car on the sloping shoulder of the road.

She got out and walked across an open area to a tall, sturdy oak that stood on the northeast corner.

This was the place. This was where Eileen Rogers's body had been found—posed rather clumsily against this tree. She and Bill had been here together six months ago. Riley started to recreate the scene in her mind.

The biggest difference was the weather. Back then it had been mid-December, and bitterly cold. A thin blanket of snow covered the ground.

Go back, she told herself. *Go back and feel it.*

She breathed deeply, in and out, until she imagined she could feel a searing coldness passing through her windpipe. She could almost see thick clouds of frost forming with her every breath.

The naked corpse had been frozen solid. It wasn't easy to tell which of the many bodily lesions were knife wounds, and which were cracks and fissures caused by the icy cold.

Riley summoned back the scene, down to every last detail. The wig. The painted smile. The eyes stitched open. The artificial rose lying in the snow between the corpse's splayed legs.

The picture in her mind was now sufficiently vivid. Now she had to do what she'd done yesterday—get a sense of the killer's experience.

Once again, she closed her eyes, relaxed, and stepped off into the abyss. She welcomed that lightheaded, giddy feeling as she slipped into the killer's mind. Pretty soon, she was with him, inside him, seeing exactly what he saw, feeling what he felt.

He was driving here at night, anything but confident. He watched the road anxiously, worried about the ice under his wheels.

37

What if he lost control, skidded into a ditch? He had a corpse on board. He'd be caught for sure. He had to drive carefully. He'd hoped his second murder would be easier than the first, but he was still a nervous wreck.

He stopped the vehicle right here. He hauled the woman's body—already naked, Riley guessed—out into the open. But it was already stiffened from rigor mortis. He hadn't reckoned on that. It frustrated him, shook his confidence. To make matters worse, he couldn't see what he was doing at all well, not even in the glare of the headlights which he directed at the tree. The night was much too dark. He made a mental note to do this in daylight next time if he possibly could.

He dragged the body to the tree and tried to put it into the pose that he'd envisioned. It didn't go at all well. The woman's head was tilted to the left, frozen there by rigor mortis. He yanked and twisted it. Even after breaking its neck, he still couldn't set it staring straight forward.

And how was he to splay the legs properly? One of the legs was hopelessly crooked. He had no choice but to get a tire iron out of his trunk and break the thigh and kneecap. Then he twisted the leg as well as he could, but not to his satisfaction.

Finally, he dutifully left the ribbon around her neck, the wig on her head, and the rose in the snow. Then he got into his car and drove away. He was disappointed and disheartened. He was also scared. In all his clumsiness, had he left any fatal clues behind? He obsessively replayed his every action in his mind, but he couldn't be sure.

He knew that he had to do better next time. He promised himself to do better.

Riley opened her eyes. She let the killer's presence fade away. She was pleased with herself now. She hadn't let herself be shaken and overwhelmed. And she'd gotten some valuable perspective. She'd gotten a sense of how the killer was learning his craft.

She only wished she knew something—anything—about his first murder. She was more certain than ever that he had killed one earlier time. This had been the work of an apprentice, but not a rank beginner.

Just as Riley was about to turn and walk back toward her car, something in the tree caught her eye. It was a tiny dash of yellow peeking out from where the trunk divided in half a little above her head.

She walked around to the far side of the tree and looked up.

"He's been back here!" Riley gasped aloud. Chills surged through her body and she glanced around nervously. Nobody seemed to be nearby now.

Nestled up in the branch of a tree staring down at Riley was a naked female doll with blond hair, posed precisely the way the killer had intended the victim to be.

It couldn't have been there long—three or four days at most. It hadn't been shifted by the wind or tarnished by rain. The murderer had returned here when he'd been preparing himself for the Reba Frye murder. Much as Riley had done, he had come back here to reflect on his work, to examine his mistakes critically.

She took pictures with her cell phone. She'd send those to the Bureau right away.

Riley knew why he'd left the doll.

It's an apology for past sloppiness, she realized.

It was also a promise of better work to come.

Chapter 9

Riley drove toward Senator Mitch Newbrough's manor house, and her heart filled with dread as it came into view. Situated at the end of a long, tree-lined drive, it was huge, formal, and daunting. She always found the rich and powerful harder to deal with than folks further down the social ladder.

She pulled up and parked in a well-manicured circle in front of the stone mansion. Yes, this family was very rich indeed.

She got out of the car and walked up to the enormous front doors. After ringing the doorbell, she was greeted by a clean-cut man of about thirty.

"I'm Robert," he said. "The Senator's son. And you must be Special Agent Riley. Come on in. Mother and Father are expecting you."

Robert Newbrough led Riley on into the house, which immediately reminded her how much she disliked ostentatious homes. The Newbrough house was especially cavernous, and the walk to wherever the Senator and his wife were waiting was disagreeably long. Riley was sure that making guests walk such an inconvenient distance was a sort of intimidation tactic, a way of communicating that the inhabitants of this house were far too powerful to tangle with. Riley also found the ubiquitous Colonial furniture and decor to be really quite ugly.

More than anything else, she dreaded what was coming next. To her, talking to victims' families was simply awful—much worse than dealing with murder scenes or even corpses. She found it all too easy to get caught up in people's grief, anger, and confusion. Such intense emotions wrecked her concentration and distracted her from her work.

As they walked, Robert Newbrough said, "Father's been home from Richmond ever since …"

He choked a little in mid-sentence. Riley could feel the intensity of his loss.

"Since we heard about Reba," he continued. "It's been terrible. Mother's especially shaken up. Try not to upset her too much."

"I'm so sorry for your loss," Riley said.

Robert ignored her, and led Riley into a spacious living room. Senator Mitch Newbrough and his wife were sitting together on a huge couch holding each other's hands.

"Agent Paige," Robert said, introducing her. "Agent Paige, let me introduce my parents, the Senator and his wife, Annabeth."

40

Robert offered Reba a seat, then sat down himself.

"First of all," Riley said quietly, "my deepest condolences for your loss."

Annabeth Newbrough replied with a silent nod of acknowledgment. The Senator just sat staring forward.

In the brief silence that followed, Riley made a quick assessment of their faces. She'd seen Newbrough on television many times, always wearing a politician's ingratiating smile. He wasn't smiling now. Riley hadn't seen so much of Mrs. Newbrough, who seemed to possess the typical docility of a politician's wife.

Both of them were in their early sixties. Riley detected that they'd both gone to painful and expensive lengths to look younger—hair implants, hair dye, facelifts, makeup. As far as Riley was concerned, their efforts had left them looking vaguely artificial.

Like dolls, Riley thought.

"I've got to ask you a few questions about your daughter," Riley said, taking out her notebook. "Were you in close touch with Reba recently?"

"Oh, yes," Mrs. Newbrough said. "We are a very close family."

Riley noted a slight stiffness in the woman's voice. It sounded like something she said a little too often, a little too routinely. Riley felt pretty sure that family life in the Newbrough home had been far from ideal.

"Did Reba say anything recently about being threatened?" Riley asked.

"No," Mrs. Newbrough said. "Not a word."

Riley observed that the Senator hadn't said a word so far. She wondered why he was being so quiet. She needed to draw him out, but how?

Now Robert spoke up.

"She'd been through a messy divorce recently. Things got ugly between her and Paul over custody of their two kids."

"Oh, I never liked him," Mrs. Newbrough said. "He had such a temper. Do you think that possibly—?" Her words trailed off.

Riley shook her head.

"Her ex-husband's not a likely suspect," she said.

"Why on earth not?" Mrs. Newbrough asked.

Riley weighed in her mind what she should and should not tell them.

"You may have read that the killer struck before," she said. "There was a similar victim near Daggett."

Mrs. Newbrough was becoming more agitated.

"What's any of this supposed to mean to us?"

"We're dealing with a serial killer," Riley said. "There was nothing domestic about it. Your daughter may not have known the killer at all. There's every likelihood that it wasn't personal."

Mrs. Newbrough was sobbing now. Riley immediately regretted her choice of words.

"Not *personal*?" Mrs. Newbrough almost shouted. "How could it be anything *but* personal?"

Senator Newbrough spoke to his son.

"Robert, please take your mother elsewhere and calm her down. I need to talk with Agent Paige alone."

Robert Newbrough obediently led his mother away. Senator Newbrough said nothing for a moment. He looked Riley steadily in the eyes. She was sure that he was accustomed to intimidating people with that stare of his. But it didn't work especially well on her. She simply returned his gaze.

At last, the Senator reached into his jacket pocket and pulled out a letter-sized envelope. He walked over to her chair and handed it to her.

"Here," he said. Then he walked back to the couch and sat down again.

"What's this?" Riley asked.

The Senator turned his gaze on her again.

"Everything you need to know," he said.

Riley was now completely baffled.

"May I open it?" she asked.

"By all means."

Riley opened the envelope. It contained a single sheet of paper with two columns of names on it. She recognized some of them. Three or four were well-known reporters on the local TV news. Several others were prominent Virginia politicians. Riley was even more perplexed than before.

"Who are these people?" she asked.

"My enemies," Senator Newbrough said in an even voice. "Probably not a comprehensive list. But those are the ones who matter. Somebody there is guilty."

Riley was completely dumbfounded now. She sat there and said nothing.

"I'm not saying that anybody on that list killed my daughter directly, face to face," he said. "But they sure as hell paid somebody to do it."

42

Riley spoke slowly and cautiously.

"Senator, with all due respect, I believe I just said that your daughter's killing probably wasn't personal. There has already been one murder nearly identical to it."

"Are you saying that my daughter was targeted purely by coincidence?" the Senator asked.

Yes, probably, Riley thought.

But she knew better than to say so aloud.

Before she could reply, he added, "Agent Paige, I've learned through hard experience not to believe in coincidences. I don't know why or how, but my daughter's death was political. And in politics, *everything* is personal. So don't try to tell me it's anything else but personal. It's your job and the Bureau's to find whoever is responsible and bring him to justice."

Riley took a long, deep breath. She studied the man's face in minute detail. She could see it now. Senator Newbrough was a thorough narcissist.

Not that I should be surprised, she thought.

Riley understood something else. The Senator found it inconceivable that anything in his life wasn't specifically about him, and him alone. Even his daughter's murder was about him. Reba had simply gotten caught between him and somebody who hated him. He probably really believed that.

"Sir," Riley began, "with all due respect, I don't think—"

"I don't want you to think," Newbrough said. "You've got all the information you need right in front of you."

They held each other's gaze for several seconds.

"Agent Paige," the Senator finally said, "I get the feeling we're not on the same wavelength. That's a shame. You may not know it, but I've got good friends in the upper echelons of the agency. Some of them owe me favors. I'm going to get in touch with them right away. I need somebody on this case who will get the job done."

Riley sat there, shocked, not knowing what to say. Was this man really that delusional?

The Senator stood.

"I'll send somebody to see you out, Agent Paige," he said. "I'm sorry we didn't see eye to eye."

Senator Newbrough walked out of the room, leaving Riley sitting there alone. Her mouth hung open with shock. The man was narcissistic, all right. But she knew there was more to it than that.

There was something the Senator was hiding.

And no matter what it took, she would find out what it was.

43

Chapter 10

The first thing that caught Riley's eye was the doll—the same naked doll she had found earlier that day in that tree near Daggett, in exactly the same pose. For a moment, she was startled to see it sitting there in the FBI forensics lab surrounded by an array of high-tech equipment. It looked weirdly out of place to Riley—like some kind of sick little shrine to a bygone non-digital age.

Now the doll was just another item of evidence, protected by a plastic bag. She knew that a team had been sent to retrieve it as soon as she'd called it in from the scene. Even so, it was a jarring sight.

Special Agent Meredith stepped forward to greet her.

"It's been a long time, Agent Paige," he said warmly. "Welcome back."

"It's good to be back, sir," Riley said.

She walked over to the table to sit with Bill and the lab tech Flores. Whatever qualms and uncertainties she might be feeling, it really did feel good to see Meredith again. She liked his gruff, no-nonsense style, and he'd always treated her with respect and consideration.

"How did things go with the Senator?" Meredith asked.

"Not good, sir," she replied.

Riley noticed a twitch of annoyance in her boss's face.

"Do you think he's going to give us any trouble?"

"I'm almost sure of it. I'm sorry, sir."

Meredith nodded sympathetically.

"I'm sure it's not your fault," he said.

Riley guessed that he had a pretty good idea of what had happened. Senator Newbrough's behavior was undoubtedly typical of narcissistic politicians. Meredith was probably all too used to it.

Flores typed rapidly, and as he did, images of grisly photographs, official reports, and news stories came up on large monitors around the room.

"We did some digging, and it turns out you were right, Agent Paige," Flores said. "The same killer did strike earlier, way before the Daggett murder."

Riley heard Bill's grunt of satisfaction, and for a second, Riley felt vindicated, felt her belief in herself returning.

But then her spirits sank. Another woman had died a terrible death. That was no cause for celebration. She had wished, actually, that she had not been right.

44

Why can't I enjoy being right once in a while? she wondered.

A gigantic map of Virginia spread out over the main flat-screen monitor, then narrowed to the northern half of the state. Flores tagged a spot high up on the map, near the Maryland border.

"The first victim was Margaret Geraty, thirty-six years old," Flores said. "Her body was found dumped in farmland, about thirteen miles outside of Belding. She was killed on June twenty-fifth, nearly two years ago. The FBI wasn't called in for that one. The locals let the case go cold."

Riley peered at the crime scene photos Flores brought up on another monitor. The killer obviously hadn't tried to pose the body. He'd just dumped her in a hurry and left.

"Two years ago," she said, thinking, taking it all in. A part of her was surprised he had been at this for so long. Yet another part of her knew that these sick killers could operate for years. They could have an uncanny patience.

She examined the photos.

"I see that he hadn't developed his style," she observed.

"Right," Flores said. "There's a wig there, and the hair was cropped short, but he didn't leave a rose. However, she was choked to death with a pink ribbon."

"He rushed through the set-up," Riley said. "His nerves got the best of him. It was his first time, and he lacked self-confidence. He did a little better with Eileen Rogers, but it wasn't until the Reba Frye killing that he really hit his stride."

She remembered something that she'd wanted to ask.

"Did you find any connections between the victims? Or between the kids of the two mothers?"

"Not a thing," Flores said. "The check of parenting groups came up empty. None of them seemed to know each other."

That discouraged Riley, but didn't altogether surprise her.

"What about the first woman?" Riley asked. "She was a mother, I take it."

"Nope," Flores said quickly, as though he'd been waiting for that question. "She was married, but childless."

Riley was startled. She was *sure* that the killer was singling out mothers. How could she have gotten that wrong?

She could feel her rising self-confidence suddenly deflate.

As Riley hesitated, Bill asked, "Then how close are we to identifying a suspect? Were you able to get anything off of those burrs from Mosby Park?"

"No such luck," Flores said. "We found traces of leather

45

instead of blood. The killer wore gloves. He seems to be fastidious. Even at the first scene, he didn't leave any prints or DNA."

Riley sighed. She had been so hopeful that she'd found something that others had overlooked. But now she felt she was striking out. They were back to the drawing board.

"Obsessive about details," she commented.

"Even so, I think we're closing in on him," Flores added.

He used an electronic pointer to indicate locations, drawing lines between them.

"Now that we know about this earlier killing, we've got the order and a better idea of his territory," Flores said. "We've got number one, Margaret Geraty, at Belding to the north here, number two, Eileen Rogers, over to the west at Mosby Park, and number three, Reba Frye, near Daggett, farther south."

As Riley looked, she saw that the three locations formed a triangle on the map.

"We're looking at an area of about a thousand square miles," Flores said. "But that's not as bad as it sounds. We're talking mostly rural areas with a few small towns. In the north you get into some big estates like the Senator's. Lots of open country."

Riley saw a look of professional satisfaction on Flores's face. He obviously loved his work.

"What I'm going to do is bring up all the registered sex offenders who live in this area," Flores said. He typed in a command, and the triangle was dotted with about two dozen little red tags.

"Now let's eliminate the pederasts," he said. "We can be sure that our killer's not one of them."

Flores typed another command, and about half of the dots disappeared.

"Now let's narrow it down to just the hardcore cases—guys who've been in prison for rape or murder or both."

"No," Riley said abruptly. "That's wrong."

All three men stared at her with surprise.

"We're not looking for a violent criminal," she said.

Flores grunted.

"Like hell we're not!" he protested.

A silence fell. Riley felt an insight forming, but it hadn't quite taken shape in her mind. She stared at the doll, which was still sitting grotesquely on the table, looking as out of place as ever.

If only you could talk, she thought.

Then she slowly began to state her thoughts.

"I mean, not *obviously* violent. Margaret Geraty wasn't raped. We already knew that Rogers and Frye weren't either."

"They were all tortured and killed," Flores grumbled.

A tension filled the room, as Brent Meredith looked worried, while Bill was staring fixedly at one of the monitors.

Riley pointed to close-up pictures of Margaret Geraty's hideously mutilated corpse.

"His first killing was his most violent," she said. "These wounds are deep and ugly—worse even than his next two victims. I'll bet your technicians have already determined that he inflicted these wounds really rapidly, one right after another."

Flores nodded with admiration.

"You're right."

Meredith looked at Riley with curiosity.

"What does that tell you?" Meredith asked.

Riley took a deep breath. She found herself slipping into the killer's mind again.

"I'm pretty sure of something," she said. "He's never had sex with another human being in his life. He's probably never even been on a date. He's homely and unattractive. Women have always rejected him."

Riley paused for a moment, collecting her thoughts.

"One day he finally snapped," she said. "He abducted Margaret Geraty, bound her, stripped her, and tried to rape her."

Flores gasped with sudden comprehension.

"But he couldn't do it!" Flores said.

"Right, he's completely impotent," Riley said. "And when he couldn't rape her, he went into a rage. He started stabbing—the closest he could get to sexual penetration. It was the first act of violence he'd ever committed in his life. My guess is he didn't even bother to keep her alive for long."

Flores pointed to a paragraph in the official report.

"Your guess is right," he said. "Geraty's body was found just a couple of days after she disappeared."

Riley felt a deepening terror at her own words.

"And he liked it," she said. "He liked Geraty's terror and pain. He liked all the cutting and stabbing. So he's made it his ritual ever since. And he's learned to take his time about it, to enjoy every minute of it. With Reba Frye, the fear and torture went on for more than a week."

A chill of silence settled over the room.

"What about the doll connection?" Meredith asked. "Why are

47

you so sure he's creating a doll?"

"The bodies sure look like dolls," Bill said. "At least the last two. Riley's right about that."

"It is about dolls," Riley said quietly. "But I don't know exactly why. There's probably some sort of revenge element here."

Finally Flores asked, "So do you think we're looking for a registered offender at all?"

"Could be," Riley said. "But not a rapist, not a violent predator. It would be somebody more innocuous, less threatening—a Peeping Tom, or a flasher, or somebody who masturbates in public."

Flores typed vigorously.

"Okay," he said. "I'll get rid of the violent offenders."

The number of red dots on the map lessened to a handful.

"So who have we got left?" Riley asked Flores.

Flores glanced at a few records, then gasped.

"I think I've got him," Flores said. "I think I've got your man. His name's Ross Blackwell. And get this. He was working in a toy store when he got caught posing dolls in kinky positions. Like they were having all kinds of weird sex. The owner called the police. Blackwell got probation, but the authorities have had their eye on him ever since."

Meredith stroked his chin thoughtfully. "Could be our guy," he said.

"Should Agent Paige and I go check on him right now?" Bill asked.

"We don't have enough to bring him in," Meredith said. "Or to get a warrant for any kind of a search. We'd better not alarm him. If he's our guy and he's as smart as we think he is, he's liable to slip through our fingers. Pay him a little visit tomorrow. Find out what he's got to say about himself. Handle him carefully."

Chapter 11

It was very dark by the time Riley got back home into Fredericksburg and, if anything, she felt her night was almost sure to get worse. She felt a spasm of déjà vu as she pulled her car in front of the large house in a respectable suburban neighborhood. She'd once shared this house with Ryan and their daughter. There were a lot of memories here, many of them good. But more than a few of them were not so good, and some were really awful.

Just as she was about to get out of the car and walk up to the house, the front door opened. April came out and Ryan stood silhouetted in the bright light of the doorway. He gave Riley a token wave as April walked away, then he stepped back into the house and closed the door.

It seemed to Riley that he shut the door quite firmly, but she knew that was probably her own mind at work. That door had closed for good some time ago, and that life was gone. But the truth was, she had never really belonged in such a bland, safe, respectable world of order and routine. Her heart was always in the field, where chaos, unpredictability, and danger reigned.

April reached the car and got into the passenger seat.

"You're late," April snapped, crossing her arms.

"Sorry," Riley said. She wanted to say more, to tell April how deeply sorry she really was, not just for this night, not just for her father, but for her whole life. Riley so badly wanted to be a better mother, to be home, to be there for April. But her work life would just not let her go.

Riley pulled away from the curb.

"Normal parents don't work all day and all night too," April said.

Riley sighed.

"I've said before that—" she began.

"I know," April interrupted. "Criminals don't take days off. That's pretty lame, Mom."

Riley drove on in silence for a few moments, wanting to talk to April, but just too tired, too overwhelmed by her day. She didn't even know what to say anymore.

"How did things go with your father?" she finally asked.

"Lousy," April replied.

It was a predictable reply. April seemed to be even more down on her father than she was on her mother these days.

Another long silence fell between them.

Then, in a softer tone, April added, "At least Gabriela's there. It's always nice to see a friendly face for a change."

Riley smiled ever so slightly. Riley really did appreciate Gabriela, the middle-aged Guatemalan woman who had worked as their housemaid for years. Gabriela was always wonderfully responsible and grounded, which was more than Riley could say about Ryan. She was glad that Gabriela was still in their lives—and still there to look after April whenever she stayed at her father's house.

During the drive home, Riley felt a palpable need to communicate with her daughter. But what could she say to break through to her? It wasn't as if she didn't understand how April felt—especially on a night like tonight. The poor girl simply had to feel unwanted, getting shuttled back and forth between her parents' homes. That had to be hard on a fourteen-year-old who was already angry about so many things in her life. Fortunately, April agreed to go to her father's house after her class each day until Riley picked her up. But today, the very first day of the new arrangement, Riley had been so very late.

Riley found herself close to tears as she drove. She couldn't think of anything to say. She was simply too exhausted. She was *always* too exhausted.

When they got home, April stalked wordlessly off to her room and shut the door noisily behind her. Riley stood in the hallway for a moment. Then she knocked on April's door.

"Come on out, sweetie," she said. "Let's talk. Let's sit down in the kitchen for a little bit, have a cup of peppermint tea. Or maybe in the backyard. It's a pretty night out. It's a shame to waste it."

She heard April's voice reply, "You go ahead and do that, Mom. I'm busy."

Riley leaned wearily against the doorframe.

"You keep saying I don't spend enough time with you," Riley said.

"It's past midnight, Mom. It's really late."

Riley felt her throat tighten and tears well up in her eyes. But she wasn't going to let herself cry.

"I'm trying, April," she said. "I'm doing my best—with everything."

A silence fell.

"I know," April finally said from inside her room.

Then all was quiet. Riley wished she could see her daughter's face. Was it possible that she heard just a trace of sympathy in those two words? No, probably not. Was it anger, then? Riley didn't think so. It was probably just detachment.

Riley went to the bathroom and took a long hot shower. She let the steam and the pounding hot droplets massage her body, which ached all over after such a long and difficult day. By the time she got out and dried her hair she felt better physically. But inside she still felt empty and troubled.

And she knew that she wasn't ready to sleep.

She put on slippers and a bathrobe and went to the kitchen. When she opened a cabinet the first thing she saw was a mostly-full bottle of bourbon. She thought about pouring herself a straight double shot of whiskey.

Not a good idea, she told herself firmly.

In her current frame of mind, she wouldn't stop with one. Through all her troubles of the last six weeks, she'd managed not to let alcohol get the best of her. This was no time to lose control. She fixed herself a cup of hot mint tea instead.

Then Riley sat down in the living room and began to pore over the folder full of photographs and information about the three murder cases.

She already knew quite a bit about the victim of six months ago near Daggett—the one they now knew to be the second of three murders. Eileen Rogers had been a married mother with two children who owned and managed a restaurant with her husband. And of course, Riley had also seen the site where the third victim, Reba Frye, had been left. She'd even visited Frye's family, including the self-absorbed Senator.

But the two-year-old Belding case was new to her. As she read the reports, Margaret Geraty began to come into focus as a real human being, a woman who had once lived and breathed. She'd worked in Belding as a CPA, and had recently moved to Virginia from upstate New York. Her surviving family aside from her husband included two sisters, a brother, and a widowed mother. Friends and relatives described her as good-natured but rather solitary—possibly even lonely.

Sipping on her tea, Riley couldn't help but wonder—what would have become of Margaret Geraty if she had lived? At thirty-six, life still held all kinds of possibilities—children, and so much else.

Riley felt a chill as another thought dawned on her. Just six weeks ago, her own life story had come fearfully close to ending up in a folder just like the one now open in front of her. Her whole

51

existence might well have been reduced to a stack of horrible photos and official prose.

She closed her eyes, trying to shake it away as she sensed the memories come flooding back. But try as she did, she could not stop them.

As she crept through the dark house, she heard a scratching below the floorboards, then a cry for help. After probing the walls, she found it—a small, square door that opened into a crawlspace under the house. She shined a flashlight inside.

The beam fell upon a terrified face.

"I'm here to help," Riley said.

"You've come!" the victim cried. "Oh, thank God you've come!"

Riley scuttled across the dirt floor toward the little cage in the corner. She fumbled with the lock for a moment. Then she pulled out her pocketknife and pried at the lock until she forced it open. A second later, the woman was crawling out of the cage.

Riley and the woman headed for the square opening. But the woman was scarcely out before a threatening male figure blocked Riley's way.

She was trapped, but the other woman had a chance.

"Run!" Riley screamed. "Run!"

Riley yanked herself back to the present. Would she ever be free from those horrors? Certainly, working on a new case involving torture and death wasn't making it easier for her.

Even so, there was one person she could always turn to for support.

She got out her phone and texted Marie.

Hey. You still awake?

After a few seconds, the reply came.

Yes. How are U?

Riley typed: *Pretty shaky. And you?*

Too scared to sleep.

Riley wanted to type something to make both of them feel better. Somehow, just texting like this didn't seem to be enough.

Do U want to talk? she typed. *I mean TALK—not just text?*

It took several long seconds before Marie replied.

No, I don't think so.

Riley was surprised for a moment. Then she realized that her voice might not always be comforting for Marie. Sometimes it

52

might even trigger awful flashbacks for her.

Riley remembered Marie's words the last time they had spoken. *Find that son of a bitch. And kill him for me.* And as she pondered them, Riley did have news that she thought Marie might want to hear.

I'm back on the job, Riley typed.

Marie's words poured out in a rush of typed phrases.

Oh good! So glad! I know it's not easy. I'm proud. U r very brave.

Riley sighed. She didn't feel so brave—not just at this moment, anyway.

Marie's words continued.

Thank U. Knowing you're working again makes me feel much better. Maybe I can sleep now. Goodnight.

Riley typed: *Hang in there.*

Then she put her phone down. She felt a bit better, too. After all, she'd accomplished something, getting back to work like this. Slowly but surely, she really was starting to heal.

Riley drank the rest of her tea, then went straight to bed. She let her exhaustion overtake her and fell asleep quickly.

Riley was six years old, in a candy store with Mommy. She was so happy about all the candy Mommy was buying for her.

But then a man walked toward them. A big, scary man. He wore something over his face—a nylon stocking, just like Mommy wore on her legs. He pulled a gun. He yelled at Mommy to give him her purse. But Mommy was so scared that she couldn't move. She couldn't give it to him.

And so he shot her in the chest.

She fell to the floor bleeding. The man snatched up the purse and ran.

Riley started screaming and screaming and screaming.

Then she heard Mommy's voice.

"There's nothing you can do, dear. I'm gone and you can't help it."

Riley was still in the candy store but she was all grown up now. Mommy was right in front of her, standing over her own corpse.

"I've got to bring you back!" Riley cried.

Mommy was smiling sadly at Riley.

"You can't," Mommy said. "You can't bring back the dead."

Riley sat up, breathing hard, startled from her sleep by a

rattling noise. She looked all around, on edge. The house was silent now.

But she'd heard something, she was sure. Like a noise at the front door.

Riley jumped to her feet, her instincts kicking in. She got a flashlight and her gun out of the dresser and moved carefully through the house toward the front door.

She peered through the small glass pane in the door, but saw nothing. All was silent.

Riley braced herself and quickly opened the door wide, shining the light outside. No one. Nothing.

As she moved the light around something on the front stoop caught her attention. A few pebbles were scattered there. Had somebody tossed them at the door, causing that rattling?

Riley wracked her brain, trying to remember if those pebbles had been there when she'd gotten home last night. In her haze, she simply couldn't be sure one way or the other.

Riley stood there for a few moments, but there was no sign of anybody anywhere.

She closed and locked the front door and headed back down the short hallway to her bedroom. As she reached the end, she was startled to see that April's bedroom door was slightly open.

Riley pulled the door open wide and looked inside.

Her heart pounded with terror.

April was gone.

Chapter 12

"April!" Riley screamed. "April!"

Riley ran to the bathroom and looked inside. Her daughter wasn't there either.

She ran desperately through the house, opening doors, looking into every room and every closet. She found nothing.

"April!" she screamed again.

Riley recognized the bitter flavor of bile in her mouth. It was the taste of terror.

At last, in the kitchen, she noticed an odd smell wafting in through an open window. She recognized that smell from long-ago college days. Her terror ebbed away, replaced by sad annoyance.

"Oh, Jesus," Riley murmured aloud, feeling immense relief.

She jerked the back door open. In the early morning light she could see her daughter, still in her pajamas, sitting at the old picnic table. April looked guilty and sheepish.

"What do you want, Mom?" April asked.

Riley strode across the yard, holding out her hand.

"Give it to me," Riley said.

April awkwardly tried to display an innocent expression.

"Give you what?" she asked.

Riley's voice choked back more sadness than anger. "The joint you're smoking," she said. "And please—don't lie to me about it."

"You're crazy," April said, doing her best to sound righteously indignant. "I wasn't smoking anything. You're always assuming the worst about me. You know that, Mom?"

Riley noticed how her daughter was hunched forward as she sat on the bench.

"Move your foot," Riley said.

"What?" April said, feigning incomprehension.

Riley pointed at the suspicious foot.

"Move your foot."

April groaned aloud and obeyed. Sure enough, her bedroom slipper had been covering a freshly crushed marijuana joint. A wisp of smoke rose from it, and the smell was stronger than ever.

Riley bent down and snatched it up.

"Now give me the rest of it."

April shrugged. "The rest of what?"

Riley couldn't quite keep her voice steady. "April, I mean it. Don't lie to me. Please."

April rolled her eyes and reached into her shirt pocket. She pulled out a joint that hadn't been lit.

"Oh, for Christ's sake, here," she said, handing it to her mother. "Don't try to tell me you're not going to smoke it yourself as soon as you get a chance."

Riley shoved both joints into her bathrobe pocket.

"What else have you got?" she demanded.

"That's it, that's all there is," April snapped back. "Don't you believe me? Well, go ahead, search me. Search my room. Search everywhere. This is all I've got."

Riley was trembling all over. She struggled to bring her emotions under control.

"Where did you get these?" she asked.

April shrugged. "Cindy gave them to me."

"Who's Cindy?

April let out a cynical laugh. "Well, you wouldn't know, would you, Mom? It's not like you know much of anything about my life. What do you care, anyway? I mean, does it make any difference to you if I get high?"

Riley was stung now. April had gone right for the jugular, and it hurt. Riley couldn't hold back the tears anymore.

"April, why do you hate me?" she cried.

April looked surprised, but hardly repentant. "I don't hate you, Mom."

"Then why are you *punishing* me? What did I ever do to deserve this?"

April stared off into space. "Maybe you ought to spend some time thinking about that, Mom."

April got up from the bench and walked toward the house.

Riley wandered through the kitchen, mechanically getting out everything she needed to make breakfast. As she took the eggs and bacon out of the refrigerator, she wondered what to do about this situation. She ought to ground April immediately. But how exactly could she do that?

When Riley had been off the job, she'd been able to keep tabs on April. But everything was different now. Now that Riley was back at work, her schedule would be wildly unpredictable. And apparently, so would her daughter.

Riley mulled over her choices as she laid strips of bacon in the pan to sizzle. One thing seemed certain. Since April would be spending so much time with her father, Riley really ought to tell Ryan what had happened. But that would open up another world of problems. Ryan was already convinced that Riley was domestically incompetent, both as a wife and mother. If Riley told him that she'd caught April smoking pot in the backyard, he'd feel absolutely sure of it.

And maybe he'd be right, she thought miserably as she pushed two slices of bread down into the toaster.

So far, Ryan and Riley had managed to avoid a custody battle over April. She knew that although he'd never admit it, Ryan was enjoying his freedom as a bachelor too much to want to be bothered with raising a teenager. He hadn't been thrilled when Riley told him that April would be spending more time with him.

But she also knew that her ex-husband's attitude could change very fast, especially if he had an excuse to blame her for something. If he found out that April had been smoking pot, he might try to take her away from Riley altogether. That thought was unbearable.

A few minutes later, Riley and her daughter were sitting at the breakfast table eating. The silence between them was even more awkward than usual.

Finally April asked, "Are you going to tell Dad?"

"Do you think maybe I should?" Riley replied.

It seemed like an honest enough reply under the circumstances.

April hung her head, looking worried.

Then April pleaded, "Please don't tell Gabriela."

The words struck Riley straight to the heart. April was more worried about their housemaid finding out than she was about what her father might think—or her own mother, for that matter.

So things have gotten this bad, Riley thought miserably.

What precious little that was left of her family life was disintegrating right before her eyes. She felt as if she were barely a mother at all anymore. She wondered if Ryan had any such feelings about being a father.

Probably not. Feeling guilty wasn't Ryan's style. She sometimes envied him his emotional indifference.

After breakfast, as April got ready for school, the house fell silent, and Riley began to obsess about the other thing that had happened that morning—*if* it had happened. What or who had caused that rattling at the front door? *Had* there been a rattling at the front door? Where had those pebbles suddenly come from?

She recalled Marie's panic over strange phone calls, and an obsessive fear was growing inside her, getting out of control. She got out her cell phone and called a familiar number.

"Betty Richter, FBI Forensics Tech," came the curt reply.

"Betty, this is Riley Paige." Riley swallowed hard. "I think you know why I'm calling."

After all, Riley had been making this exact same phone call every two or three days for the last six weeks now. Agent Richter had been in charge of closing up the details on the Peterson case, and Riley desperately wanted resolution.

"You want me to tell you that Peterson's really dead," Betty said in a sympathetic tone. Betty was the very soul of patience, understanding, and good humor, and Riley had always been grateful to have her to talk to about this.

"I know it's ridiculous."

"After all you went through?" Betty said. "No, I don't think so. But I don't have anything new to tell you. Just the same old thing. We found Peterson's body. Sure, it was burned to a cinder, but it was exactly his height and build. There's really nobody else it could have been."

"How sure are you? Give me a percentage."

"I'd say ninety-nine percent," she said.

Riley took a long, slow breath.

"You can't make that a hundred?" she asked.

Betty sighed. "Riley, I can't give you a hundred percent certainty about much of *anything* in life. Nobody can. Nobody's a hundred percent sure the sun is going to rise tomorrow morning. Earth might get smacked by a giant asteroid in the meantime, and we'll all be dead."

Riley emitted a rueful chuckle.

"Thanks for giving me something else to worry about," she said.

Betty laughed a little too. "Any time," she said. "Glad to be of help."

"Mom?" April called out, ready to go to school.

Riley ended the phone call, feeling a bit better, and prepared to go. After drop-off, she had agreed to pick up Bill today. They had a suspect to interview that fit all the demographics.

And Riley had a feeling he just might be the savage killer they were looking for.

Chapter 13

Riley turned off the engine and sat before Bill's house, admiring his pleasant two-story bungalow. She'd always wondered how he managed to keep that front lawn such a healthy green and those ornamental shrubs so immaculately trimmed. Bill's domestic life might be in turmoil, but he sure did keep a nice yard, a perfect fit for this picturesque residential neighborhood. She couldn't help wondering what all the backyards looked like in this little community so close to Quantico.

Bill came out, his wife, Maggie, appearing behind him and giving Riley a ferocious glare. Riley looked away.

Bill got in and slammed the door behind him.

"Let's get the hell out of here," he growled.

Riley started the car and pulled away from the curb.

"I take it all is not well at home," she said.

Bill shook his head.

"We had a big fight when I got home so late last night. It all started up again this morning."

He was silent for a moment, then added grimly, "She's talking about divorce again. And she wants full custody of the boys."

Riley hesitated, but then she went ahead and asked the question that was on her mind, "And I'm part of the problem?"

Bill was silent.

"Yeah," he finally admitted. "She wasn't happy to hear that we're working together again. She says you're a bad influence."

Riley didn't know what to say.

Bill added, "She says I'm at my worst when I'm working with you. I'm more distracted, more obsessed with my job."

True enough, Riley thought. She and Bill were both obsessed with their jobs.

Silence fell again as they drove. After a few minutes, Bill opened up his laptop.

"I've got some details about the guy we're going to talk to. Ross Blackwell."

He scanned the screen.

"A registered sex offender," he added.

Riley's lip curled in disgust.

"What charges?"

"Possession of child pornography. He was suspected of more but nothing was ever proved. He's in the database but no restrictions on his activity. It was ten years back, and this photo is pretty old."

Sneaky, she thought. *Maybe hard to trap.*

Bill continued reading.

"Fired from several jobs, for vague reasons. The last time he was working in a chain store in a big mall in the Beltway—really mainstream commercial stuff, and its market is mostly families with kids. When they caught Blackwell posing dolls in kinky positions, they fired and reported him."

"A man with a quirk about dolls and a record of child pornography," Riley muttered.

So far, Ross Blackwell fit the profile that she was starting to put together.

"And now?" she asked.

"He's got a job in a hobby and model shop," Bill replied. "Another chain store in another mall."

Riley was a bit surprised.

"Didn't the managers know about Blackwell's record when they hired him?"

Bill shrugged.

"Maybe they don't care. His interests seem to be entirely heterosexual. Maybe they don't figure he'll do much harm in a place that's all about model cars and airplanes and trains."

She felt a chill run through her body. Why would a guy like that even be able to get another job? This man seemed likely to be a vicious killer. Why would he be let out every day to cruise around among those who were vulnerable?

They finally made their way through the relentless traffic to Sanfield. The D.C. suburb struck Riley as a typical example of an "edge city," largely made up of malls and corporate headquarters. She found it to be soulless, plastic, and depressing.

She parked outside the huge shopping mall. For a moment, she just sat in the driver's seat and stared at the old photograph of Blackwell on Bill's laptop. There was nothing distinctive about his face, just a white guy with dark hair and an insolent expression. Now he would be in his fifties.

She and Bill got out of the car and made their way on foot through the consumers' utopia, until they saw the scale model store.

"I don't want to let him get away," Riley said. "What if he spots us and bolts?"

"We should be able to corner him inside," Bill replied. "Immobilize him and get the customers out."

Riley put one hand on her gun.

Not yet, she told herself. *Don't cause a panic if we don't have to.*

She stood there for a moment, watching the store's customers coming and going. Was one of those guys Blackwell? Was he already escaping them?

Riley and Bill walked in through the door of the model shop. Most of the space was taken up by a sprawling and detailed reproduction of a small town, complete with a running train and flashing traffic lights. Model airplanes hung from the ceiling. There wasn't a doll in sight.

Several men seemed to be working in the store, but none of them fit the image she held in her mind.

"I can't spot him," Riley said.

At the front desk Bill asked, "Do you have a certain Ross Blackwell working here?"

The man at the cash register nodded and pointed toward a rack with scale modeling kits. A short, pudgy man with graying hair was sorting the merchandise. His back was to them.

Riley touched her gun again, but left it in the holster. She and Bill spread out so they could block any escape attempt Blackwell might make.

Her heart beat faster as she approached.

"Ross Blackwell?" Riley asked.

The man turned around. He wore thick glasses and his belly protruded over his belt. Riley was especially struck by the dull, anemic pallor of his skin. She thought that he didn't seem likely to run, but her judgment of "creep" fit him just fine.

"It depends," Blackwell replied with a wide smile. "What's your business?"

Riley and Bill both showed him their badges.

"Wow, the Feds, huh?" Blackwell said, sounding almost pleased. "This is new. I'm used to dealing with the local authorities. You're not here to arrest me, I hope. Because I really thought all those weird misunderstandings were a thing of the past."

"We'd just like to ask you a few questions," Bill said.

Blackwell smirked a little and tilted his head inquiringly.

"A few questions, huh? Well, I know the Bill of Rights pretty much by heart. I don't have to talk to you if I don't want to. But hey, why not? It might even be fun. If you'll buy me a cup of coffee, I'll go along with it."

Blackwell walked toward the front desk, and Riley and Bill followed close behind him. Riley was alert for any attempt at

61

evading them.

"I'm taking a coffee break, Bernie," Blackwell called out to the cashier.

Riley could tell by Bill's expression that he was wondering if they'd gotten the right guy. She understood why he might feel that way. Blackwell didn't seem the least bit upset to see them. In fact, he seemed to be rather pleased.

But as far as Riley was concerned, this made him seem all the more amoral and sociopathic. Some of the vilest serial killers in history had displayed plenty of charm and self-assurance. The last thing she expected was for the killer to *seem* the least bit guilty.

It was only a short way to the food court. Blackwell escorted Bill and Riley straight to a coffee counter. If the man was nervous about being with two FBI agents, he didn't show it.

A little girl who was trailing along behind her mother stumbled and fell just in front of them.

"Whoops!" Blackwell cried out cheerfully. He bent over and lifted the child to her feet.

The mother said an automatic thanks, then led her daughter off by the hand. Riley watched Blackwell eye the little girl's bare legs beneath her short skirt, and she felt sick to her stomach. Her suspicion deepened.

Riley grabbed Blackwell's arm hard, but he gave her a look of bewilderment and innocence. She shook his arm and let him go.

"Get your coffee," she said, nodding to nearby the cafe counter.

"I'd like a cappuccino," Blackwell said to the young woman behind the counter. "These folks are buying."

Then, turning to Bill and Riley, he asked, "What are you two having?"

"We're fine," Riley said.

Bill paid for the cappuccino, and the three of them headed toward a table that didn't have other people seated nearby.

"Okay, so what do you want to know about me?" Blackwell asked. He seemed relaxed and friendly. "I hope you're not going to get all judgmental, like the authorities I'm used to. People are so closed-minded these days."

"Closed-minded about putting dolls in obscene poses?" Bill asked.

Blackwell looked sincerely hurt. "You make it sound so dirty," he said. "There wasn't anything obscene about it. Have a look for yourselves."

Blackwell got out his cell phone and started showing

photographs of his handiwork. They included little pornographic tableaus he had created inside of dollhouses. The little human figures were in various states of undress. They had been posed in an imaginative array of groupings and positions in different parts of the houses. Riley's mind boggled at the variety of sex acts portrayed in the pictures—some of them quite probably illegal in many states.

Looks plenty obscene to me, Riley thought.

"I was being satirical," Blackwell explained. "I was making an important social statement. We live in such a crass and materialistic culture. *Somebody's* got to make this kind of protest. I was exercising my right to free speech in a thoroughly responsible way. I wasn't abusing it. It's not like I was yelling 'fire' in a crowded theater."

Riley noticed that Bill was starting to look indignant.

"What about the little kids who stumbled across these little scenes of yours?" Bill asked. "Don't you think you were harming them?"

"No, as a matter of fact, I don't," Blackwell said rather smugly. "They get worse things out of the media every single day. There's no such thing as childhood innocence anymore. That's exactly what I was trying to tell the world. It breaks my heart, I tell you."

He actually sounds like he means it, Riley thought.

But it was obvious to her that he didn't mean it at all. Ross Blackwell didn't have a single moral or empathetic bone in his body. Riley suspected his guilt more and more with every passing moment.

She tried to read his face. It wasn't easy. Like all true sociopaths, he masked his feelings with amazing skill.

"Tell me, Ross," she said. "Do you like the outdoors? I mean like camping and fishing."

Blackwell's face lit up with a broad smile. "Oh, yeah. Ever since I was a kid. I was an Eagle Scout back in the day. I sometimes go off into the wilderness alone for weeks at a time. Sometimes I think I was Daniel Boone in a previous life."

Riley asked, "Do you like to go hunting, too?"

"Sure, all the time," he said enthusiastically. "I've got lots of trophies at home. You know, mounted heads of elks and deer. I mount them all myself. I've got a real flare for taxidermy."

Riley squinted at Blackwell.

"Do you have any favorite places? Forests and such, I mean. State and national parks."

Blackwell stroked his chin thoughtfully.

"I go to Yellowstone a lot," he said. "I suppose that's my favorite. Of course, it's hard to beat the Great Smoky Mountains. Yosemite, too. It's not easy to choose."

Bill put in, "How about Mosby State Park? Or maybe that national park near Daggett?"

Blackwell suddenly looked a bit wary.

"Why do you want to know?" he asked uneasily.

Riley knew that the moment of truth—or its opposite—had finally arrived. She reached into her purse and pulled out photographs of the murder victims, taken when they were alive.

"Can you identify any of these women?" Riley asked.

Blackwell's eyes widened with alarm.

"No," he said, his voice shaking. "I've never seen them in my life."

"Are you sure?" Riley prodded. "Maybe their names will refresh your memory. Reba Frye. Eileen Rogers. Margaret Geraty."

Blackwell seemed on the edge of sheer panic.

"Nope," he said. "I've never seen them. Never heard their names."

Riley studied his face closely for a moment. Finally, she fully understood the situation. She knew all she needed to know about Ross Blackwell.

"Thank you for your time, Ross," she said. "We'll be in touch if we need to know anything else."

Bill looked dumbfounded as he followed her out of the food court.

"What was going on back there?" he snapped. "What are you thinking? He's guilty and he knows that we're on to him. We can't let him out of our sight until we can nail him."

Riley let out a sigh of mild impatience.

"Think about it, Bill," she said. "Did you get a look at that pale skin of his? Not even a solitary freckle. That guy's scarcely spent a whole day outdoors in his life."

"So he's not really an Eagle Scout?"

Riley chuckled slightly. "Nope," she said. "And I can promise you he's never been to Yellowstone or Yosemite or the Great Smoky Mountains. And he doesn't know a thing about taxidermy."

Bill looked positively embarrassed now.

"He really had me believing him," Bill said.

Riley nodded in agreement.

"Of course he did," she said. "He's a great liar. He can make people believe he's telling the truth about anything. And he just loves to lie. He does it whenever he gets a chance—and the bigger the lies, the better."

She paused for a moment.

"The trouble is," Riley added, "he's lousy at telling the truth. He's not used to it. He loses his cool when he tries to do it."

Bill walked silently beside her for a moment, trying to take this in.

"So you're saying—?" he began.

"He was telling the truth about the women, Bill. That's why he sounded so guilty. The truth always sounds like a lie when he tries to tell it. He really and truly never saw any of those women in his life. I'm not saying he's not capable of murder. He probably is. But he didn't do *these* murders."

Bill growled under his breath.

"Damn," he said.

Riley didn't say anything the rest of the way to the car. This was a serious setback. The more she thought about it, the more alarmed she felt. The real killer was still out there, and they still didn't have a clue who or where he was. And she knew, she just knew, that he would soon kill again.

Riley was getting frustrated with her inability to figure this case out, but as she wracked her brain, it suddenly occurred to her who she needed to talk to. Right now.

Chapter 14

They were just a short distance out of Sanfield when Riley suddenly crossed two lanes and veered onto an exit ramp.

Bill was surprised. "Where are we going?" he asked.

"Belding," Riley said.

Bill stared at her from the passenger's seat, waiting for more of an explanation.

"Margaret Geraty's husband still lives there," she said. "Roy's his name, right? Roy Geraty. And doesn't he own a filling station or something?"

"Actually, it's an auto repair and supply store," Bill said.

Riley nodded. "We're going to pay him a visit," she said.

Bill shrugged doubtfully.

"Okay, but I'm not sure why," he said. "The locals did a pretty thorough job interviewing him about his wife's murder. They didn't get any leads."

Riley didn't say anything for a while. She knew all this already. Still, she felt as if there was something yet to be learned. Some sort of loose end must have been left hanging in Belding, just a short drive away through Virginia farm country. She just had to find out what it was—if she could. But she was starting to doubt herself.

"I'm rusty, Bill," Riley muttered as she drove. "For a while back there, I was really sure that Ross Blackwell was our killer. I ought to have known better at first glance. My instincts are shot."

"Don't be too hard on yourself," Bill replied. "He seemed to fit your profile."

Riley groaned under her breath. "Yeah, but my profile was wrong. Our guy wouldn't pose dolls like that—and not in a public place."

"Why not?" Bill asked.

Riley thought for a moment.

"Because he takes dolls too seriously," she said. "They hold some really deep significance for him. It's something personal. I think he'd be offended by little stunts like Blackwell's, the way he posed them. He'd consider it vulgar. Dolls aren't toys to him. They're ... I don't know. I can't quite get it."

"I know how your mind works," Bill said. "And whatever it is will come to you eventually."

Riley fell silent as she mentally replayed some of the events of the last few days. That only heightened her sense of insecurity.

66

"I've been wrong about other stuff, too," she told Bill. "I thought the killer was targeting mothers. I was sure of it. But Margaret Geraty wasn't a mother. How could I get that wrong?"

"You'll hit your stride soon," Bill said.

They reached the outskirts of Belding. It was a tired-looking little town that must have been there for generations. But the nearby farms had been bought up by wealthy families who wanted to be "gentleman farmers" and still commute to power jobs in D.C. The town was fading away and one might almost drive through it without noticing it.

Roy Geraty's auto repair and supply store was impossible to miss.

Riley and Bill got out of the car and went into the rather seedy front office. No one was there. Riley rang a little bell on the counter. They waited, but no one came. After a few minutes, they ventured into the garage. A single pair of feet poked out from beneath one vehicle.

"Are you Roy Geraty?" Riley asked.

"Yeah," came a voice from under the car.

Riley looked around. There wasn't another employee in sight. Had things gotten so bad that the owner had to do everything by himself?

Geraty came rolling out from under the car and squinted at them suspiciously. He was a bulky man in his middle to late thirties, and he was wearing oil-stained coveralls. He wiped his hands on a dirty cloth and got to his feet.

"You're not local," he said. Then he added, "Well, what can I help you with?"

"We're with the FBI," Bill said. "We'd like to ask you some questions."

"Ah, Jesus," the man growled. "I don't need this."

"It won't take long," Riley said.

"Well, come on," the man grumbled. "If we've got to talk, we've got to talk."

He led Riley and Bill into a little employee break area with a couple of banged-up vending machines. They all sat down on plastic chairs. Almost as if nobody else was there, Roy picked up a remote and turned on an old television. He fumbled around switching channels until he found an old sitcom. Then he stared at the screen.

"Just ask what you want and let's get it over with," he said. "These last few days have been hell."

Riley found it easy to guess what he meant.

"I'm sorry your wife's murder is back in the news," she said.

"The papers say there have been two more like it," Geraty said. "I can't believe it. My phone's been ringing off the hook with reporters and just plain assholes. My email inbox is flooded too. There's no respect for privacy anymore. And poor Evelyn—my wife—she's really shook up about it."

"You've remarried?" Bill asked.

Geraty nodded, still staring at the TV screen. "We tied the knot seven months after Margaret ..."

He couldn't make himself finish the sentence.

"Folks around here thought it was too fast," he said. "It didn't seem too fast to me. I'd never been lonelier in my life. Evelyn's been a gift from heaven. I don't know what would have become of me without her. I guess maybe I'd have died."

His voice grew thick with emotion.

"We've got a baby girl now. Six months old. Her name's Lucy. The joy of my life."

The sitcom laugh track on the TV erupted with inappropriate laughter. Geraty sniffed and cleared his throat and leaned back in his chair.

"Anyway, I sure can't figure what you want to ask me about," he said. "Seems to me I answered every kind of question you can think of two years ago. It didn't do any good. You couldn't catch the guy then, and you're not going to catch him now."

"We're still trying," Riley said. "We'll bring him to justice."

But she could feel the hollowness in her own words.

She paused a moment, then asked, "Do you live near here? I was wondering if we might be able to visit your house, have a look around."

Geraty knitted his brow in thought.

"Do I have to? Or do I have a choice about it?" he asked.

His question took Riley slightly aback.

"It's just a request," she said. "But it might be helpful."

Geraty shook his head firmly.

"No," he said. "I've got to draw a line. The cops practically moved into my place back in those days. Some of them were sure I'd killed her. Maybe some of you guys are thinking the same thing now. That I killed somebody."

"No," Riley reassured him. "That's not why we're here."

She saw that Bill was watching the mechanic very closely.

Geraty didn't look up. He just went on. "And poor Evelyn—

68

she's home with Lucy, and she's already a nervous wreck from all the phone calls. I won't put her through any more of it. I'm sorry, I don't mean to be uncooperative. It's just that enough is enough."

Riley could tell that Bill was about to insist. She spoke before he could.

"I understand," she said. "It's all right."

Riley felt sure that she and Bill probably were not likely to learn anything important from a visit to the Geraty home anyhow. But maybe he would answer a question or two.

"Did your wife—Margaret, your first wife—like dolls?" Riley asked cautiously. "Did she collect them, maybe?"

Geraty turned toward her, looking away from the TV for the first time.

"No," he said, looking surprised at the question.

Riley realized that no one would have asked that particular question before. Of all the theories the police might have had two years ago, dolls wouldn't have been among them. And even in the harassment he was undergoing now, no one else would have made a connection with dolls.

"She didn't like them," Geraty continued. "It wasn't like she hated them. It's just that they made her sad. She couldn't—*we* couldn't—have children, and dolls always made her think about that. They reminded her. Sometimes she'd even cry when she was around dolls."

With a deep sigh, he turned back toward the TV again.

"She was unhappy about it during those last years," he said in a low, faraway voice. "Not having kids, I mean. So many friends and relatives, having kids of their own. It seemed like everybody except us was having babies all the time, or had kids growing up. There were always baby showers to go to, mothers always asking her to help out with birthday parties. It really got her down."

Riley felt a lump of sympathy form in her throat. Her heart went out to this man who was still trying to put his life back together after an incomprehensible tragedy.

"I think that will be all, Mr. Geraty," she said. "Thanks so much for your time. And I know it's awfully late to be saying so, but I'm sorry for your loss."

A few moments later, Riley and Bill were driving away.

"A wasted trip," Riley said to Bill.

Riley looked in the rearview mirror and saw the little town of Belding vanishing behind them. The killer wasn't there, she knew. But he was somewhere in the area that Flores had shown them on

69

the map. Somewhere close. Perhaps they were driving by his trailer right now and didn't even know it. The thought tortured Riley. She could almost feel his presence, his eagerness, his urge to torture and kill that was becoming an ever more compelling need.

And she had to stop it.

Chapter 15

The man was awakened by his cell phone alarm. At first he didn't know where he was. But he knew right away that today was going to be important. It was the kind of day he lived for.

He knew that he had awakened in this strange place for a very good reason—because it was to be that kind of day. It would be a day of delicious satisfaction for him, and of sheer terror and indescribable pain for someone else.

But where was he? Still half-asleep, he couldn't remember. He was lying on a couch in a small, carpeted room, looking at a refrigerator and a microwave. Morning light streamed through a window.

He got up, opened the door to the room, and looked out into a dark hallway. He flipped on the room light beside the doorframe. Light shined out into the hallway and into an open door across the hallway. He could make out a black-upholstered medical examination table with some sterilized white paper stretched along it.

Of course, he thought. *The free medical clinic.*

Now he remembered where he was and how he'd gotten here. He congratulated himself on his stealth and cunning. Yesterday he'd arrived at the clinic late in the day, when it was especially busy. In the midst of the bustle of patients, he had asked for a simple blood pressure test. And *she* had been the nurse who tested him.

The very woman he had come here to see. The woman he had been watching for days, at her home, when she was shopping, when she came here to work.

After the blood pressure test he'd squeezed himself into a tight space deep inside a supply closet. How innocent all the staff had been. The clinic had closed and everyone had gone home without even checking the closets. Then he'd crept out and made himself at home right here, in the little staff lounge. He'd slept well.

And today was going to be a very remarkable day.

He turned the ceiling light off immediately. No one outside must know that anyone was in the building. He looked at the time on his cell phone. It was just a few minutes before seven a.m.

She would arrive any minute now. He knew this from his days of surveillance. It was her job to get the clinic ready for both physicians and patients every morning. The clinic itself didn't open until eight. Between seven and eight, she was always alone here.

71

But today was going to be different. Today she would not be alone.

He heard a car pull into the parking lot outside. He adjusted the venetian blinds just enough to look outside. It was her, all right, stepping out of the car.

He had no trouble steadying his nerves. This was not like those first two times, when he had felt so fearful and apprehensive. Ever since the third time, when everything had flowed so smoothly, he knew he had really hit his stride. Now he was seasoned and skillful.

But there was one thing he wanted to do a little differently, just to vary his routine, to make this time a little different from the others.

He was going to surprise her with a little token—his own personal calling card.

*

As Cindy MacKinnon walked through the empty parking lot, she mentally rehearsed her daily routine. After getting all the supplies in place, her first order of business would be to sign refill requests from pharmacies and make sure the appointment calendar was up to date.

Patients would be waiting outside the door by the time they opened at eight. The rest of the day would be devoted to sundry tasks, including taking vital signs, drawing blood, giving shots, making appointments, and fulfilling the often unreasonable demands of the registered nurses and physicians.

Her work here as a licensed practical nurse was hardly glamorous. Even so, she loved what she did. It was deeply gratifying to help people who otherwise couldn't afford medical care. She knew that they saved lives here, even with the basic services that they offered.

Cindy took the clinic keys out of her purse and unlocked the glass front door. She stepped inside quickly and locked the door behind her. Someone else would unlock it again at eight o'clock. Then she immediately punched in the code to deactivate the building alarm.

As she walked into the waiting area, something caught her eye. It was a small object lying on the floor. In the dim light, she couldn't make out what it was.

She switched on the overhead lights. The object on the floor was a rose.

She walked over to it and picked it up. The rose wasn't real. It was artificial, made of cheap fabric. But what was it doing there?

Probably a patient had dropped it yesterday. But why hadn't someone picked it up after the clinic closed at five p.m.?

Why hadn't *she* seen it yesterday? She had waited until the cleaning woman was finished. She had been the last to leave and she was sure the rose hadn't been there.

Then came a rush of adrenaline and an explosion of pure fear. She knew what the rose meant. She wasn't alone. She knew she had to get out. She didn't have a split second to lose.

But as she turned to run toward the door, a strong hand seized her arm from behind, stopping her in her tracks. There was no time to think. She had to let her body act on its own.

She raised her elbow and whirled around, throwing her whole weight to the side and back. She felt her elbow strike a hard but pliable surface. She heard a fierce, loud groan and felt the weight of her attacker's body tilting upon her.

Had she been lucky and hit his solar plexus? She couldn't turn around to see. There wasn't time—a few seconds, if even that.

She ran toward the door. But time slowed down, and it didn't feel like running at all. It felt like moving through thick, clear gelatin.

Finally she reached the door and tried to pull it open. But of course she had locked it after coming inside.

She groped frantically through her purse until she found her keys. Then her hands shook so badly that she couldn't hold them. They fell clattering to the ground. Time stretched out even further as she bent over and picked them up. She fumbled among the keys until she found the right one. Then she stabbed the key at the lock.

It was useless. Her hand was useless from shaking. She felt as if her body were betraying her.

At last, her eye caught a glimpse of movement outside. On the sidewalk beyond the parking lot a woman was walking her dog. Still gripping the keys, she raised her fists and pounded against the impossibly hard glass. She opened her mouth to scream.

But her voice was stifled by something tight across her mouth, pulling painfully at the corners. It was cloth—a rag or a handkerchief or a scarf. Her attacker had gagged her with merciless and implacable force. Her eyes bulged, but instead of a scream, all she could emit was a horrible groan.

She flailed her arms, and the keys fell again from her hand. She was pulled helplessly backward, away from the morning light into a

73

dark, murky world of sudden and unimaginable horror.

Chapter 16

"Do you feel kind of out of place?" Bill asked.

"Yeah," Riley said. "And I'm sure we both look it, too."

A seemingly random mix of dolls and people were seated in the leather-upholstered furniture of the ostentatious hotel lobby. The people—mostly women, but a few men—were drinking tea and coffee and chatting with one another. Dolls of sundry types, both male and female, sat among them like perfectly behaved children. Riley thought it looked like some bizarre kind of family reunion in which none of the children were real.

Riley couldn't help staring at the odd scene. With no more leads to follow, she and Bill had decided to come here, to this doll convention, hoping she might stumble upon some lead, however remote.

"Are you two registered?" he asked

Riley turned to see a security guard eyeing Bill's jacket, undoubtedly having detected his concealed weapon. The guard held his hand near his own holstered gun.

She thought that with this many people around, the guard had good reason to worry. A crazed shooter really could wreak havoc in a place like this.

Bill flashed his badge. "FBI," he said.

The guard chuckled.

"Can't say I'm surprised," he said.

"Why not?" Riley asked.

The guard shook his head.

"Because this is just about the weirdest bunch of people I ever saw in one place."

"Yeah," Bill agreed. "And they're not even all people."

The guard shrugged and replied, "You can bet that *somebody* here has done something they shouldn't have."

The man jerked his head to one side then the other, scanning the room.

"I'll be glad when it's all over." Then he strode away, looking wary and alert.

As she wandered with Bill into an adjoining hallway, Riley wasn't sure what the guard was so worried about. Generally speaking, the attendees looked more eccentric than menacing. The women in view ranged from young to elderly. Some were stern and dour looking, while others seemed open and friendly.

"Tell me again what you hope to find out here," Bill muttered.

"I'm not sure," Riley admitted.

"Maybe you're making too much of the whole doll thing," he said, clearly unhappy to be here. "Blackwell was creepy about dolls, but he wasn't the perp. And yesterday we learned that the first victim didn't even like dolls."

Riley didn't reply. Bill might well be right. But when he had showed her a brochure announcing this convention and show, she somehow couldn't help following through. She wanted to make another try.

The men Riley saw tended to look bookish and professorial, most of them wearing glasses and more than a few of them sporting goatees. None of them appeared quite capable of murder. She passed a seated woman who was lovingly rocking a baby doll in her arms and singing a lullaby. A little farther on, an elderly woman was carrying on a rapt conversation with a life-sized monkey doll.

Okay, Riley thought, *so there is a little bit of weirdness going on.*

Bill pulled the brochure out of his jacket pocket and browsed it as they walked along.

"Anything interesting happening?" Riley asked him.

"Just talks, lectures, workshops—that kind of thing. Some big manufacturers are here to bring store owners up to date on trends and crazes. And there are some folks who seem to have gotten famous in the whole doll scene. They're giving talks of one kind or another."

Then Bill laughed.

"Hey, here's a lecture with a real doozy of a title."

"What is it?"

"'The Social Construction of Victorian Gender in Period Porcelain Dolls.' It's going to start in a few minutes. Want to check it out?"

Riley laughed as well. "I'm sure we wouldn't understand a word of it. Anything else?"

Bill shook his head. "Not really. Nothing to help understand the motives of a sadistic killer, anyway."

Riley and Bill moved on into the next big open room. It was a gigantic maze of booths and tables, where every conceivable kind of doll or puppet was on exhibit. They ranged from as tiny as a single finger to life size, from antique to fresh out of the factory. Some of them were walking and some were talking, but most of them just hung or sat or stood there, staring back at the viewers who clustered in front of each one.

For the first time Riley saw that actual children were present—no boys, only small girls. Most were under their parents' immediate supervision, but a few wandered loose in unruly little groups, putting exhibitors' nerves on edge.

Riley picked up a miniature camera from a table. The attached tag claimed that it worked. On the same counter were tiny newspapers, stuffed toys, handbags, wallets, and backpacks. On the next table were doll-sized bathtubs and other bathroom fixtures.

The T-shirt station printed shirts for dolls and for full-size people, but the hair salon was for dolls only. The sight of several small carefully styled wigs gave Riley chills. The FBI had already found the manufacturers of the wigs from the murder scenes and knew that they were sold in countless stores everywhere. Seeing them lined up like this brought back images that Riley knew that other people here didn't share. Images of dead women, naked, sitting splayed like dolls, wearing ill-fitting wigs made out of doll hair.

Riley felt sure that those images would never fade from her mind. The women treated so callously, yet so carefully arranged to represent … something she couldn't quite pin down. But of course that was why she and Bill were even here.

She stepped forward and spoke to the perky young woman who seemed to be charge of the doll-hair salon.

"Do you sell these wigs here?" Riley asked.

"Of course," the woman responded. "Those are just for display, but I have brand new ones in boxes. Which one would you like?"

Riley wasn't sure what to say next. "Do you style these little wigs?" she finally asked.

"We can change the style for you. It's a very small additional charge."

"What kind of people buy them?" Riley said. She wanted to ask whether any creepy guys had been around to buy doll wigs.

The woman looked at her, wide-eyed. "I'm not sure what you mean," she said. "All kinds of people buy them. Sometimes they bring in a doll they already have to get the hair changed."

"I mean, do men often buy them?" Riley asked.

The young woman was looking distinctly uncomfortable now. "Not that I recall," she said. Then she turned abruptly away to deal with a new customer.

Riley just stood there for a moment. She felt like an idiot, accosting someone with such questions. It was as though she had thrust her own dark world into one that was supposed to be sweet and simple.

She felt a touch on her arm. Bill said, "I don't think you're going to find the perp here."

Riley could feel her face flush. But as she turned away from the doll-hair salon, she realized that she wasn't the only strange lady that the exhibitors here had to deal with. She almost walked into a woman desperately clutching a newly bought doll, weeping passionately, apparently with joy. At another table, a man and a woman had gotten into a shouting match over which of them would get to buy a particularly rare collector's item. They were engaged in a physical tug-of-war that threatened to tear the merchandise apart.

"Now I begin to see why that security guard was worried," she said to Bill.

She saw that Bill was intently watching someone nearby.

"What?" she asked him.

"Check out that guy," Bill said, nodding toward a man standing at a nearby display of large dolls in frilly dresses. He was in his mid-thirties and quite handsome. Unlike most of the other males here, he didn't look bookish or scholarly. Instead, he cut the appearance of a prosperous and confident businessman, properly dressed in an expensive suit and tie.

"He looks as out of place as we do," Bill muttered. "Why is a guy like that playing with dolls?"

"I don't know," Riley replied. "But he also looks like he could hire a real live playmate if he wanted to." She watched the businessman for a moment. He had stopped to look at a display of little girl dolls in frilly dresses. He glanced around, as if to be sure that no one was watching.

Bill turned his back to the man and leaned forward as if talking animatedly with Riley. "What's he doing now?"

"Checking out the merchandise," she said. "In a way I really don't like."

The man bent toward one doll and peered at it closely—maybe a little too closely—and his thin lips curled up into a smile. Then he again scanned the others in the room.

"Or looking for prospective victims," she added.

Riley was sure she detected a certain furtiveness in the man's manner as he fingered the doll's dress, examining the fabric in a sensuous manner.

Bill glanced at the man again. "Jesus," he murmured. "Is this guy creepy or what?"

A chilly feeling seized Riley. Rationally, she knew perfectly well that this couldn't be the murderer. After all, what were the chances of stumbling across him in public like this? Still, at that moment Riley was convinced that she was in the presence of evil.

"Don't let him get out of sight," Riley said. "If he gets weird enough, we'll ask him some questions."

But then, reality blew those dark thoughts away. A little girl about five years old came running up to the man.

"Daddy," she called him.

The man's smile widened, and his face beamed innocently with love. He showed his daughter the doll he had found, and she clapped her hands and laughed with delight. He handed it to her and she hugged it tightly. The father took out his wallet and got ready to pay the vendor.

Riley stifled a groan.

My instincts miss again, she thought.

She saw that Bill was listening to someone on his cell phone. His face looked stricken as he turned toward her.

"He's taken another woman."

Chapter 17

Riley cursed under her breath as she pulled into the parking lot beside a long, flat-roofed building. Three people wearing FBI jackets were standing outside, mingling with several local cops.

"This can't be good," Riley said. "I wish we'd gotten here before the hordes descended."

"No joke," Bill agreed.

They'd been told that a woman had been kidnapped from inside this small-town medical clinic, taken early this morning.

"At least we're getting on it faster this time," Bill said. "Maybe we stand a chance of getting her back alive."

Riley silently agreed. In the earlier cases, no one had known exactly when or where the victim was kidnapped. The women had just disappeared and later turned up dead accompanied by cryptic signs of the killer's mindset.

Maybe it will be different this time, she thought.

She was relieved that someone had witnessed enough of the crime to call 911. The local police knew about an alert for a serial kidnapper and killer, and they had called in the FBI. They were all assuming that this was the same deviant at work.

"He's still way ahead of us," Riley said. "If it's really him. This is not the kind of place I expected our perp to grab someone."

She had thought the killer would be stalking a parking garage or an isolated jogging trail. Maybe even a poorly lit neighborhood.

"Why a community clinic?" she asked. "And why in daylight? Why would he take the chance of entering a building?"

"Sure doesn't seem like a random choice," Bill agreed. "Let's get moving."

Riley parked as close to the taped-off area as she could. As she and Bill got out of the car, she recognized Special Agent in Charge Carl Walder.

"This is *really* bad," Riley muttered to Bill as they walked toward the building.

Riley didn't think much of Walder—a babyish, freckled-faced man with curly, copper-colored hair. Neither Riley nor Bill had personally worked a case under him, but he had a bad reputation. Other agents said that he was the worst kind of boss—someone who had no idea what he was doing, and was therefore all the more determined to throw his weight around and assert his authority.

To make matters worse for Riley and Bill, Walder outranked

their own team chief, Brent Meredith. Riley didn't know how old Walder was, but she was sure that he had risen up the FBI food chain too fast for his own good, or for anybody else's.

As far as Riley was concerned, it was a classic example of the Peter Principle at work. Walder had successfully risen to the level of his incompetence.

Walder stepped forward to meet Riley and Bill.

"Agents Paige and Jeffreys, I'm glad you could make it," he said.

Without niceties, Riley went right ahead and asked Walder the question that was nagging at her.

"How do we know it's the same perp that took the other three women?"

"Because of this," Walder said, holding out an evidence bag holding a cheap little fabric rose. "It was lying on the floor just inside."

"Oh, shit," Riley said.

The Bureau had been careful not to leak to the press that detail of his MO—how he'd left roses at the scenes where he'd posed the bodies. This was not the work of a copycat or of a brand new killer.

"Who was it this time?" Bill asked.

"Her name is Cindy MacKinnon," Walder said. "She's an LPN. She was abducted when she came in early to set up the clinic."

Then Walder indicated the other two agents, a young female and an even younger male. "Perhaps you've met Agents Craig Huang and Emily Creighton. They'll be joining you on this case."

Bill audibly murmured, "What the—"

Riley poked Bill in the ribs to shut him up.

"Huang and Creighton have already been briefed," Walder added. "They know as much about these murders as you do."

Riley fumed silently. She wanted to tell Walder that no, Huang and Creighton did *not* know as much as she did. Not even as much as Bill did. They couldn't know that much without having spent as much time at the crime scenes, or without having spent uncounted hours poring over evidence. They didn't have anything resembling the professional investment she and Bill had already put into this case. And she was sure that neither of these youngsters had ever summoned up the mind of a killer to get a sense of his experience.

Riley took a deep breath to stifle her anger.

"With due respect, sir," she said, "Agent Jeffreys and I have got a pretty good handle on it and we'll need to work fast. Extra help ... won't help." She'd almost said that extra help would just slow them down, but had stopped herself in time. No point in insulting the kids.

Riley detected a trace of a smirk on Walder's babyish face.

"With due respect, Agent Paige," he replied, "Senator Newbrough doesn't agree."

Riley's heart sank. She remembered her unpleasant interview with the Senator and something he had said. *"You may not know it, but I've got good friends in the upper echelons of the agency."*

Of course Walder had to be one of those "good friends."

Walder lifted his chin and spoke with borrowed authority. "The Senator says that you're having trouble grasping the full magnitude of this case."

"I'm afraid the Senator is letting his emotions run away with him," Riley said. "It's understandable, and I sympathize. He's distraught. He thinks that his daughter's killing was political or personal or both. It obviously wasn't."

Walder squinted his eyes skeptically.

"How is it obvious?" he said. "It seems obvious to me that he's right."

Riley could hardly believe her ears

"Sir, the Senator's daughter was the third woman taken out of what are now four," she said. "His time frame has been spread out over more than two years. It's purely coincidence that his daughter happened to be one of the victims."

"I beg to differ," Walder said. "And so do Agents Huang and Creighton."

As if on cue, Agent Emily Creighton piped in.

"Doesn't this kind of thing happen from time to time?" she said. "Like, sometimes a perpetrator will stage another murder before killing his intended victim? Just to make it look serial and not personal?"

"This last abduction could serve the same purpose," added Agent Craig Huang. "A final decoy."

Riley managed not to roll her eyes at the kids' naiveté.

"That's an old, old story," she said. "A work of fiction. It doesn't happen in real life."

"Well," Walder said in an authoritative tone, "it happened *this* time."

"We don't have time for this," Riley snapped. Her patience had run out. "Have we got any witnesses?"

"One," Walder said. "Greta Tedrow made the 911 call but she didn't actually see much. She's sitting inside. The receptionist is in there too, but she didn't see it happen. By the time she showed up at eight o'clock, the cops were already here."

Through the clinic's glass doors, Riley could see two women sitting in the waiting room. One was a slim woman in running clothes, with a cocker spaniel on a leash beside her. The other was large, middle-aged, and Hispanic-looking.

"Have you interviewed Ms. Tedrow?" Riley asked Walder.

"She's been too shaken up to talk," Walder said. "We're going to take her back to the BAU."

Riley actually did roll her eyes this time. Why make an innocent witness feel like a suspect? Why play the bully, as if that wouldn't shake her up even more?

Ignoring Walder's gesture of protest, she swung a door open and strode through the entrance.

Bill followed her in, but he left the interview to Riley while he checked a couple of adjoining offices, then poked around the waiting room.

The woman with the dog looked at Riley anxiously.

"What's going on?" Greta Tedrow asked. "I'm ready to answer questions. But nobody's asking me anything. Why can't I go home?"

Riley sat in a chair beside her and patted her hand.

"You will go home, Ms. Tedrow, and soon," she said. "I'm Agent Paige, and I'll ask you a few questions right now."

Greta Tedrow nodded shakily. The cocker spaniel just lay there on the floor looking up at Riley in a friendly manner.

"Nice dog," Riley said. "Very well behaved. How old is he—or is it a she?"

"It's he. Toby's his name. He's five years old."

Riley slowly held her hand toward the dog. With the animal's silent permission, she petted his head lightly.

The woman nodded an unspoken thank-you. Riley got out her pencil and notepad.

"Now take your time, don't rush," Riley said. "Tell me in your own words how it happened. Try to remember everything you can."

The woman spoke slowly and haltingly.

"I was walking Toby." She pointed outside. "We were just coming around the corner beyond the hedges, over that way. The clinic had just come into view. I thought I heard something. I looked. There was a woman in the clinic doorway. She was pounding on the glass. I think her mouth was gagged. Then someone pulled her backward out of sight."

Riley patted the woman's hand again.

"You're doing great, Ms. Tedrow," she said. "Did you see her attacker at all?"

The woman wrestled with her memory.

"I didn't see his face," she said. "I *couldn't* see his face. The light was on in the clinic, but …"

Riley could see a flash of recollection cross the woman's face.

"Oh," the woman said. "He was wearing a dark ski mask."

"Very good. What happened next?"

The woman became slightly more agitated.

"I didn't stop to think. I got out my cell phone and called 911. It seemed like a long time before I could get an operator. I was on the phone talking to the operator when a truck came tearing out from behind the building. Its tires screeched going out of the parking lot, and it turned to the left."

Riley was taking notes rapidly. She was aware that Walder and his two young favorites had come into the room and were just standing there, but she ignored them.

"What kind of truck?" she asked.

The woman knitted her forehead. "A Dodge Ram, I think. Yes, that's right. Pretty old—maybe from the late nineties. It was very dirty, but I think it was a really deep navy blue color. And it had something on its bed. Kind of like a camper, only it wasn't a camper. One of those aluminum tops with windows."

"A cap?" Riley suggested.

The woman nodded. "I think that's what they're called."

Riley was pleased and impressed by the woman's memory.

"What about a license number?" Riley asked.

The woman looked a little bit taken aback.

"I—I didn't catch it," she said, sounding disappointed with herself.

"Not even one letter or number?" Riley asked.

"I'm sorry, but I didn't see it. I don't know how I missed it."

Walder stooped down and whispered intensely in Riley's ear.

"We've *got* to take her to the BAU," he said.

He backed up a little as Riley rose to her feet.

"Thank you, Ms. Tedrow," Riley said. "That's all for now. Have the police already taken your contact information?"

The woman nodded.

"Then go home and get some rest," Riley said. "We'll be in touch again soon."

The woman walked her dog out of the clinic and headed home.

Walder looked ready to explode with rage and exasperation.

"What the hell was that all about?" he demanded. "I said we had to take her to the BAU."

Riley shrugged. "I can't imagine why we would do that," she said. "We've got to keep moving on this case and she's told us all she can."

"I want one of our hypnotists to work with her. To help her remember the license number. It's in her brain somewhere."

"Agent Walder," Riley said, trying not to sound as impatient as she felt, "Greta Tedrow is one of the most observant witnesses I've interviewed in a very long time. She said she didn't see the license plate number, didn't 'catch' it. Not even one number. That bothered her. She didn't know how she could miss it. Coming from someone with a memory as sharp as hers, that can only mean one thing."

She paused, challenging Walder to guess what that "one thing" might be. She could tell by his vacant expression that he had no idea.

"There *was* no license plate to see," she finally said. "Either the attacker had removed it or it had been muddied up and made unreadable. All she saw was a blank space where the license plate should have been. If a legible license plate had been there, that woman would have caught at least part of it."

Bill let out a snort of quiet admiration. Riley wanted to shush him, but figured that would only make matters worse. She decided to change the subject.

"Has the victim's next of kin been contacted?" she asked Walder.

Walder nodded. "Her husband. He came here for a few minutes. But he couldn't handle it. We sent him home. He lives only a few blocks away. I'll send Agents Huang and Creighton to interview him."

The two younger agents had been standing apart enthusiastically discussing something. At that moment, they turned toward Riley, Bill, and Walder. They looked very happy with themselves.

"Emily—er, Agent Creighton and I have got it figured out," Huang said. "There was no sign of a break-in, nothing resembling forced entry. That means the perp's got local connections. In fact, he knows somebody who works in this clinic. He just might work here himself."

"Somehow he got his hands on a key," Creighton put in. "Maybe he stole it, or maybe he borrowed it and copied it, something like that. And he knew the code for the alarm. He got in and out without setting it off. We'll interview the staff with that in mind."

"And we know just who we're looking for," Huang said. "Someone with some kind of grudge against Senator Newbrough."

Riley choked back her anger. These two were jumping to unfounded conclusions. Of course, they could be right. But what had they overlooked? She looked around at the clinic waiting room and adjoining hallway and a different possibility formed in her mind. She turned toward the Hispanic receptionist.

"*Perdóneme, señora,*" she said to the woman. "*Dónde está el cuarto de provisiones?*"

"*Allá,*" the woman said, pointing to a hallway door.

Riley went to the door and opened it. She looked inside, then turned to Walder and said, "I can tell you exactly how he got into the building. He came in through here."

Walder looked annoyed. By contrast, Bill looked anything but annoyed—positively delighted, in fact. Riley knew that Bill disliked Walder as much as she did. He was undoubtedly looking forward to seeing Walder get a good lesson in detective work.

The two young agents stared into the open doorway, then turned toward Riley.

"I don't get it," complained Emily Creighton.

"It's just a closet," echoed Craig Huang.

"Look at those boxes in the back," Riley said. "Don't touch anything."

Bill and Walder joined the cluster of people looking into the big supply closet. Paper supplies and bandages were stored on wide shelves. Clinicians' apparel was stacked in one area. But several large boxes on the floor looked out of place. Although everything else in the closet was arranged neatly, those boxes sat at odd angles and space was visible behind them.

"Boxes pushed away from the back wall," Bill commented. "Somebody could have hidden back in there pretty easily."

"Get the evidence crew in here," Walder snapped to the younger agents. Then he asked Riley, "What's your theory?"

Her brain was clicking away as the scenario rapidly took shape for her. She started laying it out.

"He arrived at the clinic yesterday," she said. "Probably late in the day, at some especially busy hour. In the midst of the bustle of patients, he asked the receptionist for something simple. A blood pressure test, maybe. And *she* might well have been the nurse who administered that test—Cindy MacKinnon, the woman he had been stalking, the woman he came here to abduct. He would have enjoyed that."

"You can't know that for sure," Walder said.

"No," Riley agreed. "And of course he wouldn't give his real name, but have someone check the clinic records for her services to anyone the other staff members don't recognize. In fact, we should check on everyone who was a patient here yesterday."

That would take time, she knew. But they had to follow up on every possibility as fast as they could. This man had to be stopped.

"He was here," Riley said, "mingling with all the patients. Maybe someone will remember something odd. And when no one was looking, he managed to get into this supply room."

"It isn't drug storage and I don't see anything else that would be valuable enough to steal," Bill added. "So it probably isn't watched very carefully."

"He squeezed himself into a tight space right under the bottom shelf and behind those boxes," Riley said. "The staff had no idea he was there. The clinic closed at the usual hour, and everyone went home without noticing. When he was sure that everyone had left, the perp pushed the boxes aside, crept out, and made himself at home. He waited all night. My guess is that he slept just fine."

The evidence team came in, and the agents moved aside to let them do their search for hairs, fingerprints, or anything else that might carry DNA or provide some other clue.

"You might be right," Walder muttered. "We'll also need to go over anywhere he might have been during the night. That means everywhere."

"It's the simplest solution," Riley said. "That's usually the best."

She put on her plastic gloves and went on down the hallway, looking into each room. One was a staff lounge, with a comfortable-looking couch.

"This is where he spent the night," she said with a feeling of certainty.

Walder looked inside. "Everybody stay out of this room until the team has been over it," he said, doing his best to sound efficient.

Riley returned to the waiting room. "He was already here when Cindy MacKinnon showed up this morning, right on schedule. He grabbed her."

Riley pointed toward the end of the hallway.

"Then he made off with her through the back entrance. He had his truck waiting right out there."

Riley closed her eyes for a moment. She could almost see him in her mind, a shadowy image she couldn't quite bring into focus. If he stood out someone would notice. So he wasn't extreme in appearance. Not obese, not unusually tall or short, no weird hairstyle, not marked by odd tattoos or coloring. He would be dressed in well-worn clothes, but nothing that would identify with a particular job. Old casual clothes. That would be natural to him, she thought. That was how he usually dressed.

"What is his connection with these women?" she muttered. "Where does his fury come from?"

"We'll find out," Bill said firmly.

Walder was completely silent now. Riley knew why. His protégés' overwrought theory about the abductor having an inside connection now seemed perfectly ridiculous. When Riley spoke again, it was in a tone that bordered on patronizing.

"Agent Walder, I appreciate the youthful spirit of your two agents," she said. "They're learning. They'll get good at this someday. I really believe that. But I think you'd better leave interviewing the husband to Agent Jeffreys and myself."

Walder sighed and gave her a slight, barely visible nod.

Without another word, Riley and Bill left the scene of the abduction. She had some important questions to ask the victim's husband.

Chapter 18

As she drove to the address the clinic receptionist had given her, Riley felt her usual dread at having to interview victims' families or spouses. She somehow sensed that this time was going to be even worse than usual. But the abduction was fresh.

"Maybe this time, we'll find her before he kills her," she said.

"If the evidence team can get a clue on this guy," Bill replied.

"Somehow, I doubt that he's going to turn up in any database." The image that Riley was forming in her mind wasn't of a habitual offender. This thing was deeply personal to the killer in some way that she hadn't been able to identify. She would figure it out, she was sure. But she needed to figure it out fast enough to stop the terror and agony that Cindy was going through right now. No one else should have to endure the pain of that knife … or of that darkness … of that searing flame …

"Riley," Bill said sharply, "that's it right there."

Riley jerked back to the present. She pulled the car over to the curb and looked around at the neighborhood. It was a little rundown but all the more warm and inviting because of that. It was the sort of low-rent area where young people without a lot of money could pursue their dreams.

Of course, Riley knew that the neighborhood wouldn't stay this way. Gentrification was undoubtedly scheduled to kick in any day now. But maybe that would be good for an art gallery. If the victim got back home alive.

Riley and Bill got out of the car and approached the little storefront gallery. A handsome metal sculpture was displayed in the front window behind a sign that announced "CLOSED."

The couple's apartment was upstairs. Riley rang the doorbell, and she and Bill waited for a few moments. She wondered who was going to come to the door.

When the door opened, she was relived to be greeted by the compassionate face of FBI victim specialist Beverly Chaddick. Riley had worked with Beverly before. The specialist had been in this job for at least twenty years, and she had a wonderful way dealing with distraught victims and family members.

"We need to ask Mr. MacKinnon some questions," Riley said. "I hope he's up for it."

"Yes," Beverly said. "But go easy on him."

Beverly led Bill and Riley upstairs to the little apartment. It immediately struck Riley as heartbreakingly cheerful, decorated with a marvelous clutter of paintings and sculptures. The people who lived here loved to celebrate life and all of its possibilities. Was all that over now? Her heart ached for the young couple.

Nathaniel MacKinnon, a man in his late twenties, was sitting in the combined living and dining room. His lankiness made him look all the more broken.

Beverly announced in a gentle voice, "Nathaniel, Agents Paige and Jeffreys are here."

The young man looked at Bill and Riley expectantly. His voice croaked with desperation.

"Have you found Cindy? Is she okay? Is she alive?"

Riley realized that she could say nothing helpful. She was all the more grateful that Beverly was here, and that she'd already established a rapport with the distraught husband.

Beverly sat down next to Nathaniel MacKinnon.

"Nobody knows anything yet, Nathaniel," she said. "They're here to help."

Bill and Riley sat down nearby.

Riley asked, "Mr. MacKinnon, has your wife said anything recently about feeling fearful or threatened?"

He shook his head mutely.

Bill put in, "This is a difficult question, but we have to ask. Do either you or your wife have any enemies, anybody who might wish you harm?"

The husband seemed to have trouble understanding the question.

"No, no," he stammered. "Look, there are sometimes little feuds in my line of work. But it's all just stupid little things, squabbles among artists, not people who would do something like …"

He stopped in mid-sentence.

"And everybody … *loves* Cindy," he said.

Riley detected his anxiety and uncertainty about using the present tense. She sensed that questioning this man was probably futile and possibly insensitive. She and Bill should probably cut things short and leave the situation in Beverly's capable hands.

Meanwhile, though, Riley looked around the apartment, trying to pick up the slightest trace of a clue.

She didn't need to be told that Cindy and Nathaniel MacKinnon didn't have children. The apartment wasn't big enough, and besides, the surrounding artworks were anything but childproof.

She suspected, though, that the situation was not the same as with Margaret and Roy Geraty. Riley's gut told her that Cindy and Nathaniel were childless by choice, and only temporarily. They were waiting for the right time, more money, a bigger home, a more settled lifestyle.

They thought they had all kinds of time, Riley thought.

She thought back to her early assumption that the killer targeted mothers. She wondered yet again how she could have gotten it so wrong.

Something else about the apartment was starting to dawn on her. She saw no photographs anywhere of Nathaniel or Cindy. This wasn't especially surprising. As a couple, they were more interested in the creativity of others than in pictures of themselves. They were anything but narcissistic.

Even so, Riley felt the need to get a clearer image of Cindy.

"Mr. MacKinnon," she asked cautiously, "do you have any recent photographs of your wife?"

He looked at her blankly for a moment. Then his expression brightened.

"Why, yes," he said. "I've got a new one right here on my cell phone."

He brought up the photograph on his phone and passed it along to Riley.

Riley's heart jumped up in her throat when she saw it. Cindy MacKinnon was sitting with a three-year-old girl on her lap. Both she and the child were glowing with delight as they held a beautifully dressed doll between them.

It took Riley a moment to start breathing again. The kidnapped woman, a child, and a doll. She hadn't been wrong. At least not completely. There had to be a connection between this killer and dolls.

"Mr. MacKinnon, who is the child in this picture?" Riley asked, as calmly as she could manage.

"That's Cindy's niece, Gale," Nathaniel MacKinnon replied. "Her mother is Cindy's sister, Becky."

"When was this photograph taken?" Riley asked.

The man stopped to think. "I think Cindy sent it to me on Friday," he said. "Yes, I'm sure that's when she sent it. It was at Gale's birthday party. Cindy helped her sister with the party. She left work early to help out."

Riley struggled with her thoughts, unsure for a moment just what to ask next.

"Was the doll a gift for Cindy's niece?" she asked.

Nathaniel nodded. "Gale was thrilled with it. That made Cindy so happy. She just loves to see Gale happy. The girl's almost like a daughter to her. She called me right away to tell me. That's when she sent the photograph."

Riley struggled to keep her voice steady. "It's a lovely doll. I can see why Gale was so happy with it."

She hesitated again, staring at the doll's image as though it could tell her whatever it was that she needed to know. Surely that painted smile, those blank blue eyes, held a key to her questions. But she didn't even know what to ask.

Out of the corner of her eye she could see Bill watching her intently.

Why would a brutal killer pose his victims to look like dolls?

Finally Riley asked, "Do you know where Cindy bought the doll?"

Nathaniel looked genuinely puzzled. Even Bill looked surprised. Doubtless he wondered where Riley was going with this. The truth was, Riley wasn't entirely sure yet herself.

"I've got no idea," Nathaniel said. "She didn't tell me. Is that important?"

"I'm not sure," Riley admitted. "But I think it could be."

Nathaniel was growing more agitated now. "I don't understand. What's this all about? Are you saying my wife was abducted over a little girl's doll?"

"No, I'm not saying that." Riley tried to sound calm and convincing. Of course, she realized, she *was* saying that. She thought that his wife probably was abducted over some little girl's doll, even though that made no sense at all.

Nathaniel was visibly distressed. Riley saw that Beverly Chaddick, the victim specialist who was seated nearby, was eyeing her uneasily. With a slight shake of her head, Beverly seemed to be trying to communicate that Riley needed to go easier on the distraught husband. Riley reminded herself that interviewing victims and their families was not her own forte.

I've got to be careful, she told herself. But she also felt an urgent need to hurry. The woman was in captivity. Caged or tied, that didn't matter. She didn't have long to live. Was this any time to hold back on any source of information?

"Is there any way to find out where Cindy bought it?" Riley asked, trying to speak in a gentler tone. "Just in case we do need that information."

"Cindy and I keep some receipts," Nathaniel said. "Just for tax-deductible expenses. I don't think she would have kept the receipt for a family gift. But I'll look."

Nathaniel went to a closet and took down a shoebox. He sat down again and opened the box, which was full of paper receipts. He started looking through the them, but his hands were trembling uncontrollably.

"I don't think I can do this," he said.

Beverly gently took the box away from him.

"That's all right, Mr. MacKinnon," she said. "I'll look for it."

Beverly began to rummage through the box. Nathaniel was near tears.

"I don't understand," he said in a broken voice. "She just bought a gift. It could have been anything. From anywhere. I think she was considering several possibilities, but she finally decided on a doll."

Riley felt sick to her stomach. Somehow, deciding on a doll had led Cindy MacKinnon into a nightmare. If she had decided on a stuffed animal instead, would she be at home today, alive and happy?

"Will you please explain to me what this doll business is all about?" Nathaniel insisted.

Riley knew that the man more than deserved an explanation. She could think of no gentle way to put it.

"I think—" she began haltingly. "I think that your wife's abductor—might be obsessed with dolls."

She was aware of the instant responses from the others in the room. Bill shook his head and turned his gaze downward. Beverly's head snapped up in shock. Nathaniel gazed at her with an expression of hopeless despair.

"What makes you think that?" he asked in a choked voice. "What do you know about him? What aren't you telling me?"

Riley searched for a helpful reply, but she could see an awful dawning realization in his eyes.

"He's done this before, hasn't he?" he said. "There have been other victims. Has this got something to do with—?"

Nathaniel struggled to remember something.

"Oh my God," he said. "I've been reading about it in the news. A serial killer. He killed other women. Their bodies were found in Mosby Park, and in that national park near Daggett, and somewhere around Belding."

He doubled over and began to sob uncontrollably.

"You think that Cindy's his next victim," he cried. "You think she's already dead."

Riley shook her head insistently.

"No," Riley said. "No, we don't think that."

"Then what *do* you think?"

Riley's thoughts were in turmoil. What could she tell him? That his wife was probably alive, but utterly terrified, and about to be hideously tortured and mutilated? And that the cutting and the stabbing would go on and on—until Cindy was rescued or dead, whichever came first?

Riley opened her mouth to speak, but no words at all came out. Beverly leaned forward and put one hand on Riley's arm. The specialist's face was still warm and friendly, but the fingers were quite firm.

Beverly spoke very slowly, as if explaining something to a child.

"I can't find the receipt," she said. "It's not here."

Riley understood Beverly's unspoken meaning. With her eyes, Beverly was telling her that the interview had gotten out of control, and that it was time for her to leave.

"I'll take it from here," Beverly mouthed in a barely audible whisper.

Riley whispered back to her, "Thank you. I'm sorry."

Beverly smiled and nodded sympathetically.

Nathaniel sat with his face buried in his hands. He didn't even look up at Riley as she and Bill stood up to leave.

They left the apartment and went back down the stairs to the street. They both got into Riley's car but she didn't start the engine. She felt her own tears welling up.

I don't know where to go, she thought. *I don't know what to do.*

It seemed to be the story of her life these days.

"It's dolls, Bill," she said. She was trying to explain her new theory to herself as much as to him. "It's definitely got something to do with dolls. Do you remember what Roy Geraty told us in Belding?"

Bill shrugged. "He said that his first wife—Margaret—didn't like dolls. They made her sad, he said. He said they sometimes made her cry."

"Yeah, because she couldn't have kids of her own," Riley said. "But he said something else. He said she had all kinds of friends and relatives having kids of their own. He said that she was always having to go to baby showers, and to help out with birthday parties."

Riley could see by Bill's expression that he was starting to understand now.

"So she sometimes had to *buy* dolls," he said. "Even if they did make her sad."

Riley struck the steering wheel with her fist.

"They all bought dolls," she said. "He *saw* them buying dolls. And he saw them buy the dolls in the same place, in the same store."

Bill nodded. "We've got to find that store," he said.

"Right," Riley said. "Somewhere in our thousand-plus-square-mile area, there's a doll store that all the kidnapped women went to. And he went there too. If we can find it, maybe—just maybe—we can find him."

At that moment, Bill's cell phone rang.

"Hello?" he said. "Yeah, Agent Walder, this is Jeffreys."

Riley stifled a moan. She wondered what kind of hassle Walder was about to cause them now.

She saw Bill's mouth drop open with stunned surprise.

"Jesus," he said. "Jesus. Okay. Okay. We'll be right there."

Bill ended the call and stared at Riley, dumbstruck for a few seconds.

"Walder and those kids he brought along," he said. "They've caught him."

Chapter 19

Riley and Bill arrived at the Behavioral Analysis Unit to find Walder waiting for them at the door.

"We've got him," Walder said, ushering them into the building. "We've got the guy."

Riley could hear both elation and relief in his voice.

"How?" she demanded.

"Agent Paige, you've seriously underestimated Huang and Creighton," Walder said. "After you left, the receptionist told them about a creepy guy who'd been hanging around the clinic recently. His name is Darrell Gumm. Women patients had complained about him. He was always getting too close to them, they said, not respecting their personal space. He also said some pretty unsavory things to them. And once or twice he actually sneaked into the women's restroom."

Riley mulled this over, checking it against her own assumptions about the perpetrator. *It could be him,* she thought. She felt a flutter of excitement in her throat.

Bill asked Walder, "Didn't anybody at the clinic call the police about Gumm?"

"They were letting their own security guy handle it. The guard told Gumm to stay away. At that kind of facility they do get oddballs from time to time. But Huang and Creighton picked up on the description. They realized he sounded like the guy we're looking for. They got his address from the receptionist, and we all headed over to his apartment."

"How do you know it's him?" Riley asked.

"He confessed," Walder said firmly. "We got a confession out of him."

Riley began to feel a touch of relief herself. "And Cindy MacKinnon?" she asked. "Where is she?"

"We're working on it," Walder said.

Riley's relief faded. "What do you mean, 'working on it'?" she asked.

"We've got field agents sweeping the neighborhood. We don't think he could have taken her very far. Anyhow, he'll tell us very soon. He's doing plenty of talking."

This had better be the guy, Riley thought. Cindy MacKinnon simply had to be alive. They couldn't lose yet another innocent woman to this twisted brute. His timeline was tightening up, but surely she wouldn't already be dead this soon after the abduction.

He hadn't had the pleasure of torturing her yet.

Bill asked Walder, "Where is the suspect now?"

Walder pointed the way. "We've got him over in the detention center," he said. "Come on. I'm headed there now."

Walder filled them in as they walked through the extensive BAU complex to the building where suspects were held.

"When we flashed our badges," Walder said grimly, "he invited us to come right in and make ourselves at home. Self-confident bastard."

Riley thought that sounded right. If Darren Gumm really was the perp, the agents' arrival might have been just the denouement he'd been hoping for. He might well have intended to get caught all along, after an all-too-clever, two-year game of cat and mouse with the authorities. Maybe the reward he'd been hoping for all along was fame—a lot more than fifteen minutes of fame.

The trouble was, Riley knew, he could still use his latest captive to toy with them all. And he could well be the type who would do that.

"You should have seen his place," Walder went on. "A filthy little one-room pit, with a fold-out couch and a tiny bathroom that stinks to high heaven. And on the walls, absolutely everywhere, he's got news clippings about assaults and rapes and murders from all over the country. No sign of a computer, he's completely off the grid, but I've got to say, he's got an analog database of psychopathic criminality that a lot of police departments would envy."

"And let me guess," Bill put in. "He had a cluster of stories posted up about our killings—pretty much all the information that's been made public about them for all of two years."

"He sure as hell did," Walder said. "Creighton and Huang asked him a few questions, and he acted as suspicious as hell. Finally Huang asked what he knew about Cindy MacKinnon and he clammed up. It was obvious he knew who we meant. We had enough to arrest him. And he confessed almost as soon as we got him here."

At that moment Walder led Riley and Bill into a little room with a one-way window that looked into an interrogation room.

The interrogation was already well under way. On one side of the table sat Agent Emily Creighton. Agent Craig Huang was pacing the floor behind her. Riley thought that the two young agents actually looked more capable than they had before. On the other side of the table sat Darrell Gumm. His wrists were cuffed to the tabletop.

Riley was repelled by him immediately. He was a little toad of a man, somewhere around thirty, of medium build, and somewhat pudgy. But he looked sufficiently sturdy to be a plausible physical threat, especially to defenseless women caught by surprise. His forehead sloped sharply backwards, making his skull look like that of some long extinct hominid. His chin was all but nonexistent. All in all, he certainly fit Riley's expectations. And his confession did seem to wrap things up.

"Where is she?" Creighton shouted at Gumm.

Riley could tell by the impatient crackle in Creighton's voice that she had already asked that question many times.

"Where is who?" Gumm asked in a high and unpleasant voice. His expression fairly reeked of contempt and insolence.

"Stop playing games with us," Huang said sharply.

"I don't have to say anything without a lawyer present, right?" Gumm said.

Creighton nodded. "We already told you that. We'll bring in a lawyer any time you ask for one. You keep saying you don't want one. That's your right too. You can waive your right to an attorney. Have you changed your mind?"

Gumm tilted his head and looked at the ceiling, mock-thoughtfully.

"Let me think about that. No, I don't think so. Not yet, anyway."

Huang leaned across the table toward him, trying hard to look menacing.

"I'm asking for the last time," he said. "Where did you hide the truck?"

Gumm shrugged. "And I'm *saying* for the last time—what truck? I don't own a truck. I don't even own a car. Shit, I don't even have a driver's license."

Speaking in a low voice, Walder informed Riley and Bill, "That last bit is true. No driver's license, no voter registration, no credit cards, nothing at all. He really does live off the grid. No wonder the truck didn't have a license plate. He probably stole it. But he couldn't have driven it far in the time he had. It has to be somewhere near his apartment."

Agent Creighton was scowling at Gumm now.

"You think this is funny, don't you?" she said. "You've got some poor woman tied up somewhere. You've admitted that much already. She's scared to death, and I'll bet she's hungry and thirsty

98

too. How long are you going to let her suffer? Are you really willing to let her die like that?"

Gumm snickered.

"Is this the part where you knock me around?" he asked. "Or is this when you tell me that you can get me to talk without leaving any visible marks?"

Riley had tried to keep quiet, but she couldn't contain herself any longer.

"They're not asking the right questions," she said.

She pushed past Walder and headed through the door that led into the interrogation room.

"Hold it, Agent Paige," Walder commanded.

Ignoring him, Riley charged into the room. She rushed toward the table, planted both hands on it, and leaned intimidatingly toward Gumm.

"Tell me, Darrell," she snarled. "Do you like dolls?"

For the first time, Darrell's face showed a trace of alarm.

"Who the hell are you?" he asked Riley.

"I'm somebody you don't want to lie to," Riley said. "Do you like dolls?"

Darrell's eyes darted around the room.

"I dunno," he said. "Dolls? They're cute, I guess."

"Oh, you think they're more than cute, don't you?" Riley said. "You were that kind of boy when you were little—the kind who liked to play with dolls, the kind that all the kids make fun of."

Darrell turned toward the mirror that was on his side of the one-way window.

"I know somebody's back there," he called out, sounding scared now. "Will somebody get this crazy woman away from me?"

Riley walked around the table, pushed Huang aside, and stood right next to Gumm. Then she shoved her face toward his face. He leaned back, trying to escape her gaze. But she wouldn't give him room to breathe. Their faces were only three or four inches apart.

"And you *still* like dolls, don't you?" Riley hissed, pounding her fist on the table. "Little girl dolls. You like to take their clothes off. You like to see them naked. What do you like to do with them when they're naked?"

Darrell's eyes widened.

Riley held his gaze for a long moment. She hesitated, trying to read his expression clearly. Was that contempt or disgust that turned his mouth down so sharply?

She opened her mouth to ask more, but the door to the

99

interrogation room burst open behind her. She heard Walder's stern voice.

"Agent Paige, I want you out of here right now."

"Give me just another minute," she said.

"Now!"

Riley stood over Gumm in silence for a moment. Now he just looked bewildered. She looked around and saw that Huang and Creighton were staring at her in dumbfounded disbelief. Then she turned away and followed Walder out into the adjoining room.

"What the hell was that all about?" Walder demanded. You're reaching. You don't want this case to be closed. It *is* closed. Get over it. All we've got to do now is find the victim."

Riley groaned aloud.

"I think you've got it wrong," she said. "I don't think this guy reacts to dolls the way the killer would. I need more time to be sure."

Walder stared at her for a moment, then shook his head.

"This really hasn't been your day, has it, Agent Paige?" he said. "In fact, I'd say you haven't been at your best during this whole case. Oh, you *were* right about one thing. Gumm doesn't seem to have had a connection to the Senator—neither political nor personal. Well, that hardly matters. I'm sure the Senator will be gratified that we brought his daughter's killer to justice."

It was all Riley could do to hold her temper.

"Agent Walder, with all due respect—" she began.

Walder interrupted. "And that's just your problem, Agent Paige. Your respect toward me has been severely lacking. I'm tired of your insubordination. Don't worry, I'm not going to file a negative report. You've done good work in the past and I'm giving you the benefit of the doubt now. I'm sure you're still traumatized from all you went through yourself. But you can go home now. We'll handle things from here."

Then Walder patted Bill on the shoulder.

"I'd like you to stay, Agent Jeffreys," he said.

Bill was fuming now. "If she's going, I'm going," he growled.

Bill led Riley out into the hallway. Walder stepped out of the room to watch them leave. But a short distance down the hallway, certainty caught up with Riley. The suspect's face had showed disgust, she was sure of that now. Her questions about naked dolls had not excited him. They had just confused him.

Riley was shaking all over. She and Bill continued on their way out of the building.

"He's not the guy," she uttered softly to Bill. "I'm sure of it."

Bill looked back, shocked, and she stopped and stared at him with full intensity.

"*She's* still out there," she added. "And they have no idea where she is."

*

Long after dark, Riley paced the floor at home, replaying every detail of the case in her mind. She'd even fired off emails and text messages in an effort to alert members of the Bureau that Walder had brought in the wrong man.

She had driven Bill home and been very late yet again picking up April. Riley was grateful that April hadn't made a fuss about it this time. Still subdued from the pot-smoking incident, April had even been rather pleasant as they put together a late supper and shared small talk.

Midnight came and went, and Riley felt as if her mind were going in circles. She wasn't getting anywhere. She needed someone to talk to, someone to bounce ideas off of. She thought about calling Bill. Surely he wouldn't mind getting called this late.

But no, she needed someone else—someone with insights that weren't easy to come by, someone whose judgment she'd learned to trust from past experience.

At last, she realized who that someone was.

She called a number on her cell phone and was dismayed to hear yet another recorded message.

"You've reached the number of Michael Nevins. Please leave a message at the tone."

Riley took a deep breath, then said, "Mike, could we talk? If you're there, please pick up. It's really an emergency."

No one answered. She wasn't surprised that he wasn't available. He often worked all hours. She just wished this weren't one of those times.

Finally she said, "I'm working on a bitch of a case, and I think maybe you're the only one who can help me. I'll drive up to your office first thing tomorrow morning. I hope that's okay. Like I said, it's an emergency."

She ended the call. There was nothing more she could do right now. She only hoped she could get a few hours of sleep.

Chapter 20

The chair was comfortable and the surroundings were elegant, but the soft lighting in Mike Nevins's office did nothing to raise Riley's spirits. Cindy was still missing. God only knew what was happening to her right now. Was she being tortured? The way Riley had been?

The agents sweeping the neighborhood still hadn't found her, not even after twenty-four hours. That came as no surprise to Riley. She knew they were looking in the wrong area. The problem was that neither she nor anyone else had any clues to the right area. She didn't want to wonder how far away the killer had taken her—or if she was still alive.

"We're losing her, Mike," Riley said. "With every minute that goes by, she's in more pain. She's closer to death."

"What makes you so sure they've got the wrong man?" forensic psychiatrist Michael Nevins asked her.

Always immaculately groomed and wearing an expensive shirt with a vest, Nevins had a meticulous, fussy persona. Riley liked him all the more because of it. She found him refreshing. They had first met over a decade ago, when he was a consultant on a high-profile FBI case that she worked on. His office was in D.C., so they didn't get together often. But over the years they'd often found that weaving together her instincts and his deep background knowledge gave them a unique insight into devious minds. She'd driven to see him first thing this morning.

"Where do I begin?" Riley replied with a shudder.

"Take your time," he said.

She sipped at a mug of the delicious hot tea he had given her.

"I saw him," she said. "I asked him some questions, but Walder wouldn't let me spend any time with him."

"And he doesn't fit your profile?"

"Mike, this Darrell Gumm guy is a wannabe," she continued. "He's got some kind of fanboy fantasy about psychopaths. He wants to be one. He wants to be famous for it. But he doesn't have what it takes. He's creepy, but he's not a killer. It's just that right now he gets to act out his fantasy to the hilt. It's his dream come true."

Mike stroked his chin thoughtfully. "And you don't think the real killer wants fame?"

She said, "He might be interested in fame, and he might even want it, but it's not what makes him tick. He's driven by something

102

else, something more personal. The victims represent something to him, and he enjoys their pain because of who or what they stand for. They're not chosen randomly."

"Then how?"

Riley shook her head. She wished she could put it into words better than she could.

"It's got something to do with dolls, Mike. The guy's obsessed with them. And dolls have something to do with how he targets the women."

Then she sighed. At this point, this didn't even sound very convincing to her. And yet she was sure that was the right track.

Mike was silent for a moment. Then he said, "I know that you have a talent for recognizing the nature of evil. I've always trusted your instincts. But if you're right, this suspect they're holding has got everybody else fooled. And not all FBI agents are fools."

"But some of them are," Riley said. "I can't get the woman he took yesterday out of my mind. I keep thinking about what she's going through right now." Then she blurted out the point of her visit with the psychiatrist. "Mike, could you question Darrell Gumm? You'd see through him in a second."

Mike looked startled. "They haven't called me in on this one," he said. "I checked on the case this morning and I was told that Dr. Ralston interviewed him yesterday. Apparently he agrees that Gumm's the killer. He even got Gumm to sign a written confession. The case is closed as far as the Bureau is concerned. They think that now they just need to find the woman. They're sure they'll get Gumm to talk."

Riley rolled her eyes with exasperation.

"But Ralston's a quack," she said. "He's Walder's toady. He'll come to any conclusion Walder wants."

Mike didn't say anything. He just smiled at Riley. Riley was pretty sure that Mike held Ralston in the same contempt as she did. But he was too professional to say so.

"I haven't been able to figure this one out," Riley said. "Will you at least read the files and tell me what you think?"

Mike seemed deep in thought. Then he said, "Let's talk about you a little. How long have you been back on the job?"

Riley had to think about that. This case had consumed her but it was still new.

"About a week," she said.

He tilted his head with concern. "You're pushing very hard. You always do."

"The man has killed one woman in that time and taken another. I should have stayed on the case since I first saw his work six months ago. I should never have dropped out on it."

"You were interrupted."

She knew he was referring to her own capture and torture. She had spent hours describing that to Mike and he had helped her through it.

"I'm back now. And another woman is in trouble."

"Who are you working with now?"

"Bill Jeffreys again. He's terrific but his imagination isn't as active as mine is. He hasn't come up with anything either,"

"How is that working for you? Being with Jeffreys every day?"

"Fine. Why wouldn't it be?"

Mike gazed quietly at her for a moment, then leaned toward her with an expression of concern.

"I mean, are you sure your head is clear? Are you sure you're in this game? I guess what I'm asking is—which criminal are you really after?"

Riley squinted, a little surprised by this apparent change of topic.

"What do you mean, which?" she asked.

"The new one, or the old one?"

A silence fell between them.

"I think that maybe you're actually here to talk about you," Mike said softly. "I know that you've always had trouble believing that Peterson died in that explosion."

Riley didn't know what to say. She hadn't expected this; she hadn't expected the tables to turn on her.

"That's beside the point," Riley said.

"What about your meds, Riley?" Mike asked.

Again, Riley didn't reply. She hadn't taken her prescribed tranquilizer for days. She didn't want to blunt her concentration.

"I'm not sure I like where you're going with this," Riley said.

Mike took a long sip from his mug of tea.

"You're carrying a lot of emotional baggage," he said. "You got divorced this year, and I'm aware that your feelings about that are conflicted. And of course, you lost your mother in such a horrible, tragic way all those years ago."

Riley's face flushed with irritation. She didn't want to get into this.

"We've talked about the circumstances of your own abduction," Mike went on. "You pushed the limits. You took a huge risk. Your actions were really pretty foolhardy."

"I got Marie out," she said.

"At great cost to yourself."

Riley took a long, deep breath.

"You're saying maybe I brought it on myself," she said. "Because my marriage fell apart, because of how my mother got killed. You're saying maybe I think I deserved it. So I attracted this to myself. I put myself in this situation."

Mike smiled back with a sympathetic smile.

"I'm just saying you need to take a good hard look at yourself right now. Ask yourself what's really going on inside."

Riley struggled for breath, fighting back tears. Mike was right. She had been wondering all these things. That's why his words were hitting her so hard. But she'd been ignoring those half-submerged thoughts. And it was high time she figured out if any of it was true.

"I was doing my job, Mike," she said in a choked voice.

"I know," he said. "None of it was your fault. Do you know that? It's the self-blame I worry about. You attract what you feel you deserve. You create your own life circumstances."

Riley stood, unable to hear any more.

"I wasn't taken, Doctor, because I attracted it," she said. "I was taken because there are psychos out there."

*

Riley hurried to the nearest exit, into the open courtyard. It was a beautiful summer day. She took several long, slow breaths, calming herself a little. Then she sat down on a bench and buried her head in her hands.

At that moment her cell phone buzzed.

Marie.

Her gut told her right away that the call was urgent.

Riley answered and heard nothing but convulsive gasps.

"Marie," Riley asked, concerned, "what is it?"

For a moment, Riley only heard sobs. Marie was obviously in an even worse state than she was.

"Riley," Marie finally gasped, "have you found him? Have you been looking for him? Has *anybody* been looking for him?"

Riley's spirits sank. Of course Marie was talking about Peterson. She wanted to assure her that he was really dead, killed in that explosion. But how could she say so positively when she

105

harbored doubts herself? She remembered what forensics tech agent Betty Richter had told her a few days ago about the odds that Peterson was really dead.

I'd say ninety-nine percent.

That figure hadn't given Riley any comfort. And it was the last thing Marie wanted or needed to hear right now.

"Marie," Riley said miserably, "there's nothing I can do."

Marie let out a wail of despair that chilled Riley to the bone.

"Oh, God, then it *is* him!" she cried. "It can't be anybody else."

Riley's nerves quickened. "What are you talking about, Marie? What's happened?"

Marie's words poured out in a frantic rush.

"I *told* you he'd been calling me. I cut off my landline, but somehow he's got my cell phone number. He keeps calling all the time. He doesn't say anything, he just calls and breathes, but I know it's him. Who else can it be? And he's been here, Riley. He's been to my house."

Riley's alarm mounted by the second.

"What do you mean?" she asked.

"I hear noises at night. He throws things at the door and my bedroom window. Pebbles, I think."

Riley's heart jumped as she remembered the pebbles on her own front stoop. Was it possible that Peterson was really alive? Were both she and Marie in danger all over again?

She knew she had to choose her words carefully. Marie was clearly teetering on an extremely dangerous brink.

"I'm coming to you right now, Marie," she said. "And I'll get the Bureau to look into this."

Marie let out a harsh, desperate, and bitter laugh.

"Look into it?" she echoed. "Forget it, Riley. You said it already. There's nothing you can do. You're not going to do anything. Nobody's going to do anything. Nobody *can* do anything."

Riley got in her car and put the phone on speaker so she could talk and drive.

"Stay on the phone," she said, as she started her car and headed for Georgetown. "I'm coming for you."

Chapter 21

Riley struggled against traffic while trying to keep Marie on the phone. She drove through an intersection after a yellow light switched to red; she was driving dangerously and she knew it. But what else could she do? She was in her own car, not an agency vehicle, so she had no lights and siren.

"I'm hanging up, Riley," Marie said for the fifth time.

"No!" Riley barked yet again, fighting down a surge of despair. "Stay on the phone, Marie."

Marie's voice sounded weary now.

"I can't do this anymore," she said. "Save yourself if you can, but I really can't do this. I'm through with this. I'm going to stop it all right now."

Riley felt ready to explode from panic. What did Marie mean? What was she going to do?

"You *can* do this, Marie," Riley said.

"Goodbye, Riley."

"No!" Riley shouted. "Just wait. Wait! It's all you have to do. I'll be right there."

She was driving much faster than the flow of traffic, wending among the lanes like a madwoman. Several times, other drivers honked at her.

"Don't hang up," Riley demanded fiercely. "Do you hear me?"

Marie said nothing. But Riley could hear her sobbing and keening.

The sounds were perversely reassuring. At least Marie was still there. At least she was still on the phone. But could Riley keep her there? She knew that the poor woman was plummeting into an abyss of pure animal terror. Marie no longer had a rational thought in her head; she seemed to be almost insane with fear.

Riley's own memories swarmed into her mind. Terrible days in a beastlike state in which the world of humanity simply didn't exist. Total darkness, the feeling of the very existence of a world outside of the darkness slipping away, and a complete loss of any sense of the passage of time.

I've got to fight it, she told herself.

The memories enveloped her ...

With nothing to hear or see, Riley tried to keep her other senses engaged. She felt the sour taste of fear back in her throat, rising up in her mouth until it turned into an electrical tingling on the tip of

107

her tongue. She scratched at the dirt floor she was sitting on, exploring its dampness. She sniffed the mold and mildew that surrounded her.

Those sensations were all that still kept her in the world of the living.

Then in the midst of the blackness, came a blinding light and the roar of Peterson's propane torch.

A sharp bump shook Riley out of her hideous reverie. It took her a second to realize that her car had struck against a curb and that she was in danger of veering into oncoming traffic. Horns blared.

Riley regained control of her car and looked around. She wasn't far from Georgetown.

"Marie," she shouted. "Are you still there?"

Again, she heard only a muffled sob. That was good. But what could Riley do now? She wavered. She could call for FBI help in D.C., but by the time she explained the problem and got agents sent to the address, God only knew what would happen. Besides, that would mean ending the call with Marie.

She had to keep her on the phone, but how?

How was she going to pull Marie out of that abyss? She had almost fallen into it herself.

Riley remembered something. Long ago, she had been trained in how to keep crisis callers on the line. She'd never had to use that training until now. She struggled to remember what she was supposed to do. Those lessons had been so long ago.

Part of a lesson came back to her. She was taught to do anything, *say* anything, to keep the caller talking. It didn't matter how meaningless or irrelevant it might be. What mattered was that the caller kept hearing a concerned human voice.

"Marie, there's something you need to do for me," Riley said.

"What's that?"

Riley's brain was rushing frantically, making up what to say as she went along.

"I need for you to go to your kitchen," she said. "I want you to tell me exactly what herbs and spices you've got in your rack."

Marie didn't answer for a moment. Riley worried. Was Marie in the right state of mind to go along with such an irrelevant distraction?

"Okay," Marie said. "I'm going there now."

Riley breathed a sigh of relief. Perhaps this would buy her some time. She could hear the clinking of spice jars over the phone.

Marie's voice sounded truly strange now—hysterical and robotic at the same time.

"I've got dried oregano. And crushed red pepper. And nutmeg."

"Excellent," Riley said. "What else?"

"Dried thyme. And ground ginger. And black peppercorns."

Marie paused. How could Riley keep this going?

"Have you got curry powder?" Riley asked.

After a clink of bottles, Marie said, "No."

Riley spoke slowly, as if giving life-and-death instructions—because really, she was doing exactly that.

"Well, get a pad of paper and a pencil," Riley said. "Write that down. You'll need to get it when you buy groceries."

Riley heard the sound of scribbling.

"What else have you got?" Riley asked.

Then came a deathly pause.

"This is no good, Riley," Marie said in a tone of numb despair.

Riley stammered helplessly. "Just—just humor me, okay?"

Another pause fell.

"He's here, Riley."

Riley felt a rock-hard knot in her throat.

"He's where?" she asked.

"He's in the house. I get it now. He's been here all along. There's nothing you can do."

Riley's thoughts churned as she tried to make sense of what was happening. Marie might be slipping into paranoid delusions. Riley understood this all too well from her own struggles with PTSD.

On the other hand, Marie might be telling the truth.

"How do you know that, Marie?" Riley asked, looking for an opportunity to pass a slow-moving truck.

"I hear him," Marie said. "I hear his footsteps. He's upstairs. No, he's in the front hallway. No, he's in the basement."

Is she hallucinating? Riley wondered.

It was entirely possible. Riley had heard more than her share of nonexistent noises in the days after her abduction. Even recently she sometimes couldn't trust her five senses. Trauma played awful tricks on the imagination.

"He's everywhere in the house," Marie said.

"No," Riley replied firmly. "He can't be everywhere."

Riley managed to pass a sluggish delivery truck. A sense of futility was rolling over her in what felt like tidal waves. It was a terrible feeling, almost like drowning.

When Marie spoke again, she was no longer sobbing. She sounded resigned now, even mysteriously tranquil.

"Maybe he's like a ghost, Riley. Maybe that's what happened when you blew him up. You killed his body but you didn't kill his evil. Now he can be in a whole lot of places at once. Now there's no stopping him, ever. You can't fight a ghost. Give it up, Riley. You can't do anything. I can't either. All I can do is not let the same thing happen to me again."

"Don't hang up! I need you to do something else for me."

There was a moment's silence. Then Marie said, "What? What now, Riley?"

"I need you to stay on this line, but I need you to call 911 on your landline."

Marie's voice turned into a slight growl. "Jesus, Riley. How many times do I have to tell you that I cut off my landline?"

In her confusion, Riley had forgotten. Marie actually sounded a little irritated. That was good. Anger was better than panic.

"Besides," Marie continued, "what good's it going to do to call 911? What can they do to help me? Nobody can help. He's everywhere. He'll get me sooner or later. He'll get you too. We both might as well give up."

Riley felt stymied. Marie's delusions were taking on an intractable logic of their own. And she didn't have time to persuade Marie that Peterson was not a ghost.

"We're friends, aren't we, Marie?" Riley finally said. "You once told me that you'd do anything for me. Was that true?"

Marie started crying again.

"Of course it's true."

"Then hang up and call 911. There doesn't have to be a reason. It doesn't have to do any good. Just do it because I want you too."

A long pause fell. Riley couldn't even hear Marie breathing.

"I know you want to give up, Marie. I understand. That's your choice. But *I* don't want to give up. Maybe it's stupid, but I don't. That's why I'm asking you to call 911. Because you said you'd do anything for me. And I want you to do it. I *need* you to do it. For me."

The silence continued. Was Marie even still on the line?

"Do you promise?" she asked.

The call ended with a click. Whether Marie would call for help or not, Riley couldn't leave anything to chance. She picked up her cell phone and punched in 911.

"This is Special Agent Riley Paige, FBI," she said when the operator answered. "I'm calling about a possible intruder. Someone extremely dangerous."

Riley gave the operator Marie's address.

"We'll have a team there right away," the operator said.

"Good," Riley said, and ended the call.

Riley then tried Marie's number again, but got no response.

Someone has to get there in time, she thought. *Someone has to get there right now.*

Meanwhile, she struggled against a renewed flood of dark memories. She had to get control of herself. Whatever was about to happen next, she needed to keep her wits about her.

When Marie's red brick townhouse came into view, Riley felt a surge of alarm. No emergency vehicles had yet arrived. She heard police sirens wailing in the distance. They were on their way.

Riley double-parked her car and dashed for the front door, realizing she was the first responder. When she tried the doorknob, the door swung open. But why was it unlocked?

She stepped inside and drew her gun.

"Marie!" Riley called out. "Marie!"

No answer came.

Riley knew for certain that something awful had happened here—or was happening right now. She stepped further into the front hallway.

"Marie!" she called again. The house remained silent.

The police sirens were louder now, but no help had yet arrived.

Riley was starting to believe the worst now—that Peterson had been here, and perhaps still was here.

She made her way along the dimly lit hallway. She kept calling Marie's name as she studied every door. Might he be in the closet to the left? What about the bathroom door over to the right?

If she encountered Peterson, she wouldn't be taken by him again.

She would kill the bastard once and for all.

111

Chapter 22

In spite of Riley's calls, no answer came from Marie. There were no sounds in the house other than those she made herself. The place felt empty. She made her way up the stairs and turned carefully into an open doorway.

As she turned the corner, Riley's breath stopped in her throat. She felt as if the world were collapsing beneath her.

There was Marie: suspended in mid-air, hanging by her neck from a cord tied to a light fixture on the high ceiling. An overturned stepladder lay on the floor.

Time seemed to stop as Riley's mind rejected reality.

Then her knees buckled and she caught herself against the door frame. She let out a long harsh sound.

"NOOOO!"

She dashed across the room, turned the ladder upright and scrambled up on it. She wrapped an arm around Marie's body to relieve the pressure and fingered Marie's neck, searching for any sign of a pulse.

Riley was sobbing now. "Be alive, Marie. Be alive, goddammit."

But it was too late. Marie's neck was broken. She was dead.

"Christ," Riley said, collapsing back onto the ladder. Pain surged up from somewhere deep in her abdomen. She wanted to die here, too.

As moments passed, Riley became dimly aware of sounds downstairs. The first responders had arrived. A familiar emotional mechanism kicked in. Basic human fear and grief gave way to a cold, professional efficiency.

"Up here!" she shouted.

She wiped her sleeve across her face to blot the tears.

Five heavily-armed, Kevlar-clad officers charged up the stairs. The woman in front was visibly surprised to see Riley.

"I'm Officer Rita Graham, the team chief," she said. "Who are you?"

Riley got off the ladder and flashed her badge. "Special Agent Riley Paige, FBI."

The woman looked uneasy.

"How did you get here before we did?"

"She was a friend of mine," Riley said, fully in professional mode now. "Her name was Marie Sayles. She called me. She told me something was wrong, and I was already on the way when I called 911. I didn't get here on time. She's dead."

The responder team quickly checked and confirmed Riley's declaration.

"Suicide?" Officer Graham asked.

Riley nodded. She had no doubt at all that Marie had killed herself.

"What's this?" the team leader asked, pointing at a folded notecard sitting on an end table next to the bed.

Riley looked at the card. Written in a barely legible scrawl was a message:

This is the only way.

"A suicide note?"

Riley nodded again grimly. But she knew that it wasn't the usual kind of suicide note. It wasn't an explanation, and it certainly wasn't an apology.

It's advice, Riley thought. *It's advice for me.*

The team took pictures and made notes. Riley knew that they would wait for the coroner before removing the body.

"Let's talk downstairs," Officer Graham said. She led Riley down to the living room, sat down on a chair, and gestured for Riley to sit down too.

The curtains were still drawn and no lights were on in the room. Riley wanted to throw open the curtains and let in some sunlight, but she knew better than to change anything. She sat down on the sofa.

Graham turned on a table lamp beside her chair.

"Tell me what happened," the officer said, taking out a notepad and a pencil. Although she had the toughened face of a seasoned cop, there was a sympathetic look in her eyes.

"She was the victim of an abduction," Riley said. "Almost eight weeks ago. We both were victims. You may have read about it. The Sam Peterson case."

Graham's eyes widened.

"Oh, my God," she said. "The guy who tortured and killed all those women, the guy with the blowtorch. So that was you—the agent who escaped and blew him up?"

"Right," Riley said. Then, after a pause, she said, "The trouble is, I'm not sure I really did blow him up. I'm not positive that he's dead. Marie didn't believe that he was. That's what finally got to

113

her. She just couldn't take not knowing. And maybe he *was* stalking her again."

As Riley continued her explanation, the words flowed automatically, almost as if she'd learned the whole thing by heart. She now felt completely detached from the scene, listening to herself report how this horrible thing had happened.

After helping Officer Graham get a handle on the case, Riley told her how to contact Marie's next of kin. But as she talked, anger was building beneath her professional veneer—a cold, icy anger. Peterson had claimed another victim. Whether he was dead or alive didn't matter. He'd killed Marie.

And Marie had died absolutely certain that Riley was doomed to be his next victim, whether by his hand or her own. Riley wanted to take hold of Marie and physically shake this wretched idea out of her head.

This is not *the only way!* she wanted to tell her.

But did she believe that? Riley didn't know. There seemed to be too damned much she didn't know.

The coroner arrived while Riley and Officer Graham were still talking. Graham got up and went to meet him. Then she turned to Riley and said, "I'll be upstairs for a few minutes. I'd like you to hang around and fill me in a bit more."

Riley shook her head.

"I've got to go," she said. "There's someone I need to talk to." She pulled out her card and put it down on the table. "You can get in touch with me."

The officer began to object, but Riley didn't give her a chance; she got up and walked out of Marie's dark home. She had urgent business.

*

An hour later, Riley was driving west through the Virginia countryside.

Do I really want to do this? she asked herself again.

She was exhausted. She hadn't slept well last night, and now she had been through a waking nightmare. Thank goodness she'd talked with Mike in between. He had helped steady her, but she was sure he'd never approve of what she was going to do now. She wasn't altogether sure she was fully in her right mind.

She was taking the quickest route from Georgetown to Senator Mitch Newbrough's manor house. That narcissistic politician had a lot to answer for. He was hiding something, something that might lead to the real killer. And that made him partly responsible for this new victim.

Riley knew that she was headed for trouble. She didn't care.

It was late afternoon when she pulled into the circular drive in front of the stone mansion. She parked, got out of the car, and walked up to the enormous front doors. When she rang the doorbell, she was greeted by a formally dressed gentleman—Newbrough's butler, she assumed.

"What may I do for you, ma'am?" he asked stiffly.

Riley flashed her badge at him.

"Special Agent Riley Paige," she said. "The Senator knows me. I need to talk with him."

With a skeptical look, the butler turned away from her. He raised a walkie-talkie to his lips, whispered, and then listened. The butler turned back toward Riley with a rather superior smirk.

"The Senator does not wish to see you," he said. "He's quite emphatic about it. Good day, ma'am."

But before the man could shut the doors, Riley pushed straight past him and strode on into the house.

"I'm going to notify security," the butler called after her.

"You go right ahead and do that," Riley shouted over her shoulder.

Riley had no idea where to look for the Senator. He could be anywhere in the cavernous mansion. But she figured it didn't matter. She could probably get him to come to her.

She headed into the living room where she had met with him before and plopped herself down on the huge couch. She fully intended to make herself right at home until the Senator showed himself.

Only a few seconds passed before a big man clad in a black suit stepped into the room. Riley knew by his manner that he was the Senator's security man.

"The Senator has asked for you to leave," he said, crossing his arms.

Riley didn't budge from the couch. She looked the man over, assessing just how much of a threat he really was. He was big enough to probably be able to remove her by force. But her own self-defense skills were very good. If he took her on, more than one of them was going to get pretty badly hurt, and doubtless some of the Senator's antiques would be damaged.

"I hope they told you that I'm FBI," she said, locking eyes with him. She doubted very much that he'd actually draw his weapon on an FBI agent.

Not easily intimidated, the man stared back at her. But he didn't move toward her.

Riley heard footsteps approaching behind her, and then the sound of the Senator's voice.

"What is it this time, Agent Paige? I'm a very busy man."

The security man stepped aside as Newbrough walked in front of her and stood there. His photogenic politician's smile had a sarcastic cast to it. He was silent for a moment. Riley sensed right away that they were about to engage in a battle of wills. She was determined not to move from the couch.

"You were wrong, Senator," Riley said. "There wasn't anything political about your daughter's murder—and nothing personal either. You gave me an enemies list, and I'm sure you passed along that same list to your lapdog at the Bureau."

Newbrough's smile twisted into a slight sneer.

"I take it you mean Special Agent in Charge Carl Walder," he said.

Riley knew that her choice of words was rash and that she'd live to regret it. But right now she didn't care.

"That list was a waste of the Bureau's time, Senator," Riley said. "And meanwhile another victim has been abducted."

Newbrough stood firmly rooted to his spot.

"I understand that the Bureau has made an arrest," he said. "The suspect has confessed. But he hasn't said much, has he? There's some connection to me, you can be sure of it. He'll tell all in due time. I'll make sure that Agent Walder follows through on it."

Riley tried to hide her amazement. After yet another abduction, Newbrough still considered himself to be the primary target of the killer's wrath. The man's ego was truly outrageous. His capacity to believe that *everything* was about him had no limits.

Newbrough tilted his head with seeming curiosity.

"But you seem to be blaming me somehow," he said. "I take umbrage at that, Agent Paige. It's not my fault that your own fecklessness has led to the capture of another victim."

Riley's face tingled with rage. She didn't dare reply. She'd say something far too rash.

He walked over to a liquor cabinet and poured himself a large glass of what Riley assumed to be extremely expensive whiskey. He was obviously making a point of not asking Riley if she wanted a drink.

Riley knew that it was high time for her to get to the point.

"The last time I was here, there was something you didn't tell me," she said.

Newbrough turned to face her again, taking a long sip from his glass.

"Didn't I answer all your questions?" he said.

"It's not that. You just didn't tell me something. About Reba. And I think it's time you did."

Newbrough held her in a penetrating stare.

"Did she like dolls, Senator?" Riley asked.

Newbrough shrugged. "I suppose all little girls do," he said.

"I don't mean as a little girl. I mean as an adult. Did she collect them?"

"I'm afraid I wouldn't know."

Those were the first words Newbrough had said so far that Riley truly believed. A man this pathologically self-centered knew little about anybody else's likes and interests—not even those of his own daughter.

"I'd like to talk to your wife," Riley said.

"Certainly not," Newbrough snapped. He was adopting a new expression now—one that Riley had seen him use on television. Much like his smile, this expression was carefully rehearsed, undoubtedly practiced thousands of times in a mirror. It was meant to convey moral outrage.

"You really have no decency, do you, Agent Paige?" he said, his voice shaking with calculated anger. "You come into a house of grief, bringing no comfort, no answers to a bereaved family. Instead you make veiled accusations. You blame perfectly innocent people for your own incompetence."

He shook his head in a gesture of injured righteousness.

"What a mean, cruel little woman you are," he said. "You must have brought terrible pain to a great many people."

Riley felt as if she'd been punched in the stomach. This was a tactic she hadn't been prepared for—a complete turning of the moral tables. And he'd hit her own genuine guilt and self-doubt.

He knows exactly how to play me, she thought.

She knew that she had to leave right now or she'd do something she'd regret. He was practically goading her in that direction. Without a word, she got up from the couch and walked out of the living room toward the front entrance.

She heard the Senator's voice call after her.

117

"Your career is over, Agent Paige. I want you to know that."

Riley brushed past the butler and charged out the front door. She got in her car and started to drive.

Waves of rage, frustration, and exhaustion crashed over her. A woman's life was at stake, and nobody in the world was rescuing her. She was sure that Walder was just expanding the search area around Gumm's apartment. And Riley was sure they were looking in the wrong place. It was up to her to do something. But she no longer had any idea what to do. Coming here certainly hadn't helped. Could she trust her own judgment anymore?

Riley hadn't driven for more than ten minutes before her cell phone buzzed. She looked down at it and saw that it was a text from Walder. She had no trouble guessing what it was about.

Well, she thought bitterly. *At least the Senator didn't waste any time.*

Chapter 23

When Riley reached Quantico and walked into the Behavioral Analysis Unit, both the chief and Bill were waiting for her in Walder's office. She realized that Bill must have been called in especially for this meeting.

Special Agent in Charge Carl Walder rose from his desk.

"The Senator's lapdog?" Walder said, his babyish face knotted with anger.

Riley lowered her eyes. She really had gone too far with that remark.

"I'm sorry, sir," she said.

"Sorry isn't going to cut it, Agent Paige," Walder said. "You've completely gone off the rails. What were you thinking, going to the Senator's house to confront him like that? Do you have any idea the damage you've done?"

By "damage," Riley was sure that Walder meant his own personal embarrassment. She couldn't get very worried about that.

"Have you found Cindy McKinnon yet?" she asked in a low voice.

"No, as a matter of fact, we haven't," Walder said sharply. "And frankly, you're not helping us find her."

Riley was stung.

"*I'm* not helping?" she replied. "Sir, I keep telling you, you're charging the wrong man, and you're looking in the wrong—"

Riley stopped herself in mid-sentence

Cindy MacKinnon was what mattered right now, not Riley's ongoing battles with Walder. This was no time for petty squabbling. When she spoke again, it was in a milder tone.

"Sir, even though I feel he may be withholding something, I may have been wrong to unilaterally go and see the Senator without checking with you, and I apologize. But forget about me for a moment. That poor woman's been missing for well over twenty-four hours. What if I'm right, and someone else is holding her captive? What's she going through right now? How long has she got?"

His voice cautious, Bill added, "We've got to consider the possibility, sir."

Walder sat down and said nothing for a moment. Riley could see by his expression that he, too, was concerned about the possibility. Then he spoke very slowly, giving weight to each word.

"The Bureau will handle it."

119

Riley didn't know what to say. She didn't even quite understand what Walder meant. Was he acknowledging his possible mistake? Or was he still determined not to veer from his present course?

"Sit down, Agent Paige," Walder said.

Riley sat in the chair next to Bill, who glanced at her with mounting concern.

Walder said, "I heard about what happened with your friend today, Riley."

Riley was jolted a little. She wasn't surprised that Walder knew about Marie's death. After all, word that she'd been first on the scene was sure to make its way back to the Bureau. But why was he bringing it up now? Did she detect a note of sympathy in his voice?

"What happened?" Walder asked. "Why did she do it?"

"She couldn't deal with it anymore," Riley said in a whisper.

"Couldn't deal with what?" Walder asked.

A silence fell. Riley couldn't shape an answer to that question.

"I've heard you don't think Peterson is dead," Walder said. "I guess I can understand why you can't shake that idea. But you've got to know that it doesn't make sense."

There came another pause.

"Did you tell your friend about it?" Walder asked. "Did you tell her about this obsessive idea of yours?"

Riley's face flushed. She knew what was coming next.

"She was too fragile for that, Agent Paige," Walder said. "You should have known it would make her snap. You should have used better judgment. But frankly, Agent Paige, your judgment is shot to hell. I hate to say it, but it's true."

He is blaming me for Marie's death, Riley realized.

Riley was fighting back tears now. Whether they were tears of grief or indignation, she didn't know. She had no idea what to say. Where could she begin? She hadn't planted that idea in Marie's head and she knew it. But how could she make Walder understand? How could she explain that Marie had her own reasons to doubt that Peterson was dead?

Bill spoke up again. "Sir, go easy on her, okay?"

"I think I've been going too easy on her, Agent Jeffreys," Walder said, his voice becoming stern. "I think I've been too patient."

Walder held her gaze for a long moment.

"Give me your gun and your badge, Agent Paige," he finally said.

Riley heard Bill let out a gasp of disbelief.

"Sir, this is crazy," Bill said. "We need her."

But Riley didn't need to be told twice. She rose from her chair and took out her gun and her badge. She placed them on Walder's desk.

"You can clean out your office in your own good time," Walder said, his voice steady and unemotional. "Meanwhile, you should go home and get some rest. And get back into therapy. You need it."

As Riley turned to leave the room, Bill stood up as if to go with her.

"You stay, Agent Jeffreys," Walder demanded.

Riley eyes met Bill's. With a look, she told him not to disobey. Not this time. He nodded back to her with a stricken expression. Then Riley left the office. As she walked down the hall, she felt cold and numb, wondering what to do now.

When she stepped out into the cool night air, tears finally started to flow. But she was surprised to realize that they were tears of relief, not despair. For the first time in days, she felt liberated, free from frustrating limitations.

If nobody else was going to do what had to be done, it was still up to her. But at long last, nobody was going to tell her how to do her job. She'd find the killer, and she'd save Cindy MacKinnon— no matter what it took.

*

After Riley, later again, picked up April and drove home, she found as they arrived home that she couldn't deal with fixing dinner. Marie's face still haunted her and she felt more exhausted than she had ever been.

"It's been a bad day," she told April. "A terrible day. Will you settle for grilled cheese sandwiches?"

"I'm not really hungry," April said. "Gabriela keeps me stuffed all the time."

Riley felt a deep pang of despair. *Another failure*, she thought.

But then April took another look at her mother, this time with a hint of compassion.

"Grilled cheese will be good," she said. "I'll fix them."

"Thank you," Riley said. "You're a sweetheart."

She felt her spirits lift a little. At least there would be no conflict here at home tonight. She really needed that little break.

They had a quick and quiet supper, then April went to her room to finish homework and go to bed.

As exhausted as she was, Riley felt she had little time to waste. She went to work. She opened her laptop, pulled up a map of the victims' locations, and printed out the section she wanted to study.

Riley slowly drew a triangle on the map. Its lines linked the three places where the victims had been found. The northernmost point marked where Margaret Geraty's body had been dumped in farmland two years ago. A point to the west marked where Eileen Rogers had been more carefully placed near Daggett some six months back. Finally, the point to the south marked where the killer had achieved full mastery, posing Reba Frye by a stream in Mosby Park.

Riley circled the area again and again, thinking, wondering. Another woman might soon be found dead somewhere in this area—if she wasn't dead already. There was no time to lose.

Riley hung her head. She was so tired. But a woman's life was at stake. And it now seemed to be up to Riley to save her—without official help or sanction. She wouldn't even have Bill to help her. But could she solve this case entirely on her own?

She had to try. She had to do it for Marie. She had to prove to Marie's spirit—and maybe even to herself—that suicide wasn't the only option.

Riley frowned at that triangle. It was a good guess that the victim was now being held somewhere in that area of a thousand square miles.

I've just got to look in the right place, she thought. *But where?*

She knew that she would have to condense her search area, and it wasn't going to be easy to do. At least she was familiar with some of the general area.

The uppermost part of the triangle, the point closest to Washington, was mostly upscale, rich, and privileged. Riley was all but sure that the killer didn't come from that kind of background. Besides, he had to be holding the victim in a place where no one could hear her scream. Forensics had found no sign of the other women's mouths being gagged or taped. Riley drew an X through that well-to-do area.

The two southern points were both parklands. Might the killer be holding the woman in a rented hunting cabin or on a campsite?

Riley thought it over.

No, she decided. *That would be too temporary.*

Her every instinct told her that this man operated out of his own home—perhaps a house where he had lived all his life, where he had passed an unusually miserable childhood. He would enjoy taking his victims there. Taking them home with him.

So she crossed out the park areas. What was left was primarily farmland and small towns. Riley strongly suspected that she was looking for a farmhouse somewhere in that area.

She looked again at the map on her computer, then zoomed in closely on the area under consideration. Her heart sank at the sight of a tangle of secondary roads. If she was right, the killer lived on some old dirt farm in that maze. But there were too many roads for her to search quickly by car—and besides, the farm might not even be visible from the road.

She groaned aloud with despair. The whole thing seemed more hopeless by the moment. The terrible pain of loss and failure threatened to surge up again.

But then she said aloud, "Dolls!"

She reminded herself of the conclusion she had come to yesterday—that the killer had probably spotted all of his victims in a single store that sold dolls. Where might that store be?

She drew another smaller shape on the paper map. It lay just to the east of the large triangle, and its corners marked the places where the four women had lived. Somewhere in that area, she felt pretty sure, was a store where all the women had bought dolls, and where the killer had targeted them. She would have to find that store first, before she could track down the place where he took the women.

Again, she brought up the map on her computer and zoomed in on it. The easternmost point of the smaller area wasn't very far from where Riley lived. She saw that a state road formed an arc that reached westward through several small towns, none of them wealthy or historic. They were just the sorts of towns she was looking for. And each of them undoubtedly had some kind of toy or doll store.

She printed out the smaller map, then ran another search, locating stores in every town. Finally, Riley shut down her computer. She had to get some sleep.

Tomorrow she would go out in search of Cindy MacKinnon.

Chapter 24

Dusk was falling by the time Riley pulled into Glendive. It had been a long day, and she was feeling desperate. Time was passing much too fast, and so was any possibility of finding any life-saving clues.

Glendive was the eighth town on her route. In every town so far, Riley had gone into stores that sold toys and dolls, questioning anyone who would talk to her. She felt sure that she hadn't found the store she was looking for.

Nobody in any of the stores remembered seeing the women in the photographs she had showed them. Of course, the women in question were similar in age and appearance to a dozen others that a storekeeper might meet in any given week. To make matters worse, none of the dolls Riley saw on display struck her as the likely inspiration for the arrangement of the victims.

When she drove into Glendive, Riley had an odd sense of déjà vu. The main street looked uncannily like those in most of the other towns, with a brick church flanked on one side by a movie theater and on the other side by a drug store. All these towns were starting to blur together in her exhausted mind.

What was I thinking? she asked herself.

Last night she had been desperate to sleep, and she had taken her prescription tranquilizers. That hadn't been a bad idea. But following it with a couple of shots of whiskey had been unwise. Now she had a severe headache, but she had to keep going.

As she parked her car near the store she planned to check out, she saw that daylight was waning. She sighed with discouragement. She had one more town and one more store to check out tonight. It would be at least three hours before she could get back to Fredericksburg to pick up April at Ryan's house. How many nights had she been late now?

She took out her cell phone and dialed the house number. She hoped against hope that Gabriela would answer. Instead, she heard Ryan's voice.

"What is it, Riley?" he asked.

"Ryan," Riley sputtered, "I'm terribly sorry, but—"

"You're going to be late again," Ryan said, finishing her sentence.

"Yeah," Riley said. "I'm sorry."

A silence fell.

"Look, it's really important," Riley finally said. "A woman's life is in danger. I've got to do what I'm doing."

"I've heard it before," Ryan said in a disapproving tone. "It's always a matter of life and death. Well, go ahead. Take care of it. It's just that I'm starting to wonder why you bother to pick up April at all. She might as well just stay right here."

Riley felt her throat tighten. Just as she had feared, Ryan sounded like he was gearing up for a custody fight. And it wasn't out of any sincere desire to raise April. He was too busy living it up to concern himself with his daughter. All he wanted was to cause Riley pain.

"I'll come and get her," Riley said, trying to steady her voice. "We can talk about all this later."

She ended the call.

Then she stepped out of the car and walked the short distance to the store—Debbie's Doll Boutique, it was called. She went inside and saw that the name was a little presumptuous for a store that sold pretty standard, brand-name merchandise.

Nothing quaint or fancy here, she realized.

It seemed unlikely that this was the place she was looking for. The store she had in mind had to be at least a little bit special, a place that inspired a word-of-mouth reputation that attracted customers from surrounding towns. Still, Riley had to check this one out to be absolutely sure.

Riley walked up to the counter, where a tall, elderly woman with thick glasses and birdlike features was at the cash register.

"I'm Special Agent Riley Paige, FBI," she said, once again feeling naked without her badge. So far, other clerks had been willing to talk to her without it. She hoped that this woman would as well.

Riley pulled out four photographs and put them on the counter.

"I wonder if you've seen any of these women," she said, pointing to the pictures one by one. "You probably wouldn't remember Margaret Geraty—she would have been here two years ago. But Eileen Rogers would have come here about six months ago, and Reba Frye would have bought a doll six weeks ago. This last woman, Cindy MacKinnon, would have been here late last week."

The woman peered at the pictures closely.

"Oh, dear," she said. "My eyes aren't what they used to be. Let me take a closer look."

She picked up a magnifying glass and examined the photos. Meanwhile, Riley noticed that there was someone else in the store.

He was a rather homely man of average height and build. He was wearing a T-shirt and well-worn jeans. Riley might well have overlooked him if it weren't for one important detail.

He was carrying a bunch of roses.

These roses were real, but the combination of roses and dolls could signal a killer's obsession.

The man wasn't looking at her. He had surely heard her announce herself as FBI. Was he avoiding eye contact?

Just then the woman's voice piped up.

"I don't *think* I've seen any of them," she said. "But then, like I said, I don't see at all well. And I've never been any good with faces. I'm sorry not to be of more help."

"It's all right," Riley said, putting the photos back in her purse. "Thank you for your time."

She turned to look again at the man, who was now browsing a nearby rack. Her pulse quickened.

It definitely could be him, she thought. *If he buys a doll, I'll know it's him.*

But it wouldn't do for her to stand here and watch him. If he was guilty, he wasn't likely to give himself away. He might slip away from her.

She smiled at the storekeeper and left.

Outside, Riley walked a short distance down the block and stood there waiting. Only a few minutes passed before the store's door opened and the man came out. He was still holding the roses in one hand. In the other he held a bag of newly purchased merchandise. He turned and started walking along the sidewalk, moving away from Riley.

Taking long strides, Riley walked after him. She assessed his size and build. She was slightly taller than he was, and possibly a good bit stronger. She was probably better trained. She wasn't going to let him get away.

Just as he was passing a narrow alley, the man must have heard steps behind him. He turned suddenly and glanced back at her. He stepped to one side, as though to get out of her way.

Riley pushed him sideways into the alley—pushed him hard and roughly. The space was narrow, dirty, and dim.

Startled, the man dropped both the package and the roses. The flowers scattered across the pavement. He raised an arm as though to ward her off.

She took hold of that arm and twisted it behind his back, pushing him face-first against a brick wall.

"I'm Special Agent Riley Paige, FBI," she snapped. "Where are you holding Cindy MacKinnon? Is she still alive?"

The man was shaking from head to foot.

"Who?" he asked, his voice trembling. "I don't know what you mean."

"Don't play games with me," Riley snapped, feeling more naked than ever without her badge—and especially without her gun. How was she supposed to bring this guy in without drawing a weapon? She was a long way from Quantico, and she didn't even have a partner to help her.

"Lady, I don't know what this is all about," the man said, bursting into tears.

"What are these roses for?" Riley demanded. "*Who* are they for?"

"My daughter!" the man cried out. "Her first piano recital is tomorrow."

Riley was still holding him by his right arm. The man's left hand was flat against the wall. Riley suddenly noticed something that hadn't caught her eye until now.

The man was wearing a wedding ring. She'd been all but sure that the murderer wasn't married.

"Piano recital?" she said.

"Mrs. Tully's students," he cried. "You can ask anyone in town."

Riley loosened her grip a little.

The man went on, "I bought her roses to celebrate. For when she takes her bow. I bought her a doll too."

Riley released the man's arm and walked over to where he had dropped the package. She picked it up and pulled out its contents.

It was a doll, all right—one of those teenage-girl dolls that always offended and disturbed her, all sexed up with full lips and an ample bosom. But as creepy as it was, it looked nothing like the kind of doll she'd seen near Daggett. That doll was of a little girl. So was the doll she'd seen in the picture of Cindy MacKinnon and her niece—all frilly and golden-haired and dressed in pink.

She had the wrong man. She gasped for breath.

"I'm sorry," she said to the man. "I was wrong. I'm so, so sorry."

Still shaking with shock and confusion, the man was picking up the roses. Riley bent over to help him.

"No! No!" the man exclaimed. "Don't help! Stay away! Just— get away from me!"

127

Riley turned and walked out of the alley, leaving the forlorn man to gather up his daughter's roses and doll. How could she have let this happen? Why did she go so far with it? Why had she not noticed the man's wedding ring the moment she saw him?

The answer was simple. She was exhausted, and her head was splitting. She wasn't thinking straight.

As she walked dazedly down the sidewalk, a neon storefront sign for a bar caught her eye. She wanted a drink. She felt like she needed a drink.

She went into the dimly lit place and sat down at the bar. The bartender was busy waiting on another customer. Riley wondered what the man she had just accosted was doing right now. Was he calling the police? Was she about to be apprehended herself? That would certainly be a bitter irony.

But she guessed that the man probably wouldn't call the police. After all, he'd have a hard time explaining what had happened. He might even feel embarrassed at having been attacked by a woman.

Anyway, if he had called the police, and they were on their way to get her, it wouldn't do to make a run for it. If she had to, she'd face the consequences of her actions. And maybe she deserved to be arrested. She remembered her conversation with Mike Nevins, how he'd drawn her attention to her own feelings of worthlessness.

Maybe I'm right to feel worthless, she thought. *Maybe it would have been better if Peterson had just killed me.*

The bartender stepped toward her.

"What will you have, ma'am?" he asked.

"A bourbon on the rocks," Riley said. "Make that a double."

"Coming right up," the bartender said.

She reminded herself that it wasn't like her to drink on the job. Her agonizing recovery from PTSD had been marked by occasional bouts of intense drinking, but she'd thought that was behind her.

She took a sip. The rough drink felt comforting going down.

She still had one more town to visit, and at least one more person to interview. But she needed something to calm her nerves.

Well, she thought with a bitter smile, *at least I'm not officially on duty.*

She finished the drink quickly, then talked herself out of ordering another. The toy store in the next town would close soon, and she had to get there right away. Time was running out for Cindy MacKinnon—if it hadn't run out already.

As she left the bar, Riley sensed that she was walking on the edge of a familiar abyss. She had thought she'd left all that horror, pain, and self-loathing far behind. Was it catching up with her again?

How much longer, she wondered, could she evade its deadly pull?

Chapter 25

Riley's cell phone buzzed early the next morning. She was sitting at her coffee table, looking at the map she had followed yesterday, planning a new route for today. When she saw that the call was from Bill, her nerves quickened. Would this be good or bad news?

"Bill, what's going on?"

She heard her former partner sigh miserably.

"Riley, are you sitting down?"

Riley's heart sank. She was glad that she *was* sitting down. She knew now that Bill's tone of voice could only mean one terrible thing, and she felt her muscles weaken with dread.

"They've found Cindy MacKinnon," Bill said.

"And she's dead, isn't she?" Riley said with a gasp.

Bill said nothing for a moment. But his silence answered Riley's question. Riley felt tears welling up—tears of shock and helplessness. She fought against them, determined not to cry.

"Where did they find her?" Riley asked.

"Pretty far to the west of the other victims, in the national forest, almost to the West Virginia line."

She looked at her map. "What's the nearest town?" He told her and she found the approximate location. It wasn't inside the triangle made by the other three sites where bodies had been found. But still, there must be some sort of relationship with the other sites. She couldn't quite place what it was.

Bill continued describing the discovery.

"He put her next to a cliff in an open area, no trees around it. I'm at the scene right now. It's horrible. He's getting bolder, Riley."

And acting faster, Riley thought with despair. He'd only kept this victim alive for a few days.

"So Darrell Gumm really is the wrong guy," Riley said.

"You're the only one who said so," Bill replied. "You were right."

Riley struggled to comprehend the situation.

"So has Gumm been released?" she asked.

Bill grunted with annoyance.

"Not a chance," he said. "He'll be facing obstruction charges. He's got a lot to answer for. Not that he seems to care. But we'll try to keep his name out of the news as much as we can. That amoral prick doesn't deserve the publicity."

A silence fell between them.

"Damn it, Riley," Bill said at last, "if only Walder had listened to you, maybe we could have saved her."

Riley doubted that. It wasn't as if she'd had any solid leads of her own; but maybe with all that redirected manpower, something could have been turned up in those precious hours.

"Have you got any photos?" she asked. Her heart was pounding.

"Yeah, Riley, but—"

"I know you're not supposed to show them to me. But I've got to see them. Could you send them to me?"

After a pause, Bill said, "Done."

A few moments later, Riley was looking at a series of ghastly images on her cell phone. The first was a close-up of that face she had seen in a picture just a few days back. Then the woman had been beaming with love over a happy little girl and her brand new doll. But now that face was pallid, its eyes stitched open, a hideous smile painted over its lips.

As she looked through more pictures, she saw that the display was a match for how Reba Frye's corpse had been arranged. All of the details were there. The pose was precise. The body was naked and splayed, sitting stiffly upright like a doll. An artificial rose was on the ground between her legs.

This was the killer's true signature, his message. This was the effect he'd wanted to achieve all along. He'd achieved mastery with his victims number three and four. Riley knew perfectly well he was all ready to do it again.

After looking at the pictures, Riley got back on the phone with Bill.

"I'm so sorry," she said, her voice choked with horror and sadness.

"Yeah, me too," he said. "But have you got any ideas at all?"

Riley ran the images she had just seen through her mind.

"I assume the wig and rose are the same as the others," she said. "The ribbon, too."

"Right. They look the same."

She paused again. What clues could Bill's team hope to find?

"Did you get the call early enough to check for tracks, footprints?" she asked.

"The scene was secured early this time. A ranger spotted her and called the Bureau directly. No local cops tromping around. But we didn't find anything useful. This guy is careful."

Riley thought hard for a few moments. The photos had showed

131

a woman's body sitting in the grass, leaning against a rock formation. Questions were buzzing through her mind.

"Was the body cold?" she asked.

"It was by the time we got to it."

"How long do you think it had been there?"

She could hear Bill thumbing through his notebook.

"I don't know for sure, but she was put into this pose soon after death. According to discoloration, within a few hours. We'll know more after the coroner gets to work."

Riley felt her familiar impatience well up. She wanted to get a clearer sense of the killer's chronology.

She asked, "Could he have posed her where he killed her and then brought her to the location after the body was in rigor mortis?"

"Probably not," Bill said. "I don't see anything awkward about the position. I don't think she could have already been stiff before he brought her here. Why? Do you think he brought her here and then killed her?"

Riley closed her eyes and thought hard.

Finally she said, "No."

"You're sure?"

"He killed her wherever he kept her and then brought her to the site. He wouldn't have brought her there alive. He wouldn't want to struggle with a human being in his truck or on the site."

Her eyes still shut tight, Riley reached inside herself for a sense of the killer's mind.

"He would only want to bring the raw materials for the statement he was making," she said. "Once she was dead, that's what she was to him. Like a piece of artwork, no longer a woman. So he killed her, washed her down, dried her, prepared the body just the way he wanted it, all covered with Vaseline."

The scene was starting to play out in her imagination in vivid detail.

"He got her to the location when rigor mortis was setting in," she said. "He timed it perfectly. After killing three other women, he understood just how that would work. He made the onset of rigor part of his creative process. He posed her as she hardened, little by little. He molded her like clay."

Riley found it hard to say what she saw happening next in her mind—or the killer's mind. The words came out slowly and painfully.

"By the time he'd finished sculpting the rest of her body, her chin still rested on her chest. He felt the muscles of her shoulders and neck, sensing the exact state of remaining pliability, and tilted the head up. He held it there until it stiffed. It might have taken two or three minutes. He was patient. Then he stepped back and enjoyed his handiwork."

"Jesus," Bill murmured in a hushed, shocked voice. "You're good."

Riley sighed bitterly and didn't reply. She didn't think she was good—not anymore. All she was good at was getting into a sick mind. What did that say about her? How did it do anybody any good? It certainly hadn't helped Cindy MacKinnon.

Bill asked, "How far away do you think he holds the victims while they're still alive?"

Riley did some swift mental calculations, visualizing a map of the area in her head.

"Not very far from where he posed her," she said. "Probably under two hours away."

"That still covers a lot of territory."

Riley's spirits were ebbing by the second. Bill was right. She wasn't saying a single thing that could be any help.

"Riley, we need you back on this case," Bill said.

Riley groaned under her breath.

"I'm sure Walder doesn't think so," she said.

I don't think so, either, she thought.

"Well, Walder's wrong," Bill said. "And I'm going to tell him he's wrong. I'm going to get you back on the job."

Riley let Bill's words sink in for a moment.

"It's too much of a risk for you," she said at last. "Walder's liable to fire you too if you make waves."

Bill stammered, "But—but Riley—"

"No 'buts,' Bill. If you get yourself fired, this case will never get solved."

Bill sighed. His voice was tired and resigned.

"Okay," he said. "But have you got any ideas at all?"

Riley thought for a moment. The abyss she'd been peering into for the last couple of days yawned wider and deeper. She felt what little was left of her resolve slipping away through her fingers. She'd failed, and a woman was dead.

Still, maybe there was one more thing she could do.

"I have some ideas brewing," she said. "I'll let you know."

As they ended the call, the smell of coffee and fried bacon reached Riley from the kitchen. April was in there. She'd been making breakfast ever since Riley had gotten out of bed.

133

Without even being asked! Riley thought.

Maybe spending time with her father was making her appreciate Riley, at least a little. April never liked having to be around Ryan. Whatever the reason, Riley was grateful for even the smallest comfort on a morning like this.

She sat there thinking about what to do next. She'd been planning to drive west again today, following the new route she'd mapped out. But she felt defeated, completely beaten down by this terrible turn of events. Yesterday she hadn't been at her best, and had even succumbed to that drink in Glendive. She couldn't do the same thing today, not in her present state of mind. She'd surely make mistakes. And too many mistakes had been made already.

But the location of the store was still important—maybe more important than ever. The killer would target his next victim there, if he hadn't already. Riley got on her computer and composed an email for Bill, with a copy of her map attached.

She explained to Bill which towns and which stores ought to be checked. Bill himself should probably stay focused on finding the killer's house, she wrote. But maybe he could persuade Walder to send someone else along Riley's route—as long as Walder didn't find out that it was her idea.

She sat there, staring at the map again and again, and slowly she began to spot a pattern she had not seen before. It was not that the sites related to each other, but that they were spread out in a lopsided fan from another mark on her map—the area enclosed by the four women's addresses. As she studied it, it made her more convinced than ever that the selection of victims was centered around some particular place that they all went, a particular doll store. And wherever the killer took his victims, it probably wasn't a long distance from where he first saw them.

But why hadn't she been able to find the store? Was she taking the wrong approach? Was she so stuck on a single idea that she couldn't see any other clues? Was she just imagining a pattern that was leading her completely astray?

Riley scanned her map and sent it along to Bill with her notes.

"Breakfast is ready, Mom."

As she sat down with her daughter, Riley found herself fighting back tears again.

"Thank you," she said. She began to eat silently.

"Mom, what's wrong?" April asked.

Riley was surprised at the question. Did she hear a note of concern in her daughter's voice? The girl was still pretty taciturn with Riley most of the time, but at least she hadn't been openly rude for a few days.

"Nothing's wrong," Riley said.

"That's not true," April said.

Riley said nothing in reply. She didn't want to drag April into the horrible reality of the case. Her daughter was troubled enough already.

"Was that Bill on the phone?" April asked.

Riley nodded silently.

"What did he call about?" April asked.

"I can't talk about it."

A long silence fell between them. They both kept on eating.

Finally April said, "You keep trying to get me to talk to you. That cuts both ways, you know. You never talk to me, not really. Do you ever talk to *anybody* anymore?"

Riley stopped eating and stifled a sob as it rose up in her throat. It was a good question. And the answer was no. She didn't talk to anybody at all, not anymore. But she couldn't bring herself to say so.

She reminded herself that it was Saturday, and she wasn't taking April to school. And she'd made no plans for April to stay with her father. And even though Riley wasn't going to drive west in search of clues, there was still something she had to do.

"April, I've got to go somewhere," she said. "Will you be okay here by yourself?"

"Sure," April said. Then, in a truly sad voice, she asked, "Mom, could you at least tell me where you're going?"

"I'm going to a funeral."

Chapter 26

Riley arrived at the parlor in Georgetown shortly before Marie's service was scheduled to begin. She dreaded funerals. To her, they were worse than arriving at a crime scene with a freshly murdered body. They always got inside her gut in some terrible way. Yet Riley felt she still owed something—she wasn't sure what—to Marie.

The funeral parlor had a facade of prefab brick panels and white columns on the front portico. She entered a carpeted, air-conditioned foyer that led into a hallway wallpapered in muted pastel colors gauged to be neither depressing nor cheery. The effect backfired on Riley, adding to her feeling of despair. She wondered why funeral homes couldn't just be the gloomy and uninviting places they really ought to be, like mausoleums or morgues, with none of this phony sanitization.

She passed several rooms, some with caskets and visitors, others empty, until she arrived where Marie's service was to be held. At the far end of the room she saw the open casket, made out of burnished wood with a long brass handle along the sides. Perhaps two dozen people had showed up, many of them seated, some of them mingling and whispering. Bland organ music was being pumped into the room. A small viewing line was passing the coffin.

She got in line and soon found herself standing beside the coffin, looking down at Marie. For all of Riley's mental preparation, it still gave her a jolt. Marie's face was unnaturally passive and serene, not twisted and agonized, as it had been when she was hanging from that light fixture. This face was not stressed and fearful, as it had been when they had talked in person. It seemed wrong. Actually, it seemed worse than wrong.

She quickly moved past the coffin, noticing a somewhat elderly couple sitting in the front row. She assumed that they were Marie's parents. They were flanked by a man and woman closer to Riley's age. She took them to be Marie's brother and sister. Riley reached back into memories of conversations with Marie and recalled that their names were Trevor and Shannon. She had no idea what Marie's parents' names were.

Riley thought of stopping to offer the family her condolences. But how would she introduce herself? As the woman who rescued Marie from captivity, only to find her corpse later? No, surely she was the last person they wanted to see right now. It was best to leave them to grieve in peace.

As she made her way to the back of the room, Riley realized that she didn't recognize a single person there. That seemed strange and terribly sad. After all their countless hours of video chatting and their single face-to-face meeting, they didn't have one friend in common.

But they did have one terrible enemy in common—the psychopath who had held them both. Was he here today? Riley knew that killers commonly visited the funerals and graves of victims. Deep down, as much as she owed it to Marie, she also had to admit that that was the real reason she had come here today. To find Peterson. It was also why she was carrying a concealed weapon—her personal Glock that she normally kept boxed in her car trunk.

As she walked toward the back of the room, she scanned the faces of those already seated. She had glimpsed Peterson's face in the glare of his torch, and she'd seen pictures of him. But she'd never gotten a really good look at him face to face. Would she recognize him?

Her heart pounded as she looked at all the faces suspiciously, searching for a murderer in each one. They all soon became a blur of grief-stricken faces, staring back puzzlingly at her.

Seeing no obvious suspects, Riley sat down in an aisle seat in the back row, separated from anyone else, where she could watch anyone who entered or exited.

A young minister stepped up to a podium. Riley knew that Marie hadn't been religious, so the minister must have been her family's idea. The stragglers sat down, and everybody became quiet.

In a hushed and rather professional-sounding voice, the minister began with familiar words.

"'Even though I walk through the valley of the shadow of death, I will fear no evil, for you are with me; your rod and your staff, they comfort me.'"

The minister paused for a moment. In the brief silence, a single phrase echoed through Riley's mind …

"I will fear no evil."

Somehow, it struck Riley as a grotesquely inappropriate thing to say. What did it even mean to "fear no evil"? How could it possibly be a good idea? If Marie had been more fearful months ago, more wary, maybe she wouldn't have fallen into Peterson's clutches at all.

This was definitely a time to be fearful of evil. There was

137

plenty of it out there.

The minister began to speak again.

"My friends, we have gathered here to mourn the loss and celebrate the life of Marie Sayles—daughter, sister, friend, and colleague ..."

The minister then launched into a boilerplate homily about loss, friendship, and family. Although he described Marie's "passing" as "untimely," he made no mention of the violence and terror that had haunted the last weeks of her life.

Riley quickly tuned out his sermon. As she did, she remembered the words in Marie's suicide note.

"This is the only way."

Riley felt a knot of guilt swelling inside of her, growing so large that she almost couldn't breathe. She wanted to rush up to the front of the room, push the minister aside, and confess to the congregation that this was all, all her own fault. She had failed Marie. She had failed everyone who loved Marie. She had failed herself.

Riley fought back the urge to confess, but her unease started to take on a brutal clarity. First there had been the funeral home's prefab bricks, silly white columns, and pastel-colored wallpaper. Next had been Marie's face, so unnatural and waxy in the coffin. And now here was the preacher, gesturing and talking like some kind of toy, a miniature automaton, and the congregation of little heads bobbing as he spoke to them.

It's like a doll house, Riley now realized.

And Marie was posed in the coffin—not a real corpse, but a pretend one, in a pretend funeral.

Horror cascaded over Riley. The two murderers—Peterson and whoever had killed Cindy MacKinnon and the others—merged together in her mind. It didn't matter that the pairing was completely groundless and irrational. She couldn't disentangle them. They became one to her.

It seemed as though this well-crafted funeral was the monster's final touch. It announced that there would be many more victims and many more funerals to follow.

As she sat there, Riley noticed out of the corner of her eyes someone slip in quietly to the service and sit on the other end of the back row. She turned her head slightly to see who had arrived in the middle of the service and saw a man dressed casually, wearing a baseball cap drawn low, shielding his eyes. Her heart beat faster. He looked large and strong enough to be the one who overpowered her

138

when he caught her. His face was hard, jaws clenched, and she thought that he had a guilty look about him. Could it be the killer she was looking for?

Riley realized that she was almost hyperventilating. She slowed her breathing down until her head cleared. She had to restrain herself from leaping up and arresting the latecomer. The service was obviously coming to a close, and she couldn't disrupt it and disrespect Marie's memory. She had to wait. What if it wasn't him?

But then, to her surprise, he suddenly got to his feet and quietly left the room. Had he spotted her?

Riley jumped up and followed him. She sensed heads turn at her sudden commotion, but that didn't matter now.

She trotted through the funeral parlor hallway toward the front entrance, and as she threw open the front door, she saw that the man was walking briskly away along the city sidewalk. She drew her handgun and charged after him.

"FBI!" she shouted. "Stop right there!"

The man whirled around to face her.

"FBI!" she repeated, once again feeling naked without her badge. "Keep your hands where I can see them."

The man facing her looked utterly baffled.

"ID!" she demanded.

His hands were shaking—whether from fear or indignation, Riley couldn't tell. He fished out a wallet with a driver's license and as she scanned it, she saw it identified him as a Washington resident.

"Here's my ID," he said. "Where's yours?"

Riley's resolution started to slip away. Had she ever seen this man's face before? She wasn't sure.

"I'm an attorney," the man said, still very shaken. "And I know my rights. You'd better have a good reason for pulling a gun on me for no reason. Right here on a city street."

"I'm Agent Riley Paige," she said. "I need to know why you were attending that funeral."

The man looked at her more closely.

"Riley Paige?" he asked. "The agent who rescued her?"

Riley nodded. The man's face suddenly sagged with despair.

"Marie was a friend," he said. "Months ago, we were close. And then this terrible thing happened to her and …"

The man choked back a sob.

"I'd lost touch with her. It was my fault. She was a good friend, and I didn't stay in touch. And now I'll never get a chance to …"

The man shook his head.

"I wish I could go back and do everything differently. I just feel so bad about it. I couldn't even make it all the way through the funeral. I had to leave."

This man was feeling guilty, Riley realized, and in pain. For reasons very much like her own.

"I'm sorry," Riley said softly, deflated, lowering her gun. "I really am. I will find the bastard who did this to her."

As she turned to walk away, she heard him call out in a perplexed tone.

"I thought he was already dead?"

Riley didn't reply. She left the bereaved man standing on the sidewalk.

And as she walked away, she knew exactly where she needed to go. A place where no one else on earth, except Marie, could possibly understand.

*

Riley drove through city streets that transitioned from Georgetown's elegant homes to a ramshackle neighborhood in a once-thriving industrial area. Many buildings and stores were abandoned, and the local residents were poor. The deeper she drove, the worse it became.

She finally parked along a block that consisted entirely of condemned row houses. She got out of the car and quickly found what she was looking for.

Two vacant homes flanked a broad, barren area. Not very long ago, three deserted houses had stood here. Peterson had lived as a squatter in the middle house, using it as his secret lair. It had been the perfect spot for him, too separated from living inhabitants for anyone to hear the screams coming from beneath the house.

Now the space had been leveled flat, all evidence of the houses cleared away, and grass was starting to grow there. Riley tried to visualize what it had looked like when the houses had been there. It wasn't easy. She'd only been here once when the houses were standing. And then it had been night.

As she walked into the clearing, memories started to come back to her ...

Riley had been trailing him all day and into the night. Bill had been called away on an unrelated emergency, and Riley had unwisely decided to follow the man here alone.

She watched him enter the wretched little house with boarded up windows. Then, just a few moments later, he left again. He was on foot, and she didn't know where he was going.

She briefly considered calling for backup. She decided against it. The man had gone away, and if the victim was really inside that house, she couldn't leave her alone and in torment for another minute. She walked up onto the porch and squeezed her way between boards that only partially blocked the doorway.

She turned on her flashlight. The beam reflected against at least a dozen tanks of propane gas. It was no surprise. She and Bill knew that the suspect was obsessed with fire.

Then she heard a scratching below the floorboards, then a weak cry ...

Riley paused the flow of memories. She looked around. She felt sure—uncannily sure—that she was now standing on the very spot that she both dreaded and sought. It was here where both she and Marie had been caged in that dark and filthy crawlspace.

The rest of the story was still raw in her mind. Riley had been captured by Peterson when she set Marie free. Marie had staggered a couple of miles in a state of complete shock. By the time she was found, she had no idea where she had been held captive. Riley was left alone in the dark to find her own way out.

After a seemingly endless nightmare, tormented repeatedly by Peterson's torch, Riley had gotten loose. When she did, she had beaten Peterson nearly unconscious. Every blow gave her a great sense of vindication. Maybe those blows, that small vindication, she reflected, had allowed her to heal better than Marie.

Then, crazed and maddened with fear and exhaustion, Riley had opened all the tanks of propane. As she fled the house, she threw a lighted match back inside. The explosion threw her all the way across the street. Everyone was amazed that she'd survived.

Now, two months after that explosion, Riley stood looking around at her grim handiwork—a vacant space where nobody lived or was likely to live for a long time. It seemed like a perfect image of what her life had become. In a way, it seemed like the end of the road—at least for her.

A sickening feeling of vertigo came over her. Still standing in that grassy spot, she felt as if she were falling, falling, falling. She tumbled straight into that abyss that had been yawning open for her. Even in broad daylight, the world seemed terribly dark—even darker than it had been in that cage in that crawlspace. There seemed to be no bottom to the abyss, and no end to her fall.

Riley recalled once again Betty Richter's assessment of the odds that Peterson had been killed.

I'd say ninety-nine percent.

But that nagging one percent somehow rendered the other ninety-nine meaningless and absurd. And besides, even if Peterson really had died, what difference did it make? Riley remembered Marie's awful words on the phone on the day of her suicide.

Maybe he's like a ghost, Riley. Maybe that's what happened when you blew him up. You killed his body but you didn't kill his evil.

Yes, that was it. She had been fighting a losing battle all her life. Evil, after all, haunted the world, as surely as it did this place where she and Marie had suffered so horribly. It was a lesson she should have learned as a little girl, when she couldn't stop her mother from being murdered. The lesson was hammered home by Marie's suicide. Rescuing her had been pointless. There was no point in rescuing anybody, not even herself. Evil would prevail in the end. It was just as Marie had told her over the phone.

You can't fight a ghost. Give it up, Riley.

And Marie, so much braver than Riley had known, finally took matters into her own hands. She'd explained her choice in five simple words.

This is the only way.

But that was not courage, to take your life own life. That was cowardice.

A voice broke through Riley's darkness.

"You all right, lady?"

Riley looked up.

"What?"

Then, slowly, she realized that she was on her knees in a vacant city lot. Tears were running down her face.

"Should I call someone for you?" the voice asked. Riley saw that a woman had stopped on the nearby sidewalk, an older woman in shabby clothes but with a concerned look on her face.

Riley got her sobbing under control and rose to her feet, and the woman shuffled off.

Riley stood there, numb. If she couldn't put an end to her own horror, she knew a way that she could numb herself against it. It wasn't courageous, and it wasn't honorable, but Riley was past caring. She wasn't going to resist it any longer. She got into her car and drove toward home.

Chapter 27

Hands still shaking, Riley reached into a kitchen cabinet for the bottle of vodka she'd stashed, the one she promised she would never touch again. She unscrewed the bottle cap and tried to pour it quietly into a glass, so that April wouldn't hear. Since it looked so much like water, she hoped she could drink it openly without lying about it. She didn't want to lie. But the bottle gurgled indiscreetly.

"What's going on, Mom?" April asked from behind her at the kitchen table.

"Nothing," Riley answered.

She heard April groan a little. She could tell that her daughter knew what she was doing. But there was no pouring the vodka back into the bottle. Riley wanted to throw it away, she really did. The last thing she wanted to do was drink, especially in front of April. But she had never felt so low, so shaken. She felt as if the world were conspiring against her. And she really needed a drink.

Riley slipped the bottle back into the cabinet, then went to the table and sat down with her glass. She took a long sip, and it burned her throat in a comforting way. April stared at her for a moment.

"That's vodka, isn't it, Mom?" she said.

Riley said nothing, guilt creeping over her. Did April deserve this? Riley had left her at home all day, calling occasionally to check up on her, and the girl had been perfectly responsible and had stayed out of trouble. Now Riley was the one being furtive and reckless.

"You got mad at me for smoking pot," April said.

Riley still said nothing.

"Now is when you're supposed to tell me that this is different," April said.

"It *is* different," Riley said wearily.

April glared.

"How?"

Riley sighed, knowing her daughter was right, and feeling a deepening sense of shame.

"Pot's illegal," she said. "This isn't. And—"

"And you're an adult and I'm a kid, right?"

Riley didn't reply. Of course, that was exactly what she had been starting to say. And of course, it was hypocritical and wrong.

"I don't want to argue," Riley said.

"Are you really going to start into this kind of thing again?" April said. "You drank so much when you were going through all those troubles—and you never even told me what it was all about."

Riley felt her chin clench. Was it from anger? What on earth did she have to be angry with April about, at least right now?

"There are some things I just can't tell you," Riley said.

April rolled her eyes.

"Jesus, Mom, why not? I mean, am I *ever* going to be grown up enough to learn the awful truth about what you do? It can't be much worse that what I imagine. Believe me, I can imagine a lot."

April got up from her chair and stomped over to the cabinet. She pulled down the vodka bottle and started to pour herself a glass.

"Please don't do that, April," Riley said weakly.

"How are you going to stop me?"

Riley got up and gently took the bottle away from April. Then she sat down again and poured the contents of April's glass into her own glass.

"Just finish eating your food, okay?" Riley said.

April was tearing up now.

"Mom, I wish you could see yourself," she said. "Maybe you'd understand how it hurts me to see you like this. And how it hurts that you never tell me anything. It just hurts so much."

Riley tried to speak but found that she couldn't.

"Talk to somebody, Mom," April said, beginning to sob. "If not to me, to somebody. There must be *somebody* you can trust."

April fled into her room and slammed the door behind her.

Riley buried her face in her hands. Why did she keep failing so badly with April? Why couldn't she keep the ugly parts of her life separate from her daughter?

Her whole body heaved with sobs. Her world had spun completely out of control and she couldn't form a single coherent thought.

She sat there until the tears stopped flowing.

Taking the bottle and the glass with her, she went into the living room and sat on the couch. She clicked on the TV and watched the first channel that came up. She had no idea what movie or TV show she'd happened upon, and she didn't care. She just sat there staring blankly at the pictures and letting the meaningless voices wash over her.

But she couldn't stop the images flooding through her mind. She saw the faces of the women who had been killed. She saw the blinding flame of Peterson's torch moving toward her. And she saw Marie's dead face—both when Riley had found her hanging and when she'd been so artfully displayed in the coffin.

145

A new emotion started to crawl along her nerves—an emotion that she dreaded above all others. It was fear.

She was terrified of Peterson, and she could feel his vengeful presence all around her. It didn't much matter whether he was alive or dead. He'd taken Marie's life, and Riley couldn't shake the conviction that she was his next target.

She also feared, perhaps even more, the abyss that she was falling into now. Were the two really separate? Hadn't Peterson caused this abyss? This was not the Riley she knew. Did PTSD ever have an end?

Riley lost track of time. Her whole body buzzed and ached with her multifaceted fear. She drank steadily, but the vodka wasn't numbing her at all.

She finally went to the bathroom and combed the medicine cabinet and found what she was looking for. Finally, with shaking hands, she found it: her prescription tranquilizers. She was supposed to take one at bedtime, and to never mix it with alcohol.

With shaking hands, she took two.

Riley went back to the living room couch and stared at the TV again, waiting for the medication to take effect. But it wasn't working.

Panic seized her in an icy grip.

The room seemed to be spinning now, making her feel nauseous. She closed her eyes and stretched out on the couch. Some of the dizziness went away, but the darkness behind her eyelids was impenetrable.

How much worse can things get? she asked herself.

She knew right away that it was a stupid question. Things were going to get worse and worse and worse for her. Things would never ever get better. The abyss was bottomless. All she could do was surrender to the fall and give herself over to cold despair.

The pitch-blackness of intoxication folded itself around her. She lost consciousness and soon began to dream.

Once again, the white flame of the propane torch cut through the darkness. She heard someone's voice.

"Come on. Follow me."

It wasn't Peterson's voice. It was familiar, though—extremely familiar. Had somebody come to her rescue? She rose to her feet and began to follow whoever was carrying the torch.

But to her horror, the torch cast its light on one corpse after another—first Margaret Geraty, then Eileen Rogers, then Reba

Frye, then Cindy MacKinnon—all of them naked and horribly splayed. Finally the light fell on Marie's body, suspended in mid-air, her face horribly contorted.

Riley heard the voice again.

"Girl, you sure as hell botched things up."

Riley turned and looked. In the sizzling glare, she saw who was holding the torch.

It wasn't Peterson. It was her own father. He was wearing the full dress uniform of a Marine colonel. That struck her as odd. He'd been retired for many years now. And she hadn't seen or spoken to him in more than two years.

"I saw some bad shit in 'Nam," he said with a shake of his head. "But this really makes me sick. Yeah, you botched it bad, Riley. Of course I learned long ago not to expect anything from you."

He waved the torch so that it shone on one last body. It was her mother, dead and bleeding from the bullet wound.

"You might as well have shot her yourself, for all the good you did her," her father said.

"I was just a little girl, Daddy," Riley wailed.

"I don't want to hear any of your damn excuses," her father barked. "You never brought a single human soul a moment of joy or happiness, you know that? You never did anybody a lick of good. Not even yourself."

He turned the knob of the torch. The flame went out. Riley was in pitch-darkness again.

Riley opened her eyes. It was night, and the only light in the living room came from the TV. She remembered her dream clearly. Her father's words kept ringing in her ears.

You never brought a single human soul a moment of joy or happiness.

Was it true? Had she failed everybody so miserably—even the people she loved most?

You never did anybody a lick of good. Not even yourself.

Her mind was foggy and she couldn't think straight. Maybe she couldn't bring anybody any real joy and happiness. Maybe there was simply no real love inside of her. Maybe she wasn't capable of love.

On the verge of despair, reeling for a crutch, Riley recalled April's words.

Talk to somebody. Somebody you can trust.

147

In her drunken haze, not thinking clearly, almost automatically Riley tapped a number on her cell phone. After a few moments, she heard Bill's voice.

"Riley?" he asked, sounding more than half-asleep. "Do you know what time it is?"

"I've got no idea," Riley said, slurring her words badly.

Riley heard a woman ask groggily, "Who is that, Bill?"

Bill said to his wife, "I'm sorry, I've got to take this."

She heard the sound of Bill's footsteps and a door closing. She guessed that he was going somewhere to talk privately.

"What's this all about?" he asked.

"I don't know, Bill, but—"

Riley stopped for a moment. She felt herself on the brink of saying things that she'd regret—maybe forever. But somehow she couldn't pull herself back.

"Bill, do you think you could get away for a while?"

Bill let out a growl of confusion.

"What are you talking about?"

Riley drew a deep breath. What *was* she talking about? She was finding it hard to collect her thoughts. But she knew that she wanted to see Bill. It was a primal instinct, an urge she could not control.

With what little awareness she had left she knew she should say *I'm sorry* and hang up. But fear, loneliness, and desperation overtook her, and she plunged ahead.

"I mean…" she continued, slurring her words, trying to think coherently, "just you and me. Spend some time together."

There was only silence on the line.

"Riley, it's the middle of the night," he said. "What do you mean *spend time together*?" he demanded, his irritation clearly rising.

"I mean…" she began, searching, wanting to stop, but unable to. "I mean…I think about you, Bill. And not just at work. Don't you think about me, too?"

Riley felt a terrible weight crushing upon her as soon as she had said it. It was wrong, and there was no taking it back.

Bill sighed bitterly.

"You're drunk, Riley," he said. "I'm not going to meet you anywhere. You're not going to drive anywhere. I've got a marriage I'm trying to save, and you … well, you've got your own problems. Pull yourself together. Try to get some sleep."

Bill ended the call abruptly. For a moment, reality seemed to hang in a state of suspension. Then Riley was seized by a horrible clarity.

"What have I done?" she whimpered aloud.

In but a few moments, she had thrown away a ten-year professional relationship. Her best friend. Her only partner. And probably the most successful relationship of her life.

She'd been sure that the abyss she'd fallen into had no bottom. But now she knew she was wrong. She'd hit the bottom, and shattered the floor. Still, she was falling. She didn't know if she'd ever be able to get up again.

She reached for the vodka bottle on the coffee table—she didn't know whether to drink the last of its contents or to pour it out. But her hand-eye coordination was completely shot. She couldn't take hold of it.

The room swam around her, there came a crash, and everything went black.

Chapter 28

Riley opened her eyes, then squinted, shielding her face with her hand. Her head was splitting, her mouth dry. The morning light from the window was blinding and painful, reminding her uncannily of the white flash of Peterson's torch.

She heard April's voice say, "I'll take care of that, Mom."

There came a slight rattling and the glare diminished. She opened her eyes.

She saw that April had just closed the venetian blinds, shutting out the direct sunlight. She came over to the couch and sat down beside where Riley still lay. She picked up a cup of coffee and offered it to her.

"Careful, it's hot," April said.

Riley, the room spinning, slowly eased herself into a sitting position and reached for the mug. Handling the cup gingerly, she took a small sip. It was hot, all right. It burned both her fingertips and her tongue. Still, she was able to hold it, and she took another sip. At least the pain gave her a feeling of coming to life again.

April was staring off into space.

"Are you going to want some breakfast?" April asked in a distant, vacant voice.

"Maybe later," Riley said. "I'll fix it."

April smirked a bit sadly. Doubtless she could see that Riley was in no condition to fix much of anything.

"No, I'll do it," April said. "Just let me know when you feel like eating."

They both fell silent. April kept on staring elsewhere. Humiliation gnawed at Riley's gut. She vaguely remembered her disgraceful phone call to Bill last night, then her last thoughts before passing out—that hideous knowledge that she'd truly hit rock bottom. And now, to make matters worse, her daughter was here to witness her ruin.

Still sounding distant, April asked, "What are you planning to do today?"

It seemed both an odd question and a good one. It was time for Riley to make plans. If this was rock bottom, she needed to start pulling herself out.

She flashed back to her dream, her father's words, and as she did, she realized it was time to confront some of her demons.

Her father. The darkest presence of her life. The one who had always lingered in the back of her consciousness. The driving force, she sometimes felt, behind all the darkness she had manifested in her life. He, of all people, was the one she needed to see. Whether it was a primal urge for a father's love, her urge to face head-on the darkness in her life, or a desire to shake off being haunted by her dream, she did not know. But the urge consumed her.

"I think I'll drive out to see Grandpa," she said.

"Grandpa?" she asked, shocked. "You haven't seen him for years. Why would you go see him? I think he hates me."

"I don't think so," Riley said. "He's always been too busy hating me."

Another silence fell, and Riley sensed that her daughter was gathering her resolve.

"I want you to know something," April said. "I dumped out the rest of the vodka. There wasn't much left. I also poured out the whiskey you still had in the cabinet. I'm sorry. I guess it was none of my business. I shouldn't have done that."

Tears came to Riley's eyes. This was surely the most grown-up and responsible thing she'd ever known April to do.

"No, you should have," Riley said. "It was the right thing to do. Thank you. I'm sorry I couldn't do it myself."

Riley wiped away a tear and gathered up her own resolve.

"I think it's time we really talked," Riley said. "I think it's time I told you some of the things you've wanted me to tell you." She sighed. "But it won't be pleasant."

April finally turned and looked at her, anticipation in her eyes.

"I really wish you would, Mom," she said.

Riley took a long, deep breath.

"A couple of months back, I was working on a case," she said. Relief poured through her as she began to tell April about the Peterson case. She realized that this was much too long overdue.

"I got too eager," she continued. "I was by myself and I came across a situation, and I wasn't willing to wait. I didn't call for backup. I thought I could take care of it by myself."

April said, "That's what you do all the time. You try to take care of everything alone. Without me even. Without even talking to me."

"You're right."

Riley steeled herself.

"I got Marie out of captivity."

Riley hesitated, then finally plunged ahead. She heard her own voice shaking.

151

"I got caught," she continued. "He held me in a cage. There was a torch."

She broke down crying, all her pent-up terror rushing to the surface. She was so embarrassed, but couldn't stop.

To her surprise, she felt April's reassuring hand on her shoulder, and heard April crying herself.

"It's okay, mom," she said.

"They couldn't find me," Riley continued, between sobs. "They didn't know where to look. It was my fault."

"Mom, nothing's your fault," April said.

Riley wiped away her tears, trying to get a hold of herself.

"Finally, I got away finally. I blew up the place. They say the man is dead. That he can't hurt me now."

There came a silence.

"Is he?" April asked.

Riley so desperately wanted to say yes, to reassure her daughter. But instead she found herself saying:

"I don't know."

The silence thickened.

"Mom," April said, a new tone to her voice, one of kindness, of compassion, of strength, one Riley had never heard before, "you saved someone's life. You should be so proud of yourself."

Riley felt a new dread as she slowly shook her head.

"What?" April asked.

"That's where I was yesterday," Riley said. "Marie. Her funeral."

"She's dead!?" she asked, flabbergasted.

Riley could only nod.

"How?"

Riley hesitated. She didn't want to say it, but she had no choice. She owed April the whole truth. She was done withholding things.

"She killed herself."

She heard April gasp.

"Oh, Mom," she said, crying. "I'm so, so sorry."

They both cried for a long, long time, until finally they settled into a relaxed silence, each spent.

Riley took a deep breath, leaned over, and smiled at April, pulling the hair off her wet cheeks with love.

"You'll have to understand that there will be things I can't tell you," Riley said. "Either because I can't tell anybody, or because it wouldn't be safe for you to know, or maybe just because I don't think you should be thinking about them. I have to learn how to be the mother here."

"But something as big as this," April said. "You should have told me. You're my mother, after all. How was I supposed to know what you were going through? I'm old enough. I can understand. "

Riley sighed.

"I guess I thought you had enough to worry about. Especially with Dad and I splitting up."

"The split wasn't as hard as having you not talk to me," April countered. "Dad's always ignored me except when he felt called upon to give orders. But you—it's like suddenly you weren't there anymore."

Riley took April's hand and squeezed it tightly.

"I'm sorry," Riley said. "For everything."

April nodded.

"I'm sorry too," she said.

They hugged, and as Riley felt April's tears flow down her neck, she vowed to be different. She vowed to make a change. When this case was behind her, she would become the mother she always wanted to be.

Chapter 29

Riley drove reluctantly into the heart of her early childhood. What she expected to find there she didn't know. But she knew this was a crucial errand—for herself, anyway. She braced herself at the idea of seeing her father. Yet she knew she needed to face him.

Sloping all around her were the Appalachian Mountains, far to the south of her recent investigations. The trip down here had been a tonic in some ways, and with the windows down, she was beginning to feel better. She'd forgotten how beautiful the Shenandoah Valley was. She found herself steering upward through rocky passes and alongside flowing streams.

She passed through a typical mountain town—little more than a cluster of buildings, a gas station, a grocery store, a church, a handful of houses, a restaurant. She remembered how she'd spent her earliest childhood years in a town much like this.

She also remembered how sad she'd been when they'd moved to Lanton. Mother had said it was because it was a university town and had a whole lot more to offer. That had reset Riley's life expectations when she was still very young. Might things have gone better if she'd been able to spend her whole life in this simpler and more innocent world? A world where her mother wasn't likely to get gunned down in a public place?

The town disappeared behind her in multiple curves of the mountain roads. After a few miles, Riley turned off onto a winding dirt road.

Before too long she arrived at the cabin her father had bought after retiring from the Marines. A battered old utility vehicle was parked nearby. She hadn't been here in more than two years, but she knew the place well.

She parked and got out of her car. As she walked toward the cabin, she breathed in the clean forest air. It was a beautiful sunny day, and at this altitude the temperature was cool and pleasant. She basked in the splendid quiet, broken by nothing more than bird songs and the rustle of leaves in the breeze. It felt good to be surrounded on all sides by deep forest.

She walked toward the door, past a tree stump where her father cut his firewood. There was a pile of wood nearby—his only source of heat in colder weather. He also lived without electricity, but spring water was piped into the cabin.

Riley knew that this simple life was a matter of choice, not poverty. With his excellent benefits, he could have retired anywhere he'd liked. He'd chosen here, and Riley couldn't blame him. Maybe someday she'd do the same. Of course, a substantial pension looked markedly less likely, now that she'd lost her badge.

She pushed at the door and it opened freely. Out in these parts, there was little to fear from intruders. She stepped inside and looked around. The spare but comfortable single room was dim, with several unlit gas lanterns here and there. The pine paneling gave off a warm and pleasant woody smell.

Nothing had changed since the last time she'd been here. There were still no mounted deer heads or any other signs of game animals. Her father killed more than his share of animals, but solely for food and clothing.

The quiet was broken by a gunshot outside. She knew it wasn't deer season. He was probably shooting at smaller game—squirrels, crows, or groundhogs. She left the cabin and walked uphill past the smokehouse where he stored his meat, then followed a trail into the woods.

She passed by the covered spring that his fresh water came from. She arrived at the edge of what remained of an old apple orchard. Small lumpy fruit hung from the trees.

"Daddy!" she called out.

No reply came. She pushed on into the overgrown orchard. Soon she saw her father standing nearby—a tall, gangly man wearing a hunting cap and a red vest and holding a rifle. Three dead squirrels lay at his feet.

He turned his lined, hard, weathered face toward her, looking not the least bit surprised to see her—and not the least bit pleased.

"You shouldn't be up here without a red vest, girl," he growled. "Lucky thing I didn't shoot you dead."

Riley didn't reply.

"Well, there's nothing out here to shoot now," he said irritably, unloading his gun. "You've run them all off, with your yelling and crashing through the brush. At least I've got squirrels for dinner."

He started to walk downhill toward his cabin. Riley followed after him, barely able to keep up with his long, swift strides. After years of retirement, he still walked with his old military bearing, his whole body coiled like a huge steel spring.

When they got to the cabin, he didn't invite her in, nor did she expect him to. Instead, he tossed the squirrels into a basket by the door, then walked over to the stump near the woodpile and sat there. He took off his cap, revealing gray hair that was still cropped short, Marine-style. He didn't look at Riley.

With no place else to sit, Riley plopped down on the front steps.

"It looks nice inside your cabin," she said, trying to find something to talk about. "I see you're still not mounting trophies."

"Yeah, well," he said with smirk, "I never took trophies when I killed in 'Nam. I'm not going to start now."

Riley nodded. She'd heard this remark often, always delivered with his typical grim humor.

"So what are you doing here?" her father asked.

Riley started to wonder. What on earth had she expected from this hard man, so incapable of basic affection?

"I've got some troubles, Daddy," she said.

"With what?"

Riley shook her head and smiled sadly. "I don't know where to start," she said.

He spit on the ground.

"It was a damn fool thing you did, getting caught by that psychopath," he said.

Riley was surprised. How did he know? She'd had no communication with him for a year.

"I thought you lived completely off the grid," she said.

"I get into town from time to time," her father said. "I hear things."

She almost said that her "damn fool thing" had saved a woman's life. But she quickly remembered—that wasn't true at all, not in the long run.

Still, Riley found it interesting that he knew about this. He'd actually gone to the trouble to find out something that had happened to her. What else might he know about her life?

Probably not much, she thought. *Or at least nothing I've done right according to his standards.*

"So did you fall to pieces after that whole thing with the killer?" he asked.

Riley bristled at this.

"If you mean did I suffer from PTSD, yes, I did."

"PTSD," he repeated, chuckling cynically. "I can't even remember just what those damn letters stand for. Just a fancy way of saying you're weak, as far as I'm concerned. I never suffered from this PTSD thing, not after I got home from the war, not after all the stuff I saw and did and got done to me. Don't see how anybody gets away with using that as an excuse."

156

He fell silent, looking off into space as if she weren't there. Riley figured this visit wasn't going to end well. She might as well talk a little about what was going on in her life. He wouldn't have anything encouraging to say about it, but at least it would make conversation.

"I'm having trouble with a case, Daddy," she said. "It's another serial killer. He tortures women, strangles them, and poses them outdoors."

"Yeah, I heard about that too. Poses them naked. Sick business." He spit again. "And let me guess. You're at odds with the Bureau about it. The powers-that-be don't know what they're doing. They won't listen to you."

Riley was startled. How did he guess?

"It was the same with me in 'Nam," he said. "The brass didn't seem to even get that they were fighting a damn war. Christ, if they'd left it up to the likes of me, we'd have won it. Makes me sick to think about it."

Riley heard something in his voice that she hadn't heard often—or at least had seldom noticed. It was regret. He actually felt regret about not winning the war. It didn't matter that he was in no way to blame. He felt responsible.

As Riley studied his face she realized something. She looked like him, more than she'd looked like her mother. But it was more than that. She *was* like him—not just in her horrible way with relationships, but with her cussed determination, her overweening sense of responsibility.

And that wasn't altogether a bad thing. In this rare moment of felt kinship, she wondered if maybe he really could tell her something she needed to know.

"Daddy, what he does—it's so ugly, leaving bodies naked and so horribly posed, but—"

She stopped, trying to find the right words.

"The places he leaves them are always so beautiful—forests and creeks, natural scenes like that. Why do you suppose he picks such places do something so ugly and evil?"

Her father's eyes turned inward. He seemed to be exploring his own thoughts, his own memories, talking as much about himself as about anybody else.

"He wants to start all over again," he said. "He wants to go all the way back to the beginning. Isn't it the same with you? Don't you just want to go back to where you started and begin all over again? Go back to where you were a kid? Find the place where

157

everything went wrong and make life go all different?"

He paused for a moment. Riley remembered her thoughts driving here—how sad she'd been as a little girl when she'd had to leave these mountains. There really was some elemental truth in what her father was saying.

"That's why *I* live here," he said, slipping deeper into reverie.

Riley sat there quietly, taking this in. Her father's words started to bring something into focus. She'd long assumed that the killer kept and tortured the women in his childhood home. It hadn't occurred to her that he chose that setting for a reason—to somehow reach back into his past and change everything.

Still not looking at her, her father asked, "What does your gut tell you?"

"It's something to do with dolls," Riley said. "It's something that the Bureau's not getting. They're chasing after everything wrong. He's obsessed with dolls. That's the key somehow."

He grunted and shuffled his feet.

"Well, you just keep following that gut of yours," he said. "Don't let the bastards tell you what to do."

Riley was dumbstruck. It wasn't as if he were paying her a compliment. It wasn't as if he meant to be nice. He was the same irascible jerk he'd always been. But somehow, he was saying exactly what she needed to hear.

"I'm not going to quit," she said.

"You'd damn well better not quit," he snarled in a whisper.

There was nothing more to say. Riley got to her feet.

"It was good to see you, Daddy," she said. And she actually halfway meant it. He didn't reply, just sat there looking at the ground. She got into her car and drove away.

As she drove, she realized that she felt different from when she'd come—and in some odd way, much better. Something, she felt, had been resolved between them.

She also knew something that she hadn't known before. Wherever the killer lived, it wasn't in some tenement, some sewer, or even some wretched, rundown shack out in the woods somewhere.

It was going to be a place of beauty—a place where beauty and horror were poised equally, side by side.

*

A little while later, Riley was sitting at the counter in a cafe in the town nearby. Her father had offered her nothing to eat, which was no surprise, and now she was hungry and needed some nutrition for the drive home.

Just when the waitress set her bacon, lettuce, and tomato sandwich on the counter in front of her, Riley's cell phone buzzed. She looked to see who was calling, but there was no identification. She took the call warily.

"Is this Riley Paige?" asked a woman with an efficient voice.

"Yes," Riley said.

"I've got Senator Mitch Newbrough on the line. He wants to speak with you. Could you hold, please?"

Riley felt a jolt of alarm. Of all the people she did *not* want to hear from, Newbrough was at the top of her list. She had the urge to end the call without another word, but then thought better of it. Newbrough was already a powerful enemy. Making him hate her even more wasn't a good idea.

"I'll hold," Riley said.

A few seconds later, she heard the Senator's voice.

"Senator Newbrough here. I'm talking to Riley Paige, I assume."

Riley didn't know whether to be furious or terrified. He was talking as if she were the one calling him.

"How did you get this number?" she asked.

"I get things when I want them," Newbrough said in a typically cold voice. "I want to talk to you. In person."

Riley's dread mounted. What possible reason could he have for wanting to see her? This couldn't be good. But how could she say no without making things worse?

"I could drop by your house," he said. "I know where you live."

Riley almost asked how he knew her address. But she reminded herself that he'd already answered that question.

"I'd rather we just took care of this right now on the phone," Riley said.

"I'm afraid that's not possible," Newbrough said. "I can't talk about it on the phone. How soon can you meet me?"

Riley felt herself in the grip of Newbrough's powerful will. She wanted to refuse, but somehow couldn't make herself do so.

"I'm out of town right now," she said. "I won't be getting home until much later. Tomorrow morning I drive my daughter to school. We could meet in Fredericksburg. Maybe in a coffee shop."

"No, not a public place," Newbrough said. "It needs to be

159

somewhere less conspicuous. Reporters tend to follow me around. They get all over me whenever they get a chance. I'd rather stay off their radar. How about Quantico, the BAU headquarters?"

Riley couldn't keep a note of bitterness out of her voice.

"I don't work there anymore, remember?" she said. "You should know that better than anybody."

There came a brief pause.

"Do you know the Magnolia Gardens Country Club?" Newbrough asked.

Riley sighed at the absurdity of the question. She certainly didn't move in those kinds of circles.

"I can't say I do," she said.

"It's easy to find, about halfway between Quantico and my farm. Be there at ten-thirty a.m."

Riley liked this less and less. He wasn't asking, he was giving an order. After wrecking her career, what business did he have demanding anything of her?

"Is that too early?" Newbrough asked when Riley didn't reply.

"No," Riley said, "it's just that—"

Newbrough interrupted, "Then be there. It's members only, but I'll notify them to let you in. You'll want to do this. You'll see that it's important. Trust me."

Newbrough ended the call without saying goodbye. Riley was flabbergasted.

"Trust me," he'd said.

Riley might have found it funny if she weren't so unnerved. Next to Peterson and whatever other killer she was trailing, Newbrough was possibly the person she least trusted in the world. She trusted him even less than she did Carl Walder. And that was really saying something.

But she didn't appear to have any choice. He had something to tell her, she could feel it. Something, she sensed, that might even lead to the killer.

Chapter 30

Riley neared the Magnolia Gardens Country Club and was stopped at a little white building at the gate. A green and white striped boom barrier blocked the way, and a uniformed security guard holding a clipboard stepped out of the building and walked up to the driver's side of her car.

Riley opened the window.

"Your name?" the guard said brusquely.

Riley was not at all certain about the protocol needed to get into the club, but Newbrough had said he'd let them know she was coming.

"I'm Riley Paige," she said. Then she stammered, "I'm a, uh, guest of Senator Newbrough."

The guard scanned the list, then nodded.

"Go on in," he said.

The boom gate lifted and Riley drove on through.

The entry lane wound through the namesake gardens, extremely luxurious, colorful, and fragrant this time of year. At last she pulled up at a brick building with white columns. Unlike those on the funeral parlor she'd visited recently, these columns were the real thing. Riley felt as if she'd stumbled upon some sort of nineteenth-century Southern plantation.

A valet hurried up to her car, gave her a card, and took her keys. He drove the car away.

Riley stood alone in front of the grand entrance, feeling as out of her element as she had at the Senator's home. Dressed in casual jeans, she wondered if she'd even be allowed to enter. Wasn't there some kind of a dress code in places like this? It was a good thing her jacket draped loosely over her shoulder holster.

A uniformed doorman stepped out to meet her.

"Your name, ma'am?" he asked.

"Riley Paige," she said, wondering if he'd ask for some sort of identification.

The doorman glanced at his own list. "Right this way, ma'am," he said.

He escorted her inside, down a long corridor, and to a small, private dining room. She had no idea whether to tip the doorman or not. But then, she had no idea how much the man was paid. Might he make more than she did as an FBI agent? She thought it possible that offering a tip might be more gauche than not tipping him at all.

It seemed best not to take chances.

"Thank you," she said to the man.

He nodded, showing no sign of disappointment, and went back the way they'd come.

The room was small but by far the most posh dining area she'd ever ventured into. There were no windows, but the single painting on the wall was an original oil of the namesake gardens she's passed outside.

The single table was set with silver, china, crystal, and linen. She chose a plush covered chair that faced the door and sat down. She wanted to see Senator Newbrough when he arrived.

If he arrives, she thought. She had no real reason to think he wouldn't. But this whole situation seemed so unreal, she didn't know what to expect.

A white-suited waiter came in and placed a tray with cheeses and a variety of crackers on her table.

"Would you like something to drink, ma'am?" he asked politely.

"Just water, thanks," Riley said. The waiter went out and within seconds popped back in with a crystal pitcher of water and two matching glasses. He poured water for her and left the pitcher and the other glass on the table.

Riley sipped at her water. She had to admit to herself that she enjoyed the feel of the elegant glass in her hand. She only had to wait a minute or two before the Senator arrived, looking every bit as cold and severe as he had before. He closed the door behind him and sat down on the opposite side of her table.

"I'm glad you came, Agent Paige," he said. "I've brought something for you."

Without further ceremony, Newbrough placed a thick, leather-bound notebook on the table. Riley stared at it warily. She remembered the list of enemies that Newbrough had given her the first time they'd met. Was this going to be something equally problematic?

"What is this?" she asked.

"My daughter's diary," Newbrough said. "I picked it up at her house after she was ... found. I took it because I didn't want anyone to see it. Mind you, I don't know what's in it. I've never read it. But I'm quite sure it includes things that I'd rather not have become public knowledge."

Riley didn't know what to say. She had no idea why he might want her to have this. She could tell that Newbrough was weighing

162

whatever he was about to say next carefully. From the first time she met with him, she'd been sure that he'd been withholding information from her. She tingled with expectancy that he might now tell her what that was.

Finally he said, "My daughter was having trouble with drugs during the last year of her life. Cocaine, heroin, Ecstasy, all kinds of hard stuff. Her husband put her on that route. It was one of the reasons her marriage failed. Her mother and I had been hoping she was pulling out of it when she died."

Newbrough paused, staring at the diary.

"At first I thought that her death was somehow connected with all that," he said. "The users and dealers in her circle were an unsavory bunch. I didn't want it to get out. You understand, I'm sure."

Riley wasn't at all sure that she did understand. But she was certainly surprised.

"Drugs had nothing to do with your daughter's murder," she said.

"I realize that now," Newbrough said. "Another woman was found dead, wasn't she? And doubtless there will be more victims. It appears that I was wrong in thinking this had anything to do with me or my family."

Riley was stunned. How often did this incredibly egotistical man ever admit that he was wrong about anything?

He patted the diary with his hand.

"Take this with you. It might have some information to help you with your case."

"It's not *my* case anymore, Senator," Riley said, allowing a trace of her bitterness to emerge. "I think you know that I was fired from the Bureau."

"Oh, yes," Newbrough said, tilting his head thoughtfully. "My mistake, I'm afraid. Well, it's nothing I can't fix. You'll be reinstated. Give me a little time with it. Meanwhile, I hope you can make use of this."

Riley was overwhelmed by the gesture. She took a deep breath.

"Senator, I believe I owe you an apology. I—I wasn't at my best the last time we met. I'd just been to a friend's funeral, and I was distraught. I said some things I shouldn't have."

Newbrough nodded in silent acceptance of her apology. It was apparent that he wasn't going to apologize to her, as much as she knew that she deserved it. She had to be content with his admission that he'd made a mistake. At least he was trying to make amends.

163

That mattered more than an apology, anyway.

Riley picked up the diary without opening it.

"There's just one thing I'd like to know, Senator," she said. "Why are you giving this to me and not to Agent Walder?"

Newbrough's lips twisted into a slight semblance of a smile.

"Because there's one thing I've learned about you, Agent Paige," he said. "You're nobody's lapdog."

Riley couldn't reply. This sudden respect from a man who otherwise seemed to only have regard for himself simply stunned her.

"And now perhaps you'd like some lunch," the Senator said.

Riley thought it over. As grateful as she was for Newbrough's change of heart, she still felt far from comfortable around him. He remained a cold, brittle, and unpleasant man. And besides, she had work to do.

"If you don't mind, I think I'd better excuse myself," she said. Indicating the diary, she added, "I need to start making use of this right away. There's no time to lose. Oh—and I promise not to let anything I find here become public."

"I appreciate that," Newbrough said.

He politely rose from his chair as Riley left the room. She exited the building and handed the ticket to the valet. While she waited for him to fetch her car, she opened the diary.

As she flipped through its pages, she saw right away that Reba Frye had written quite a bit about her illicit drug use. Riley also got the immediate impression that Reba Frye was a very self-absorbed woman who seemed to be obsessed with petty resentments and dislikes. But after all, wasn't that the whole point of a diary? It was a place where one had every right to be self-absorbed.

Besides, Riley thought, even if Reba had been as narcissistic as her father, she certainly didn't deserve such a terrible fate. Riley felt a chill as she remembered the photos she'd seen of the woman's corpse.

Riley continued flipping through the diary. Her car pulled up on the gravel driveway, but she ignored the valet, mesmerized. She stood there, hands trembling, and read all the way through to the end, desperate for any mention of the killer, of anything, any clue at all. But she was crestfallen to find none.

She began to lower the heavy book, feeling crushed. She couldn't stand another dead end.

Just then, as she lowered it, a small piece of paper, tucked between two pages, began to slip out of the book. She caught it and studied it, curious.

As she examined it, her heart suddenly slammed in her chest.
In utter shock, she dropped the diary.
She was holding a receipt.
To a doll store.

Chapter 31

There it was. After all the dead ends, Riley could barely believe what she was holding. At the top of the handwritten receipt was the name and address of the store: Madeline's Fashions in Shellysford, Virginia.

Riley was stumped. It didn't sound like a doll or toy store.

On her cell phone she found the website for Madeline's Fashions. It was, oddly, a women's clothing shop.

But she looked closer and saw that they also dealt in collectible dolls. They could only be viewed by appointment.

A chill ran up Riley's spine.

This has got to be the place, she thought.

She picked up the diary and with shaking hands, flipped through the pages to find the entry for the date on the receipt. There it was:

Just bought the perfect little doll for Debbie. Her birthday's not for a month, but she's so hard to shop for.

There it was, in plain English. Reba Frye had bought a doll for her daughter at a store in Shellysford. Riley felt certain that all the other victims had bought dolls there, too. And that that was where the murderer had first spotted them.

Riley pulled up a map on her phone, and it showed Shellysford a hour's drive away. She had to get there as soon as she possibly could. For all she knew, the murderer had already spotted another victim.

But she needed to get some information in the works. And she needed to make a painful phone call that she'd put off too long already.

She took her keys from the baffled valet, jumped in her car, and pulled out, her tires screeching on the club's manicured drive. As she sped past the gate, she punched in Bill's cell phone number, wondering if he'd bother to answer. She couldn't blame him if he never wanted to speak to her again.

To her relief, Bill's voice came over the phone.

"Hello," he said.

Riley's heart jumped. She didn't know whether to be relieved or terrified to hear his voice.

"Bill, this is Riley," she said.

"I know who this is," Bill replied.

A silence fell. This wasn't going to be easy. And she knew she didn't deserve for it to be easy.

"Bill, I don't know how to start," she said. Her throat swelled with emotion and she found it hard to speak. "I'm so, so terribly sorry. It's just that—well, everything had gotten so bad, and I just wasn't in my right mind, and—"

"And you were drunk," Bill said, interrupting.

Riley sighed miserably.

"Yes, I was drunk," she said. "And I apologize. I hope you can forgive me. I'm so sorry."

Another silence came.

"Okay," Bill finally said.

Riley's heart sank. She knew Bill better than she knew anybody else in the world. So she could hear a world of meaning in those two blunt syllables. He wasn't forgiving her, and he wasn't even accepting her apology—at least not yet. All he was doing was acknowledging that she *had* apologized.

Anyway, now was no time to be hashing it out. There was a far more urgent matter to take care of.

"Bill, I've got a lead," she said.

"What?" he asked in a stunned voice.

"I found the store."

Bill sounded worried now.

"Riley, are you out of your mind? What are you doing, still working this case? Walder *fired* you, for God's sake."

"Since when have I ever waited for permission? Anyway, it looks like I'm going to be reinstated."

Bill snorted with disbelief.

"Who says?"

"Newbrough."

"What are you talking about?" Bill asked, sounding more and more agitated. "Christ, Riley, you didn't go to his house again, did you?"

Riley thoughts became jangled. There was too much to explain. She had to stick to the basics.

"No, and he was different this time," she said. "It was weird, and I can't get into it right now. But Newbrough gave me some new information. Bill, Reba Frye bought a doll at a store in Shellysford. I've got proof. I've got the name of the store."

"That's crazy," Bill said. "We've had agents scouring that whole area. They've been to every town out there. I don't think they

167

even found a doll store in Shellysford."

Riley was finding it harder and harder to contain her own excitement.

"That's because there isn't one," she said. "It's a clothing store that sells dolls, but you can only see them by appointment. Madeline's Fashions, it's called. Are you at the BAU right now?"

"Yes, but—"

"Then get somebody checking into the place. Get whatever you can on everybody who's ever worked there. I'm going there right now."

Bill's voice was loud and frantic.

"Riley, don't! You've got no authorization. You don't even have a badge. And what if you find the guy? He's liable to be dangerous. And Walder took your gun."

"I've got my own gun," Riley said.

"But you won't be able to detain anybody."

With a growl of determination, Riley said, "I'll do whatever I have to do. Another life might be at stake."

"I don't like this," Bill said, sounding more resigned now.

Riley ended the phone call and stepped on the gas.

*

Bill sat in his office staring dumbly at his cell phone. He realized that his hands were shaking. He wasn't sure why. Anger and frustration? Or was it from fear for Riley, for whatever reckless thing she was about to do?

Her drunken phone call two nights ago had left him confused and devastated. It was something of a cliché that law enforcement partners often felt closer to one another than to their own spouses. And Bill knew that it was true. For a long time, he'd felt closer to Riley than he'd ever felt to anyone in his life.

But there was no room for romance in their line of work. Complications or hesitations on the job could have deadly results. He'd always kept things professional between them and always trusted Riley to do the same. But now she had broken that trust.

Well, she was obviously aware of her mistake. But what had she meant when she said she would be reinstated? Would they work together again? He wasn't sure if he wanted to. Was the dynamic and comfortable professional rapport they'd long shared ruined forever?

But he couldn't worry about all of that now. Riley had asked him to check on the employees of a store. He'd pass that request on, but not to Carl Walder. Bill got on the phone and called the extension for Special Agent Brent Meredith. Meredith wasn't in the proper chain of command on this case, but Bill knew he could count on him to get the job done.

He planned to keep the call short and efficient. He had to drive to Shellysford right now and he only hoped he could get there before Riley Paige did something really stupid.

Like get herself killed.

Chapter 32

Riley's heart was pounding in anticipation as she pulled into the little town of Shellysford. Madeline's Fashions was easy to spot. It was in plain view on the main street, and its name was displayed across the front window. Shellysford was a bit more upscale than she'd expected. Some apparently historic buildings had been kept in good repair, and the main street verged on elegance. The rather chic-looking clothing store fit in well with its prosperous surroundings.

Riley parked at the curb in front of the store, got out of her car, and took in her surroundings. She immediately noticed that one of the store's window mannequins was actually holding a doll—a princess in a pink dress, wearing a sparkly tiara. The agents combing this town, though, may have easily have taken this as mere window dressing. Only a small sign in the window suggested otherwise: *Collectible Dolls Shown By Appointment.*

A bell above the door rang as Riley walked inside, and the woman at the counter glanced in her direction. She looked middle-aged but remarkably youthful, and her graying hair was full and healthy.

Riley weighed her options. Without her badge, she had to be careful. True, she'd managed to get other retailers to talk to her without it. But she absolutely did not want to spook this woman.

"Excuse me," Riley said. "Are you Madeline?"

The woman smiled. "Well, my name is actually Mildred, but I go by Madeline. I like it better. And it sounds better for the name of a store. 'Mildred's Fashions' just wouldn't have the same ring." The woman chuckled and winked. "It wouldn't draw quite the clientele I'm aiming for."

So far so good, Riley thought. The woman was open and talkative.

"Lovely place," Riley said, looking around. "But seems like a lot of work for one person. Have you got any help? Surely you don't do all this by yourself."

The woman shrugged.

"Mostly I do," she said. "Sometimes I've got a teenage girl who works the register while I help customers. This is a quiet day, though. There was no need for her to come in."

Still considering the right approach, Riley walked over to a clothing rack and fingered some of the merchandise.

"Beautiful outfits," she said. "Not many stores carry dresses like these."

Madeline looked pleased.

"No, you're not likely to find anything like them elsewhere," she said. "They're all high fashion, but I buy them from outlets when styles have been discontinued. So by big city standards, these would be yesterday's fashion." Then with another wink and a grin, she added, "But in a little town like Shellysford—well, they might as well be the latest thing."

Madeline pulled a lavender-colored cocktail dress off the rack.

"You'd look wonderful in this," she said. "It's perfect for your coloring—and for your personality too, I suspect."

Riley didn't think so. In fact, she couldn't see herself wearing any of the store's rather posh outfits. Still, she was sure that this dress would have been more appropriate at the country club than what she was now wearing.

"Actually," Riley said, "I was hoping to look at some of your dolls."

Madeline looked slightly surprised.

"Did you make an appointment?" she asked. "If you did, it seems to have slipped my mind. And how did you find out about our doll collection?"

Riley pulled the receipt out of her handbag and showed it to Madeline.

"Someone gave this to me," Riley said.

"Oh, a referral," Madeline said, obviously pleased. "Well, I can make an exception, then."

She walked to the back of the store and opened a wide folding door, and Riley followed her into a small back room. Its shelves were lined with dolls, and a couple of racks standing on the floor were filled with doll accessories.

"I started this little side business a few years back," Madeline said. "I had the opportunity to buy out the stock of a manufacturer that went out of business. The owner was a cousin of mine, so when they closed down I got a special deal. I'm happy to pass on those savings to my customers."

Madeline picked up a doll and looked it over proudly.

"Aren't they lovely?" she said. "Little girls love them. Their parents too. And these dolls are no longer being made, so they're truly collectibles, even though they're not antiques. And look at all these costumes. Any of my dolls can wear any of these outfits."

Riley scanned the rows of dolls. They looked much alike, although their hair color varied. So did their clothes, which included

171

modern dress, princess gowns, and historical outfits. Among the accessories, Riley saw doll furniture to go with each style. The prices of the dolls were all above a hundred dollars.

"I hope you understand why I don't keep this section open," Madeline explained. "Most of my walk-in clients aren't shopping for dolls. And just between you and me," she added, lowering her voice to a whisper, "many of these smaller items are awfully easy to steal. So I'm careful about who I show all this to."

Fluffing up a doll's dress, Madeline asked, "By the way, what is your name? I like to know the names of all my customers."

"Riley Paige."

Then Madeline squinted with an inquisitive smile.

"And who was the customer who referred you?" she asked.

"Reba Frye," Riley said.

Madeline's face darkened.

"Oh, dear," she said. "The state senator's daughter. I remember when she came in. And I heard about ..." She fell silent for a moment. "Oh, dear," she added, shaking her head sadly.

Then she looked at Riley warily.

"Please tell me you're not a reporter," she said. "If so, I must ask you to leave. It would be terrible publicity for my store."

"No, I'm an FBI agent," Riley said. "And the truth is, I'm here to investigate Reba Frye's murder. I met with her father, Senator Newbrough, just a little while ago. He gave me this receipt. That's why I'm here."

Madeline looked more and more uneasy.

"Would you show me your badge?" she asked.

Riley held back a sigh. She had to bluff her way through this somehow. She had to lie at least a little.

"I'm off duty," she said. "We don't carry badges when we're off duty. It's standard procedure. I just came here on my own time to find out whatever I could."

Madeline nodded sympathetically. She seemed to believe her— or at least not to disbelieve her. Riley tried not to show her relief.

"What can I do to help?" Madeline asked.

"Just tell me anything you can about that day. Who else came in to work? How many customers came in?"

Madeline held out her hand. "May I see the receipt? For the date, I mean."

Riley handed her the receipt.

"Oh, yes, I remember," Madeline said as she looked at it. "That was a crazy day, several weeks ago."

Riley's attention quickened.

"Crazy?" Riley asked. "How so?"

Madeline knitted her brow as she recollected.

"A collector came in," she said. "He bought twenty dolls at once. I was surprised that he had the money. He didn't look all that rich. He was just a rather sad-looking older man. I gave him a special price. Things were really a mess while my girl and I rang up all that merchandise. We're not used to that kind of business. Everything was in turmoil for a little while there."

Riley's mind clicked away, putting this information together.

"Was Reba Frye in the store at the same time as this collector?" she asked.

Madeline nodded. "Why yes," she said. "Now that you mention it, she was here right then."

"Do you keep a record of your customers?" Riley asked. "With contact information?"

"Yes, I do," Madeline said.

"I need to see the man's name and address," Riley said. "It's very important."

Madeline's expression grew more wary.

"You said the Senator gave you this receipt?" she asked.

"How else could I have gotten it?" Riley asked.

Madeline nodded. "I'm sure that's true, but still …"

She paused, struggling with her decision.

"Oh, I'm sorry," she blurted, "but I can't do it—let you look at the records, I mean. You don't even have any identification, and my customers deserve their privacy. No, really, Senator or no Senator, I can't let you look at it without a warrant. I'm sorry, but it just doesn't seem right to me. I hope you understand."

Riley took a long breath as she tried to assess the situation. She didn't doubt that Bill would show up here as soon as he could. But how soon would that be? And would the woman still insist on seeing a warrant? How much more time might that involve? For all Riley knew, someone's life might be hanging in the balance right that very minute.

"I understand," Riley said. "But is it okay if I just look around here a bit? I might find some clues."

Madeline nodded. "Of course," she said. "Take as long as you like."

A distraction tactic quickly took shape in Riley's mind. She began to browse among the dolls while Madeline tidied up some of the accessories. Riley reached up onto a high shelf as if trying to fetch down a doll. Instead, she managed to knock a whole row of dolls off the shelf.

"Oh!" Riley said. "I'm so sorry!"

She backed away in the clumsiest manner she could muster. She collided with a rack of accessories and knocked them all over.

"Oh, I'm so, so sorry!" Riley said again.

"It's all right," Madeline said with more than a note of irritation. "Just—just let me take care of it."

Madeline started to pick up the scattered merchandise. Riley hastily left the room and headed for the front desk. Glancing to make sure that Madeline wasn't watching her, Riley dived behind the desk. She quickly spotted a ledger book on a shelf under the cash register.

Her fingers shaking, Riley thumbed through the ledger. She quickly found the date, the name of the man, and his address. She didn't have time to write it down, so she committed it to memory.

She had just stepped out from behind the counter when Madeline returned from the back room. Madeline looked genuinely suspicious now.

"You'd really better leave," she said. "If you come back with a warrant, I'll be able to help. I certainly want to help the Senator and his family in any way I can. I feel terrible about all they're going through. But right now—well, I think you should leave."

Riley made a beeline toward the front door.

"I—I understand," she stammered. "I'm terribly sorry."

She rushed to her car and got in. She took out her cell phone and called Bill's number.

"Bill, I've got a name!" she almost shouted when he answered. "His name is Gerald Cosgrove. And I've got his address."

Remembering carefully, Riley recited the address to Bill.

"I'm only a few minutes away," Bill said. "I'll call in his name and address, see what kind of information the Bureau can turn up. I'll get back to you right away."

Bill ended the phone call. Riley fidgeted, waiting impatiently. She looked back at the store and noticed that Madeline was standing near the window, looking out at her suspiciously. Riley couldn't blame Madeline for her mistrust. Her behavior just now had been more than a little odd.

Riley's cell phone buzzed. She answered it.

"Bingo," Bill said. "The guy's a registered sex offender. The address you gave me isn't far. You're maybe a little closer to him than I am."

"I'm driving there right now," Riley said, stepping on the gas.

"For Christ's sake, Riley, don't go in there alone!" he barked back. "Wait for me outside. I'll get there as soon as I can. Do you hear me?"

Riley ended the call and drove away. No, she could not wait.

*

Less than fifteen minutes later, Riley pulled up to a dusty, isolated lot. A shabby-looking mobile home sat in the middle of it. Riley parked her car and got out.

An old car was parked on the street in front of the lot, but Riley didn't see any sign of the truck the witness described after Cindy MacKinnon's abduction. Of course, Cosgrove might well be keeping it somewhere else. Or perhaps he had dumped it for fear that it might be traced.

Riley shuddered when she saw a couple of sheds with padlocked doors at the back of the lot. Was that where he had kept the women? Was he holding one right now, torturing her and preparing to kill her?

Riley looked around, taking in the area. The lot wasn't completely isolated. There were a few houses and mobile homes not far away. Even so, it seemed likely that no one live near enough to hear a woman screaming in one of those sheds.

Riley drew her gun and approached the trailer. It was set up on a permanent foundation, and it looked like it had been there for many years. Some time ago, someone had planted a flower bed alongside the trailer to make it look more like a regular house. But now the bed was overrun with weeds.

So far, the place matched her expectations. She felt certain that she'd come to the right place.

"It's all over for you, you bastard," she murmured under her breath. "You'll never take another victim."

When she reached the trailer, she banged on the metal door.

"Gerald Cosgrove!" she yelled. "This is the FBI. Are you in there?"

There was no answer. Riley edged her way up onto the cinderblock steps and peered through the door's little window. What she saw inside chilled her to the bone.

The place seemed to be packed full of dolls. She didn't see a living soul, just dolls of all shapes and sizes.

Riley shook the door handle. It was locked. She banged on the door again. This time she heard a man's voice.

"Go away. Leave me alone. I didn't do anything."

Riley thought she heard someone scrambling around inside. The trailer door was designed to open outward, so she couldn't kick it in. She fired her gun at the locked handle. The door fell open.

Riley burst into the small main room. She was momentarily dazzled by the sheer number and array of dolls. There must have been hundreds of them. They were simply everywhere—on shelves, on tables, and even on the floor. It took a moment for her to see a man among them, cowering on the floor against a partition wall.

"Don't shoot," Cosgrove pleaded, his hands raised and shaking. "I didn't do it. Don't shoot me."

Riley sprung at him and yanked him to his feet. She spun him around and pulled one hand behind his back. She holstered her handgun and got out her cuffs.

"Give me your other hand," she said.

Shaking from head to foot, he obeyed without hesitation. Riley quickly had him cuffed and sitting awkwardly in a chair.

He was a weak-looking man in his sixties with thin gray hair. He cut a pathetic figure, sitting there with tears running down his face. But Riley wasted no pity on him. The spectacle of all these dolls was enough to tell her that he was a sick, twisted man.

Before she could ask any questions, she heard Bill's voice.

"Jesus, Riley. Did you blow open this door?"

Riley turned and saw Bill stepping into the trailer.

"He wouldn't open up," Riley said.

Bill growled under his breath. "I thought I told you to wait outside," he said.

"And I thought you knew better than to think I would," Riley said. "Anyway, I'm glad you're here. This looks like our guy."

The man was wailing now.

"I didn't do it! It wasn't me! I did my time! I put all that stuff behind me!"

Riley asked Bill, "What did you find out about him?"

"He did some time for attempted child molestation. Nothing since—until now."

This made good enough sense to Riley. This monstrous little man had undoubtedly moved on to bigger prey—and to greater cruelty.

"That was years ago," the man said. "I've been good ever since. I take my meds. I don't get those urges anymore. It's all in the past. You've made a mistake."

Bill asked in a cynical tone, "So you're an innocent man, eh?"

"That's right. Whatever you think I did, it wasn't me."

"So what's with all the dolls?" Riley asked.

Through his tears, Cosgrove smiled brokenly.

"Aren't they beautiful?" he said. "I collected them little by little. I got lucky a few weeks back, found this great store over in Shellysford. So many dolls and so many different dresses. I spent my whole Social Security check right there and then, bought as many as my money could get me."

Bill shook his head. "I sure as hell don't want to know what you do with them," he said.

"It's not what you think," Cosgrove said. "They're like my family. My only friends. They're all I've got. I just stay home with them. It's not like I can afford to go anywhere. They treat me right. They don't judge me."

Again, Riley worried. Was Cosgrove holding a victim right now?

"I want to check your sheds out back," she told him.

"Go ahead," he said. "There's nothing there. I've got nothing to hide. The keys are right over there."

He nodded toward a bunch of keys hanging next to the wounded door. Riley walked over and grabbed them.

"I'm going out there for a look," she said.

"Not without me, you're not," Bill said.

Together, Bill and Riley used Bill's cuffs to fasten Cosgrove to his refrigerator door. Then they stepped outside and walked around the trailer. They opened the first shed's padlock and looked inside. There was nothing in there except a garden rake.

Bill stepped into the shed and looked around.

"Nothing," he said. "Not even any sign of blood."

They walked over to the next shed, unlocked it, and looked inside. Aside from a rusty hand lawnmower, the shed was completely empty.

"He must have held them somewhere else," Bill said.

Bill and Riley went back to into the trailer. Cosgrove was still sitting there, gazing wretchedly at his family of dolls. Riley found him a troubling sight—a man with no real life of his own, and certainly no future.

Still, he struck her as an enigma. She decided to ask him a couple of questions.

"Gerald, where were you last Wednesday morning?"

"What?" Cosgrove replied. "What do you mean? I don't know.

I don't remember Wednesday. Here, I guess. Where else would I be?"

Riley gazed at him with increasing curiosity.

"Gerald," she said, "what day is today?"

Cosgrove's eyes darted around in desperate confusion.

"I—I don't know," he stammered.

Riley wondered—could it possibly be true? Did he not know what day it was? He sounded perfectly sincere. He certainly didn't seem bitter or angry. She saw no fight in him at all. Just fear and desperation.

Then she sternly reminded herself not to let him take her in. A true psychopath could sometimes fool even a seasoned veteran with a total lie.

Bill unfastened Cosgrove from the refrigerator. Cosgrove was still cuffed behind his back.

Bill barked out, "Gerald Cosgrove, you're under arrest for the murders of three women ..."

Bill and Riley escorted him roughly out of the trailer as Bill continued with the victims' names and Cosgrove's rights. Then they shoved him to the car Bill had driven here—a well-equipped Bureau vehicle with mesh caging between the back and front seats. Riley and Bill pushed him into the back seat. They strapped and cuffed him in securely. Afterwards they both just stood for a moment without saying a word.

"Damn it, Riley, you did it," Bill muttered with admiration. "You caught the bastard—even without your badge. The Bureau's going to welcome you back with open arms."

"Do you want me to ride with you?" Riley asked.

Bill shrugged. "Naw, I've got him under control. I'll get him into custody. You just take your own car back."

Riley decided not to argue, wondering if Bill still harbored resentment toward her for the other night.

As she watched Bill pull away, Riley wanted to congratulate herself on her success, and her redemption. But any feeling of satisfaction evaded her. Something kept nagging at her. She kept hearing her father's words.

You just keep following that gut of yours.

Little by little as she drove, Riley started to realize something.

Her gut was telling her that they'd gotten the wrong man.

Chapter 33

The next morning Riley drove April to school, and as she dropped her off, that gut feeling was still nagging at her. It had bothered her all night, not letting her sleep.

Is he the guy? she kept asking herself.

Before April got out of the car, she turned to her with an expression of genuine concern.

"Mom, what's wrong?" she asked.

Riley was a little taken aback by the question. She and her daughter seemed to have entered into a whole new phase of their relationship—a much better one than they'd had before. Still, Riley wasn't used to having April worry about her feelings. It felt good, but strange.

"It shows, huh?" Riley said.

"It sure does," April said. She gently held her mother's hand. "Come on. Tell me."

Riley thought for a moment. That feeling of hers still wasn't easy to put into words.

"I…" she began, then trailed off, unsure what to say. "I'm not sure I arrested the right man."

April's eyes widened.

"I'm…not sure what to do," Riley added.

April took a long breath.

"Don't doubt yourself, Mom," April replied. "You do it a lot. And you always wish you hadn't. Isn't that what you always tell me, too?"

April smiled, and Riley smiled back.

"I'll be late if I don't get to class," April said. "We can talk about this later."

April kissed Riley on the cheek, got out of the car, and dashed toward school.

Riley sat there, thinking. She didn't drive away immediately. Instead, she called Bill.

"Anything?" she asked when she got him on the line.

She heard Bill heave a long sigh.

"Cosgrove is a strange character," he said. "Right now he's a real mess—exhausted and depressed, and crying a lot. I think he'll probably crack soon. But …"

Bill paused. Riley sensed that he, too, was struggling with doubt.

"But what?" Riley asked.

"I don't know, Riley. He seems so disoriented, and I'm not sure even knows what's going on. He slips in and out of reality. Sometimes he doesn't seem to understand that he's been arrested. Maybe all those meds he's taking are messing him up. Or maybe it's just plain old psychosis."

Riley's own doubts kicked in again.

"What is he telling you?" she asked.

"Mostly, he just keeps asking for his dolls," Bill said. "He's worried about them, like they're children or pets that he shouldn't leave at home alone. He keeps saying they can't do without him. He's completely docile, not the least bit belligerent. But he's not giving us any information. He's not saying anything about the women, or whether he's holding one right now."

Riley turned Bill's words over in her mind for a moment.

"So what do you think?" she finally asked. "Is he the one?"

Riley detected growing frustration in Bill's voice.

"How could he not be? I mean, everything points to him and nobody else. The dolls, the criminal record, everything. He was in the store the same time as her. What more could you ask for? How could we have got it wrong?"

Riley said nothing. She couldn't argue. But she could tell that Bill was struggling with his own instincts.

Then she asked: "Did somebody run a search on Madeline's past employees?"

"Yeah," Bill said. "But that didn't lead anywhere. Madeline always hires high school girls to work the register. She's been doing it pretty much since she's been in business."

Riley groaned with discouragement. When were they going to get a break in this case?

"Anyway," Bill said, "a bureau psychologist will interview Cosgrove today. Maybe he can get some insights, tell us where we stand."

"Okay," Riley said. "Keep me in the loop."

She ended the phone call. Her car engine was running, but she still hadn't driven away from the school. Where was she going to go? If Newbrough really was trying to get her reinstated, he hadn't gotten it done yet. She still didn't have a badge—or a job.

I might as well go home, she thought.

But as soon as she started driving, her father's words came rushing back again.

You just keep following that gut of yours.

180

Right now, her gut was telling her loud and clear that she needed to get back to Shellysford. She didn't know exactly why, but she just had to.

*

The bell above the fashion store door rang as Riley walked inside. She saw no customers. Madeline looked up from her work at the front desk and frowned. Riley could see that the shop owner was not at all happy to see her again.

"Madeline, I'm sorry about yesterday," Riley said, walking to the desk. "I was so clumsy, and I'm sorry. I hope I didn't actually break anything."

Madeline folded her arms and glared at Riley.

"What do you want this time?" she asked.

"I'm still struggling with this case," Riley said. "I need your help."

Madeline didn't reply for a few seconds.

"I still don't know who you are, or even if you're FBI," she said.

"I know, and I don't blame you for not trusting me," Riley pleaded. "But I did have Reba Frye's receipt, remember? I could only have gotten it from her father. He really did send me here. You know that much is true."

Madeline shook her head warily.

"Well, I guess that must mean something. What do you want?"

"Just let me look at the doll collection again," Riley said. "I promise not to make a mess this time."

"All right," Madeline said. "But I'm not leaving you alone."

"That's fair," Riley said.

Madeline went to the back of the store and opened the folding doors. As Riley moved in among the dolls and accessories, Madeline stood in the doorway watching her like a hawk. Riley understood the woman's misgivings, but this scrutiny wasn't good for her concentration—especially since she really didn't know what she ought to be looking for.

Just then the bell above the front door rang. Three rather boisterous customers burst into the store.

"Oh, brother," Madeline said. She hurried back into the dress store to tend to her customers. Riley had the dolls all to herself, at least for the moment.

She studied them closely. Some were standing, but others were

181

seated. All of the dolls were decked out in dresses and gowns. But even though they were clothed, the seated dolls were in exactly the same pose as the naked murder victims, their legs splayed stiffly. The killer had obviously taken his inspiration from this kind of doll.

But that wasn't enough for Riley to go on. There had to be some other clue lurking here.

Riley's eyes fell on a row of picture books on a lower shelf. She stooped down and began to pull them off the shelf one by one. The books were beautifully illustrated adventure stories about little girls who looked exactly like the dolls. The dolls and the girls on the covers even wore the same dresses. Riley realized the books and the dolls were originally meant to be sold together as a set.

Riley froze at the sight of one book cover. The girl had long blond hair and wide-open bright blue eyes. Her pink and white ball gown had a spray of roses draped across the skirt. She had a pink ribbon in her hair. The book was titled *A Grand Ball for a Southern Belle*.

Riley's skin crawled as she looked more closely at the girl's face. Her eyes were bright blue, opened extremely wide, with enormous black lashes. Her lips, shaped into an exaggerated smile, were thick and bright pink. There was no doubt about it. Riley knew for certain that the killer was fixated on this very image.

At that moment, the bell rang again as the three customers left the store. Madeline trotted to the back room, visibly relieved that Riley hadn't caused any damage. Riley showed her the book.

"Madeline, do you have the doll that goes with this book?" she asked.

Madeline looked at the cover, then scanned the shelves.

"Well, I must have had several of them at one time or another," she said. "I don't see any of them right now." She thought for a moment, then added, "Now that I think of it, I sold the last of those a long time ago."

Riley could barely keep her voice from shaking.

"Madeline, I know you don't want to do this. But you've *got* to help me look for names of people who might have bought this doll. I can't begin to tell you how important this is."

Madeline now seemed to sympathize with Riley's agitation.

"I'm sorry, but I can't," she said. "It's not that I don't want to, but I can't. It's been ten or fifteen years now. Even my ledger doesn't go back that far."

Riley's spirits fell. Another dead end. She had taken it as far as she could possibly take it. Coming here had been a waste of time.

Riley turned to go. She crossed the store and opened the door, and as the fresh air hit her, something struck her. The smell. The fresh air outside made her realize how stale the air was in here. Not stale, but…pungent. It seemed out of place in a frilly, feminine store like this. What was it?

Then Riley realized. Ammonia. But what did that mean?

Follow your gut, Riley.

Halfway out the door, she stopped and turned, looking back at Madeline.

"Did you mop the floors today?" she asked.

Madeline shook her head, puzzled.

"I use a temp agency," she said. "They send over a janitor."

Riley's heart pounded faster.

"A janitor?" she asked, her voice barely above a whisper.

Madeline nodded.

"He comes in during our morning hours. Not every day. Dirk is his name."

Dirk. Riley's heart pounded and her skin grew cold.

"Dirk what?" she asked.

Madeline shrugged.

"I'm afraid I don't know his last name," she replied. "I don't write his checks. The temp agency might, but it's a rather slipshod outfit, really. Dirk's not very reliable, if you want to know the truth."

Riley took long slow breaths to steady her nerves.

"Was he here this morning?" she asked.

Madeline nodded mutely.

Riley approached her, and summoned all her intensity.

"Madeline," she urged, "whatever you do, do *not* let that man back in your store. Ever again."

Madeline staggered back with shock.

"Do you mean he's—?"

"He's dangerous. Extremely dangerous. And I've got to find him right away. Do you have his phone number? Do you have any idea where he lives?"

"No, you'd have to ask the temp agency," Madeline said in a fearful voice. "They'll have all his information. Here, I'll give you their business card."

Madeline rummaged around on her desk and found a card for the Miller Staffing Agency. She handed it to Riley.

"Thank you," Riley said with a gasp. "Thank you so much."

Without another word, Riley rushed out of the store and got in

183

the car and tried calling the temp office. The phone rang and rang. There was no voicemail.

She made a mental note of the address and started to drive.

*

The Miller Staffing Agency was a mile away on the other side of Shellysford. Housed in a brick storefront building, it looked like it had been in business for many years.

As Riley went inside, she saw that it was a decidedly low-tech operation that hadn't kept up with the times. There was only one nearly obsolete computer in sight. The place was pretty crowded, with several would-be workers filling out application forms at a long table.

Three other people—clients, apparently—were crowded around the front desk. They were complaining loudly and all at once about problems they were having with the agency's employees.

Two longhaired men worked at the desk, fending off complainers and trying to keep up with phone calls. They looked like twenty-something slackers, and they didn't appear to be managing things at all well.

Riley managed to push her way to the front, where she caught one of the young men between phone calls. His nametag said "Melvin."

"I'm Agent Riley Paige, FBI," she announced, hoping that in the confusion, Melvin wouldn't ask to see her badge. "I'm here on a murder investigation. Are you the manager?"

Melvin shrugged. "I guess."

From his vacant expression, Riley guessed that he was either stoned or not very bright, or possibly both. At least he didn't seem to be worried about seeing any ID.

"I'm looking for the man you've got working at Madeline's," she said. "A janitor. His first name is Dirk. Madeline doesn't seem to know his last name."

Melvin muttered to himself, "Dirk, Dirk, Dirk … Oh, yeah. I remember him. 'Dirk the Dick,' we used to call him." Calling out to the other young man, he asked, "Hey, Randy, whatever happened to Dirk the Dick?"

"We fired him," Randy replied. "He kept showing up late for jobs, when he bothered to show up at all. A real pain in the ass."

"That can't be right," Riley said. "Madeline says he's still working for her. He was just there this morning."

Melvin looked puzzled now.

"I'm sure we fired him," he said. He sat down at the old computer and began some kind of a search. "Yeah, we sure did fire him, about three weeks ago."

Melvin squinted at the screen, more puzzled than before.

"Hey, this is weird," he said. "Madeline keeps sending us checks, even though he's not working anymore. Somebody should tell her to stop doing that. She's blowing a lot of money."

The situation was becoming clearer to Riley. Despite being fired and no longer getting paid, Dirk still kept going to work at Madeline's. He had his own reasons for wanting to work there—sinister reasons.

"What's his last name?" Riley asked.

Melvin's eyes roamed about the computer screen. He was apparently looking at Dirk's defunct employee records.

"It's Monroe," Melvin said. "What else do you want to know?"

Riley was relieved that Melvin wasn't being too scrupulous about sharing what ought to be confidential information.

"I need his address and phone number," Riley said.

"He didn't give us a phone number," Melvin said, still looking at the screen. "I've got an address, though. Fifteen-twenty Lynn Street."

By now, Randy had taken interest in the conversation. He was looking over Melvin's shoulder at the computer screen.

"Hold it," Randy said. "That address is completely bogus. The house numbers on Lynn Street don't go anywhere near that high."

Riley wasn't surprised. Dirk Monroe obviously didn't want anyone to know where he lived.

"What about a Social Security number?" she asked.

"I've got it," Melvin said. He wrote the number down on a piece of paper and handed it to Riley.

"Thanks," Riley said. She took the paper and walked away. As soon as she set foot outside, she called Bill.

"Hey, Riley," Bill said when he answered. "I wish I could give you some good news But our psychologist interviewed Cosgrove, and he's convinced that the man is not capable of killing anyone, let alone four women. He said—"

"Bill," she interrupted. "I've got a name—Dirk Monroe. He's our guy, I'm sure of it. I don't know where he lives. Can you run his Social? Now?"

Bill took the number and put Riley on hold. Riley paced up and down the sidewalk anxiously as she waited. Finally Bill came back

185

on the line.

"I've got the address. It's a farm about thirty miles west of Shellysford. A rural road."

Bill read her the address.

"I'm going," Riley said.

Bill sputtered.

"Riley, what are you talking about? Let me get some backup there. This guy's dangerous."

Riley felt her whole body tingle with an adrenaline rush.

"Don't argue with me, Bill," she said. "You ought to know better by now."

Riley ended the call without saying goodbye. Already, she was driving.

Chapter 34

When the farmhouse came into view, Riley felt jarred in a way that she hadn't expected. It was as if she'd driven into an oil painting of an ideal rural America. The white wood-frame house was nestled cozily in a small valley. The house was old, but obviously kept in decent condition.

A few outbuildings were scattered on the nearby grounds. They were not in as good repair as the house. Neither was a large barn that looked ready to collapse. But those structures looked all the more charming because of their dilapidation.

Riley parked a short distance from the house. She checked the gun in her holster and got out of the car. She breathed in the clear, clean country air.

It shouldn't be this lovely here, Riley thought. And yet she knew that it made perfect sense. Ever since she'd talked to her father, she'd dimly realized that the killer's lair might well be a place of beauty.

Still, there was a kind of danger here that she hadn't prepared herself for. It was the danger of being lulled by the sheer charm of her surroundings, of letting down her guard. She had to remind herself that a hideous evil coexisted with this beauty. She knew she was about to find herself face to face with the true horror of the place. But she had no idea just where she'd find it.

She turned and looked all around. She didn't see any truck on the grounds. Either Dirk was out driving somewhere, or the truck was inside one of the outbuildings or the barn. The man himself could be anywhere, of course—in one of the outbuildings, possibly. But she decided to check the house first.

A noise startled her, and her peripheral vision caught a flurry of rapid movement. But it was only a handful of loose chickens. Several hens were pecking the ground nearby. Nothing else moved except tall blades of grass and leaves on the trees as a gentle breeze blew through them. She felt utterly alone.

Riley approached the farmhouse. When she arrived at the steps, she drew her gun, then walked up on the porch. She knocked on the front door. There was no response. She knocked again.

"I've got a delivery for Dirk Monroe," she called out. "I need a signature to leave it."

Still no response.

Riley stepped off the porch and began to circle the house. The windows were too high to see into, and she found that the back door

187

was also locked.

She returned to the front door and knocked again. There was still only silence. The door lock was a simple, old-fashioned type for a skeleton key. She carried a little lock-picking set in her handbag for just such situations. She knew that the hook of a small flat tension wrench would do the trick.

She slipped her gun back into its holster and found the wrench. She inserted it into the lock, then groped and twisted it until the lock rotated. When she turned the doorknob the door swung open. Drawing her gun again, she walked inside.

The interior had much the same picturesque quality as the landscape outside. It was a perfect little country home, remarkably neat and clean. There were two big soft chairs in the living room with white crocheted pieces on the arms and back.

The room made her feel as though friendly family members might step out at any second to welcome her, to invite her to make herself at home. But as Riley studied her surroundings, that feeling waned. This house actually did not look as if it were lived in at all. Everything was just too neat.

She remembered her father's words.

He wants to start all over again. He wants to go all the way back to the beginning.

That's exactly what Dirk was trying to do right here. But he was failing, because his life had somehow been hopelessly flawed from the start. Surely he knew that and was tormented by it.

Instead of finding his way back into a happier childhood, he'd trapped himself in an unreal world—a display that might be in some historical museum. A framed cross-stitch embroidery even hung on the living room wall. Riley stepped closer to look at it.

The little stitched x's made up the image of a woman in a long gown and holding a parasol. Beneath her were embroidered words …

A Southern Belle is always
gracious
courteous
genteel …

The list went on, but Riley didn't bother to read the rest. She got the message that mattered to her. The stitchery was nothing more wishful thinking. Obviously, this farm had never been a plantation. No so-called Southern belle had ever lived here, sipping sweet tea and ordering servants about.

Still, the fantasy must be dear to someone who lived here—or had lived here in the past. Maybe that someone had once bought a doll—a doll that represented a Southern belle in a storybook.

Listening for any sound, Riley moved quietly into the hallway. On one side, an arched doorway opened into a dining room. Her sense of being in a past time grew even stronger. Sunlight streamed in through lace curtains hanging over the windows. A table and chairs were positioned perfectly, as if awaiting a family dinner. But like everything else, the dining room looked as though it hadn't been used for a long time.

A large old-fashioned kitchen was on the other side of the hallway. There, too, everything was in its proper place, and there was no sign of recent use.

Ahead of her, at the end of the hall, was a closed door. As Riley moved in that direction, a cluster of framed photographs on the wall drew her attention. She examined them as she edged by. They appeared to be ordinary family photos, some black and white, some in color. They reached far back in time—perhaps as long as a century.

They were just the sort of pictures one might find in any home—parents, elderly grandparents, children, and the dining room table laden with feasts of celebration. Many of the images were faded.

A picture that didn't look more than a couple of decades old appeared to be a boy's school picture—a cleaned-up student with a new haircut and a stiff, unfelt smile. The picture to the right of it was a woman hugging a girl in a frilly dress.

Then, with a slight shock, Riley noticed that the girl and the boy had exactly the same face. They were actually the same child. The girl with the woman wasn't a girl at all, but the schoolboy wearing a dress and a wig. Riley shuddered. The expression on the costumed boy's face told her that this was not a case of a harmless dress-up or comfortable cross-dressing. In this photograph, the child's smile was anguished, wretched—even angry and hateful.

The final snapshot showed the boy at about age ten. He was holding a doll. The woman stood behind the boy, smiling a smile that glowed with entirely misplaced, uncomprehending joy. Riley leaned closer to view the doll and gasped.

There it was—a doll that matched the picture on the book in the store. It was exactly the same, with long blond hair, bright blue eyes, roses, and pink ribbons. Years ago, the woman had given the boy this doll. She must have forced it upon him, expecting him to cherish and love it.

The tortured expression on the boy's face told the real story. He couldn't fake a smile this time. His face was knotted with disgust and self-loathing. This picture captured the moment when something broke apart in him, never to be made whole again. Right then and there, the image of the doll fastened itself onto his unhappy young imagination. He couldn't shake it off, not ever. It was an image that he was recreating with dead women.

Riley turned away from the pictures. She moved toward the closed door at the end of the hall. She swallowed hard.

There it is, she thought.

She was sure of it. That door was the barrier between the dead, artificial, unreal beauty of this country home and the hideously ugly reality that crept behind it. That room was where the false mask of blissful normalcy fell away once and for all.

Holding her gun in her right hand, she opened the door with her left hand. The room was dark, but even in the dim light from the hall, she could see that it was completely unlike the rest of the house. The floor was littered with debris.

She found a light switch to the side of the door and flicked in on. A single overhead bulb revealed a nightmare spread out before her. The first thing that registered on her mind was a metal pipe standing in the middle of the space, bolted to the floor and to the ceilings. Bloodstains on the floor marked what happened there. The unheeded screams of women echoed through her mind, nearly overwhelming her.

No one was inside the room. Riley steadied herself and stepped forward. The windows were boarded up, and no sunlight entered. The walls were pink, with storybook images painted on them. But they were defaced by ugly smears.

Pieces of a child's furniture—frilly chairs and stools really meant for a little girl—were overturned and broken. Scraps of dolls had been thrown everywhere—amputated limbs and heads and snatches of hair. Small doll wigs were nailed to the walls.

Heart pounding with fear, with rage, remembering her own captivity too well, Riley stepped deeper into the room, mesmerized by the scene, by the fury, by the agony that she sensed here.

There came a sudden rustle behind her, and suddenly, the lights went out.

Riley, panic-stricken, spun around to fire her gun but missed her chance. Something heavy and hard struck her arm an agonizing blow. Her weapon went skittering into the darkness.

Riley tried to dodge the next blow, but a rigid, weighty, object glanced across her head, cracking noisily against her skull. She fell and scrambled toward a dark corner of the room.

The blow kept echoing between her ears. Concussive sparkles flickered in the darkness of her mind. She'd been hurt and she knew it. She struggled to hold onto consciousness, but it felt like sand slipping between her fingers.

There it was again—that hissing white flame cutting through the darkness. Little by little, the shimmering light revealed who was carrying it.

This time it was Riley's mother. She was standing right in front of Riley, the fatal bullet wound bleeding in the middle of her chest, her face pale and dead-looking. But when her mother spoke, it was with Riley's father's voice.

"Girl, you're doing this all wrong."

Riley was seized by nauseating dizziness. Everything kept spinning. Her world made no sense at all. What was her mother doing, holding this awful instrument of torture? Why was she speaking with her father's voice?

Riley cried out, "Why aren't you Peterson?"

Suddenly, the flame was extinguished, leaving only lingering traces of phantom light.

Again, she heard her father's voice growling in pitch-blackness.

"That's your trouble. You want to take on all the evil in the world—all at the same time. You've got to make your choice. One monster at a time."

Her head still swimming, Riley tried to grasp that message.

"One monster at a time," she murmured.

Her consciousness ebbed and flowed, taunting her with bursts of lucidity. She saw that the door was slightly ajar and a man was silhouetted there against the dim hallway light. She couldn't make out his face.

He held something in his hand—a crowbar, she now realized. He seemed to be in his stocking feet. He must have been somewhere in the house all along, waiting for the right moment to come and take her by surprise.

Her arm and her head hurt horribly. She felt a sticky, liquid warmth on the side of her skull. She was bleeding, and bleeding badly. She struggled against unconsciousness.

She heard the man laugh, and the laughter wasn't a familiar voice. Her thoughts became hopelessly confused. It wasn't Peterson's voice, so cruel and mocking in that darkness. And where was his torch? Why was everything so different?

She groped about in her mind for the truth of her situation.

It's not Peterson, she told herself. *It's Dirk Monroe.*

She whispered aloud to herself, "One monster at time."

This monster was bent on killing her.

She clawed around on the floor. Where was her gun?

The man moved toward her, swinging the crowbar with one hand, slicing the air with it. Riley got halfway to her feet before he landed a blow across her shoulder and knocked her down again. She braced herself for another blow, but then heard the sound of the crowbar falling to the floor.

Something was looped around her left foot, pulling her. He'd gotten a rope around that foot and was dragging her slowly across the floor, through the litter and toward the pipe in the middle of the room. It was the place where four women had already suffered and died.

Riley tried to probe his thoughts. He hadn't scouted her or chosen her. He'd never seen her buying one of those dolls he so deeply loathed. Even so, he intended to make the most of her arrival. He was going to make her his next victim. He was determined to make her suffer. She was going to die in pain.

Even so, Riley caught a glimmer of impending justice. Bill and a team would get here soon. What would Dirk do when the FBI stormed the house? He'd kill her, of course, and instantly. He'd never allow her to be rescued. But he was doomed all the same.

But why did Riley have to be his last victim? She saw faces of people she loved—April, Bill—even her father. Now Riley knew she shared with him a stubborn bond of dark wisdom, a comprehension of limitless evil in the world. She thought of the work she lived each day to do, and slowly, a new determination rose up in her. She wouldn't let him claim her easily. She'd die on her own terms, not his.

She groped around the floor with her hand. She found something solid—not part of a doll, but something hard and sharp. She gripped the handle of the knife. It was surely the very knife he'd used on four women.

Time slowed down to a mind-numbing crawl. She realized that Dirk had just passed the rope around the central pipe. Now he was pulling her foot up against it.

He was turned away from her, too sure that she was defeated already. His mind was occupied with tying her to the post—and on what he would do to her then.

His unwariness gave Riley a moment, and one moment only, before he turned back her way. Still prone on the floor, she wrenched her body into a seated position. He noticed this and started to turn, but she moved quicker. She wrestled her free right foot beneath her, then rose up to face him.

She plunged the knife into his stomach, then drew it out and stabbed him again and again. She heard him shriek and moan. She kept stabbing madly until she blacked out.

Chapter 35

Riley opened her eyes. Her whole body was in pain, especially her shoulder and her head. Bill's face filled her vision. Was she dreaming?

"Bill?" she asked.

He smiled, looking relieved. He was holding something soft against her head, staunching the flow of blood.

"Welcome back," he said.

Riley realized that she was still in the room, with the post nearby. She was seized by a moment of panic.

"Where's Dirk?" she asked.

"Dead," Bill said. "You gave him just what he deserved."

Riley still wondered if she was dreaming.

"I've got to see," she gasped. She managed to turn her head. She saw Dirk stretched out across the floor face down in a pool of his own blood. Eyes opened. Unblinking.

Bill turned her head back toward him.

"Don't try to move," he said. "You're hurt pretty bad. You're going to be okay. But you've lost a lot of blood."

A spasm of nauseated dizziness told her that Bill was right. She managed to whisper five words before she lost consciousness again.

"One monster at a time."

Chapter 36

Special Agent Brent Meredith shut the thick manila envelope stuffed with photographs and written reports with a note of satisfied finality. Riley felt the same satisfaction, and she was sure that Bill and Flores did too. They were all seated at the table in the Behavioral Analysis Unit conference room. If only Riley weren't bandaged up and hurting all over, the moment would have felt perfect.

"So Dirk's mother wanted a daughter instead of a son," Meredith said. "She tried to turn him into a Southern belle. That was probably just the tip of the iceberg. God knows what else he went through as a kid."

Bill leaned back in his chair.

"Let's not give him too much sympathy," he said. "Not everybody with a lousy childhood turns into a murderous sadist. He made his own choices."

Meredith and Flores nodded in agreement.

"But does anybody know whatever happened to Dirk's mother?" Riley asked.

"Records show that she died five years ago," Flores said. "His father disappeared long before that, when Dirk was still a baby."

A sober silence settled over the group. Riley understood exactly what it meant. She was in the presence of three people whose lives were devoted to destroying evil. Even in their satisfaction, the specter of more evil, and much more work to do, hung over all of them. It would never be over. Not for them.

The door opened, and Carl Walder walked in. He was all smiles.

"Great work, everybody," he said. He slid Riley's gun and badge across the table toward her. "These belong to you."

Riley smiled a wry smile. Walder was not going to apologize, much less acknowledge any fault of his own. But that was just as well. Riley didn't know just how she'd respond if he actually said he was sorry. Probably not gracefully.

"By the way, Riley," Walder said. "The Senator called me this morning, and he sends you his best wishes for your recovery, and his thanks. He seems to think the world of you."

Riley now had to stifle her amusement. That call, she was sure, was exactly why Walder was giving her back her gun and her badge. She remembered one of the last things Newbrough had said to her.

"You're nobody's lapdog."

The same thing could never be said of Carl Walder.

"Stop by my office soon," Walder said. "Let's talk promotion. An administrative position, maybe. You deserve it."

Without another word, Walder left the office. Riley heard her companions breathe a shared sigh of relief that he was gone so quickly.

"You should think about it, Riley," Meredith said.

Riley chuckled.

"Can you really see me in an administrative job?"

Meredith shrugged.

"You've more than paid your dues. You've done more tough field work than most agents do in a lifetime. Maybe you should become an instructor. You'd be great at training agents, with your experience and insight. What do you think?"

Riley thought it over. What would she really have to teach young agents? Her instincts were all she had, and as far as she knew, instincts couldn't be taught. There was no way to train people to follow their gut. They either had it or they didn't.

Besides, did she really wish her own gut instincts on anybody? She lived too much in terror of her own thoughts, haunted by her troubling capacity to grasp an evil mind. It was a hard thing to live with.

"Thanks," Riley said, "but I like it just where I am."

Meredith nodded, and rose from his chair. "Well, let's call it a day. Get some rest, folks."

The meeting broke up, and Riley and Bill found themselves walking down the hall together silently. They left the building and sat down together on a bench outside. Whole minutes passed. Neither of them seemed to know what to say. There was too much to say.

"Bill," she asked tentatively, "do you think we can be partners again?"

After a pause, Bill said, "What do you think?"

They turned and looked into each other's eyes. Riley could see lingering pain in Bill's face. The wound she'd inflicted with her drunken phone call still hadn't healed. It was going to take a long time.

But she now knew something else—something that had long been true, but that she'd never let herself admit before. Her bond to Bill was intense and powerful, and he almost certainly felt the same.

It was no longer a secret that they could keep from themselves. There was no way for them to go back to their former ways.

Their partnership was over. They both knew it. Neither one of them had to say it aloud.

"Go home, Bill," Riley said gently. "Try to put things back together with your wife. You've got your kids to think of."

"I will," Bill said. "But I hope I don't lose you—your friendship, I mean."

Riley patted his hand and smiled.

"There's no chance of that," she said.

They both got up from the bench and walked away to their cars.

*

"What's on your mind, Mom?" April asked.

Riley and April had been sitting in the living room long into the night watching television. Earlier that evening, Riley had told April all that had happened—or at least all that she felt she could tell her.

Riley hesitated before answering April's question. But she knew that she had to say it aloud. Besides, April knew about it already. It wasn't a secret. It was just something Riley couldn't shake off her mind.

"I killed a man today," Riley said.

April looked at her with love and concern.

"I know," she said. "What does that feel like?"

"It's hard to put into words," Riley said. "It's terrible. It's something no one has a right to do—not ever, really. But sometimes it's the only thing."

Riley paused. "I feel something else," she said. "I'm not sure I should say it."

April laughed quietly. "I thought we weren't going to do the silent thing anymore, Mom."

Riley steadied herself and said, "I feel alive. God help me, it makes me feel alive. And any day now, I know that some woman will walk into Madeline's store and buy a doll and never be in any danger. I'm just ... well, I'm just happy for her. I'm glad that I could give her that, even if she'll never know it."

Riley squeezed April's hand.

"It's late, and you've got school tomorrow," she said.

April kissed her mother on the cheek.

"Goodnight, Mom," she said, then went to her bedroom.

197

Riley felt a new wave of pain and exhaustion. She realized that she'd better get to bed or she'd fall asleep right there on the couch.

She picked herself up and walked toward her bedroom. She was already in her nightgown, and she didn't bother to stop at the bathroom to brush her teeth. She just wanted to go straight to bed.

When she entered her bedroom and turned on the light, something caught her eye immediately. Her heart skipped a beat.

There, in her bed, was something awry.

It was a handful of small pebbles.